D1630790

THE
LIFE SHE
WANTS

MEL SHERRATT

bookouture

Published by Bookouture in 2021

An imprint of Storyfire Ltd.
Carmelite House
50 Victoria Embankment
London EC4Y 0DZ

www.bookouture.com

ISBN: 978-1-80314-004-9
eBook ISBN: 978-1-80314-003-2

Thanks to all my loyal and friendly readers – I literally couldn't do this without you.

PROLOGUE

We stand together in the silence of the night, in the clearing in the woods. Our breathing is the only thing I can hear.

We are as one, but only because we've agreed to cover up what happened.

It wasn't supposed to end like this. When is killing someone ever a satisfactory conclusion? This was just a momentary lapse of concentration. A burst of anger. A fist of infuriation. Hands squeezing something they shouldn't have.

But now the body is buried. We've hidden the crime. If anyone finds out, we'll make up lies and pretend it never happened. No one will ever know the truth.

Because I won't let them find out.

PART ONE

ONE

Juliette Ansell pulled the collar of her coat in, the biting wind making her shiver. Her gloved hand was snug, her husband Danny's wrapped tightly around it as they walked along the South Bank of the Thames. London was looking bleak but the day was ending early, lights lit up everywhere as a new year began.

The question hung over them as they dodged the crowds. It was the second of January. She suspected lots of people were probably in the swing of making plans. Getting a new job, writing a book, having a baby. Planning a wedding, a big birthday, a holiday. Making and breaking resolutions, setting out goals for the next twelve months.

Juliette and Danny were making plans too, but they were reluctant to leave the previous year behind. Juliette's youngest sister had got married; her older sister had found a new job. Her dad's cancer had gone into remission, and her mum was getting better by the week after a recent fall left her with a broken leg. Danny's brother had come home from the army and there had been many family reunions. Two of their friends, who they never even expected to become a couple, got engaged. Danny's parents had celebrated their golden wedding anniversary.

Everything was looking good for their family now.

Except *they* weren't a family any more.

Their daughter, Emily, had died last summer. She had been fine one day and gone two days later. They'd noticed the telltale signs of meningitis quite early on but the disease had ravaged her tiny body and, in the end, it had given up.

Emily was three weeks shy of her fifth birthday. That day itself had gone by in a blink. Who would want to celebrate the birth and death of their child at the same time?

Now, they bought coffee and doughnuts. Spying an empty bench, they sat down, looking over the water. There was a peaceful calm about it and despite the cold it was enjoyable. The buildings along the riverside were impressive, as well as familiar. Westminster Bridge and the London Eye to their left. Blackfriars Bridge to their right. People were wrapped up warm wherever they looked.

Juliette originated from Tamworth but had always loved London. Yet when Emily died, everything around her became familiarly painful. Grief overwhelmed her at every turn. Driving by the park Emily walked past to get to school. Anastasia, Emily's friend's house two streets away. The café on the main road where they took breakfast most Sunday mornings.

Then there was everyone they knew. The mums from the school run and play dates. The people in the local pub and the restaurants they frequented. Neighbours and friends. Danny's work colleagues. It was all a bit too much.

As they'd spent their first Christmas without her, they'd discussed moving out of the city. They had options. They could sell up here completely or do it half and half, buying a small flat and a property out of the city so that Danny could commute. The first choice had been favourable the more they discussed it.

'What do you think?' Danny asked as he gazed out over the river.

Juliette sipped her coffee before answering. 'What do *you* think?' She turned to look at him and they shared a smile. It was as if neither of them wanted to say out loud what they wanted to do.

'Okay, I'll go first.' Danny turned towards her a little. 'I think we should move to the Midlands. We'll be nearer to my family as well as yours. We'll buy a cottage and take a lease out on a flat. You move in, I'll look for a job up there and commute until I do.'

Juliette looked at him, the man she had loved since she was eighteen. Seventeen years they had been together, the last ten of those as a married couple. She loved Danny with all her heart. But something was missing. They both knew it. They needed to start again. Where the memories wouldn't haunt them as much on a daily basis.

'And you'll visit Emily?' she asked, her voice low and breaking with emotion. Emily had been cremated, but her ashes were in their local cemetery.

'Of course! And you can stay with me whenever you wish. It will give us the chance to try out the best of both worlds. See if we like being country bumpkins before we throw in the towel completely.'

Juliette still wasn't sure. She was ninety per cent there, but not yet fully committed.

'There are too many reminders of what could have been,' Danny said. 'I know in time the grief will get easier and the memories will always be here.' He pointed first to his head, then his heart.

Juliette swallowed the lump in her throat and nodded, deciding there and then. 'I think we should do it.'

Danny moved closer to her, wrapping an arm around her shoulders and drawing her in close. 'If we hate it, we can move to another part of London on our return.'

'Do you think we'll hate it?'

He paused. 'No. Do you?'

She paused too. 'No.'

'Then we'll do it. We won't probably move until spring anyway. Deal?'

She looked up at him. He leaned over and kissed her gently.

'Deal,' she replied.

They sat in companionable silence, watching the world go by.

Juliette was glad now they'd made a decision. It was something to concentrate on. Christmas had been a bad time, the pain seeping in with every new December day. Now the new year would start with optimism, plans for the future. It wasn't as if they were moving on from Emily. They were doing it to help them heal, forget their sorrow. Make new memories.

It was the right thing to do, she was sure.

TWO

Nothing could have prepared Juliette for the feeling of overwhelm that crashed through her as she and Danny drew up outside their new home. You couldn't get anything more picturesque either. Yet it was what she'd left behind to move here that gave her a gut punch as they drove through the gates.

Over the past few months, they had visited properties in the Midlands to see what their money would buy them. They'd finally secured a small rental flat for Danny and had their eye set on a cottage. It had been the end of June before the sale had completed. It was a big move and they'd wanted to be prepared, but they were here at last.

'Ready for our adventure?' Danny leaned over to squeeze her hand as she tried to contain her tears.

'Hmm-hmm,' was all she managed to reply.

Abbey Cottage was on the outskirts of both the Staffordshire Moorlands and Stoke-on-Trent. The village of Mapleton was a mere five minutes' walk, where there were shops of all kinds along a terraced high street.

The cottage was set almost at the top of a hill. The view was the thing that had drawn them to it. From the kitchen there were rolling hills and fields, horses in the distance. They'd been told the lane itself was quiet except for the odd tractor and car. They were off the beaten track, enough to be secluded but equally near enough to civilisation to feel semi-rural. Even though they were hoping they'd adapt to country life, it was the mixture they both needed after living in the capital for most of their lives.

Losing Emily last year had been hard for them both but luckily Juliette's business working as an online bookkeeper was portable. Danny was an architect, well sought after in the capital. Hopefully something would open up here too, but they hadn't wanted that to stop them. Danny was to commute to London during the week and come home at weekends. It was an hour and half by train.

'Still in love with it?' Danny asked before getting out of the car.

'Oh, yes,' Juliette admitted. The property needed a little work but it was liveable and workable around that. The previous owner had moved into residential care seven years ago and the house, although checked on by two sons, hadn't been lived in since then. However, once the owner died, the sons renovated a lot of the property themselves. Some parts were great, some not to their taste but definitely fine to live with until they could afford to change them.

Juliette got out of the car, stretching her arms in the air for a moment, stiff after such a long journey. The removal van was a few minutes behind them, after stopping to refuel, and for now it was peaceful as she surveyed her new surroundings.

She closed her eyes and listened to the chattering of birds. She couldn't hear anything else. It both unnerved and soothed her. It would take a while to get accustomed to missing the lull of traffic that would send her to sleep. The voices shouting, the horns beeping. Sounds of life going on.

There were only two houses for a few hundred metres: theirs and their closest neighbours. The double-fronted stone cottage was set off from the road and quite a way back. At the front of the garden was a large hedgerow that separated them from the lane. A cobbled driveway led to several outbuildings and a double garage at the side of the property. To the rear were three acres of garden and fields.

Juliette still couldn't imagine walking out of the house into so much greenery. Their old home in London had been landscaped with decking to minimise the work they'd have to do keeping it tidy. Here if they didn't employ a gardener, she recognised it would take them both the best part of a day to make a dip in it. She made a mental note to check if there was someone local to hire.

Danny reached for her hand and they went inside through a wooden door that needed a shoulder to budge it. She sniffed the air. There wasn't a hint that the property had been empty for so long. It smelled of fresh paint, the walls having been replastered throughout after asbestos had been found on a survey. Everything had had to be stripped out and redone before the bank would grant them a mortgage, luckily at the vendor's cost. There was dust everywhere but only a few days' worth. Someone had been in and cleaned it in readiness for them, which was extremely kind and rare having moved from London where they never even spoke to their neighbours.

She walked a few steps forward into the kitchen, a large sunny room at the back of the house overlooking their garden and the field. Cream Shaker units and a large fridge-freezer and Aga in matching shades of red. An island to sit four and space for a large pine table in front of it, overlooking the garden.

Juliette's heart went into her mouth as she thought of her daughter. Emily would have loved it here. Memories were portable but would it be more painful not to see their daughter running from room to room here? She had no idea but had to believe that it was the right thing for them to do. The property would make an excellent home for a new family, even if she was thirty-five now. Danny was forty-two and there was still time to try again.

Upstairs in the back bedroom, she paused at the window. This would be ideal for a nursery if they were blessed with another child. The sun filtering in made it feel bright and welcoming.

Behind her, she heard movement and turned to see Danny pop

his head around the door. 'The removal van is here. Let's find the tea box. I'm desperate for a brew.'

'When are you ever not?' she teased, following him down the stairs and outside.

'Hi there,' a voice shouted. They turned to see a man in the garden to their right. He looked to be in his mid-forties. 'I'm Richard. Welcome to the neighbourhood.'

'Hi.' Danny waved. 'I'm Danny, and this is my wife, Juliette. It's nice to meet you.'

'Likewise. I'll leave you to it for now. I'm sure you have lots to do.'

'Yes, we'll be... oh, he's gone.'

'Perhaps he keeps himself to himself.' Juliette shrugged.

'Knowing our luck, he's probably the neighbourhood watch foreman.'

'I hope not.'

'Well, at least there'll be someone watching over you while I'm away during the week.'

'I'm quite capable of looking after myself.' Juliette slapped him playfully.

As the removal men came towards them with the first of a gazillion boxes, Juliette breathed in deeply. A new start was going to be great. And what better place than here.

THREE

From behind the curtains, Sarah spotted the man coming out of the house, followed by the woman. It would be strange seeing people in the property. It had been empty for the two years she'd been living here. Richard had told her the previous owner, an elderly woman, had died several years ago now and her family had inherited it. He'd often spoken to them when they'd shown up for a quick recce but nothing about their grand plans to refurbish the property had ever materialised. And then the For Sale board had gone up, surprising them both.

She stood watching them for a while, seeing them going in and out of the house. They looked to be in their mid-to-late thirties. She could see no children, unless they were inside, glad if that were the case. She wasn't sure how she would cope if there were youngsters to contend with too. And Richard would be a nightmare to live with as well.

'What are you doing?' Richard came up behind her, making her jump.

'Seeing what's happening next door.'

Richard stood beside her, not at all bothered that he'd be seen. He towered several inches above her, the sense of foreboding engulfing her. She waited for his snide comments to start, but he took her by surprise.

'They look decent. I hope they keep themselves to themselves.'

'I'm sure they—'

'Don't get any clever ideas.' He turned his head to stare at her, waiting to see if she would react. Instead she moved away to go downstairs. She wasn't in the mood for an argument.

'It's nearly lunch,' she said. 'I'll make sandwiches. Will ham and cheese be okay?'

He nodded. 'Bring them out to the garden. We can sit outside for fifteen minutes.'

Sarah trotted off quickly. So that was his game. The property next door was set further up the hill so they could always be seen in their garden. It was all show for the new neighbours.

In the kitchen, she cut thick slices of brown bread, fresh from the village that morning, and spread butter over it. Then she added cheese, being sure not to hang any of it over the sides of the bread. She topped it with ham and added a dash of dressing before stacking them into sandwiches. The bread was cut diagonally, the sandwiches placed on top of each other on the plate. Richard liked the simple things to be correct.

She made builder's tea, strong with two sugars for Richard, and coffee for herself. She lay everything on a tray and took it out onto a decked area through the French doors. The sun was beating down and she stood for a moment to relish its warmth on her skin.

'Come now.' Richard clicked his fingers as he sat down. 'I'm starving.'

She placed the tray down, spread its contents over the table and sat opposite him. There was a twenty-five-year age gap between them, yet in some respects Richard seemed much younger. His hair was dark, a thick, full head of it and when he smiled his eyes twinkled inside hooded lids. He often had facial hair, a small goatee that he kept well-trimmed, but right now he was clean-shaven.

Yet it was those eyes that she'd been drawn to. Dark sapphire with hints of coal when he was at his most dangerous.

'Have you spoken to either of them yet?' Sarah asked, curious to know who was living so close to them now.

'I said hello. We can do the friendly neighbour thing later.' Richard picked up a sandwich. 'We'll have to be very careful what we tell them. You do realise that?'

'Of course.' Behind her, she could hear voices but she wouldn't look. They ate in silence and then Richard raised his hand.

'Someone's waving at us,' he said. 'Turn and wave too.'

Sarah did as she was told. The couple were standing together but moved apart again. It was just a small greeting but it was friendly. It would be lovely to have someone so close to talk to, even if Richard would never allow her to mix and make friends.

'They seem nice,' she said, turning back to him. 'They'll most probably keep to themselves.'

'They can see too much,' he muttered. 'I might have to let the hedge grow higher.'

'We're pretty private here though, don't you think?' Sarah couldn't bear the barrier being raised.

'I *think* you should clear this mess away.' Richard stood up, his chair dragging across the flags. 'Get inside now. It's enough that you've been seen.'

Sarah piled the tray with the dirty dishes and took them into the house. There was no modern kitchen with a dishwasher for her. The kitchen was an old farmhouse style but purely because it was over twenty years old. She rinsed everything quickly, dried it and put it away.

She checked her watch: one thirty-five. She had a whole afternoon ahead of her. What she would give to be able to sit in the garden and read a book. But she couldn't do that now there were people next door.

She wondered how much it would change their lives. Richard was right, they would have to be careful. Equally, this could be

Sarah's chance to change things, slowly but surely. For now, she
would bide her time and hopefully get to know them better.
Garner their trust.

With a sigh, she made her way upstairs to enjoy what little
time she had left of the afternoon.

FIVE

2015

'I can't believe we've come this far for a painting,' I said. 'What is it with this bloke, anyway? And how can you afford it?'

'It's for our parents, and we've all chipped in. It's something they've wanted for ages and not many couples get to their twenty-fifth wedding anniversary without killing each other.'

Martin, my friend, grinned at me. He'd been smoking and his breath smelt like potato peelings but at least I'd got an afternoon off.

Martin and I worked at the local biscuit factory. It was a bugger of a job for low pay and awful conditions and we both hated it. Today we were on late shifts so I'd offered to ride from Derby to Mapleton, to keep him company.

Martin and I weren't an item. We were just really good friends. Besides, he was dating Mandy Pilkington and I loved teasing her. She hated that he wanted to spend time with me; she got so jealous it was laughable. So once I found out she didn't want to go and see some 'crappy pictures', I jumped at the chance. My life was so exciting – not.

We drove there in Martin's Mini, small and compact and falling apart. I was surprised it got us there and back to be honest. It was a death trap, a tin can on wheels. But it was Martin's pride and joy. He loved all things retro – and the Mini was definitely older than us.

The air in the car was hotter than it was outside. I wound down the window and thrust my hand out, waving it about in the breeze.

'So who is he, the artist?' I over-pronounced the word *artist* to prove I didn't believe he would be good.

'He's called Richard Sykes-Morgan. I doubt you'll have heard of him.'

'Sounds like a ponce to me.'

'He's really good. I scoured the internet for someone who would draw a bespoke piece. Richard came highly recommended and when I saw some of the pieces he's created, I knew my mum would fall in love with one in particular.'

'What of?'

'Wait and see.'

Twenty minutes later, almost at the top of a hill, we turned into a gateway and pulled up in front of a stone farmhouse, with a large garden and what looked like a forest behind it. I reckoned the house must date back a fair few years.

'Wow.' Martin whistled. 'Some property.'

'Indeed. He must be doing well for himself.'

A man came striding towards us as we got out of the car. I stretched my back after sitting cramped for so long and then raised a hand to my eyes to shield them from the sun.

'Hi, I'm Richard.' He offered his hand to Martin, then did the same to me. 'Right then, let me show you what I have.'

I let the men walk slightly in front of me as I studied Richard's physique. He was built like a rugby player, most probably in his late thirties. I fell in love with him there and then.

Close up, he wasn't much taller than me and his face was gorgeous. He had these twinkling eyes and a cheeky grin that made him look younger than he was. I found out later that he was nearly forty to my twenty. I had no idea at the time of his previous relationships either. Well, you don't, do you? You just take at face value everything someone says to you.

He led us into a studio that was almost as large as the factory unit I was working in. He beckoned us over to a canvas covered in a white cloth, removing it with a 'ta-da' which made me giggle.

'What do you think?' His eyes were as wide as a child's waiting for approval from a parent. I must admit to gasping when I looked. It was an image of a young girl on the rocks by the sea. Beside her, a teenage boy was showing her a starfish. The image was simple but extremely emotive as they gazed at each other with wonder in their eyes. I had to admit, for a wedding anniversary present it was perfect.

'This is incredible.' Martin's eyes were as wide as Richard's. 'Mum will love it.' He reached for a wad of notes from his pocket and counted it out on the workbench. Richard's eyes were on me and I blushed at his stare. I smiled shyly and he returned it.

When Martin got to five hundred pounds, I could barely disguise my astonishment. I had no idea paintings would go for that much. I lived in a council house on a rough estate. My dad did a runner when I was little and there was only me and my sister left with my mum. So five hundred pounds was so much money.

'Leave it at that,' Richard said, still looking my way.

'You said five fifty on the phone.'

'It's fine.'

Martin beamed and handed him the money. 'Thanks very much.'

'Aren't you forgetting something?' I said, arms folded at Martin's stupidity.

Both men looked at me, waiting to be enlightened.

'That's never going to fit in the Mini.'

'Sure it will,' Martin said, although looking doubtful.

'If it won't, I'll deliver it,' Richard said. 'It's for a special occasion. It's no problem. Here, take my contact details regardless.' He handed me a business card. I looked at it.

Richard Sykes-Morgan. Artist.

I could feel him staring at me again and I looked up. Somehow in that moment, I knew he would ask me out. We had a connection, something I couldn't explain.

True to my thoughts, the Mini was not the transport vehicle Martin should have chosen. But there had been no one else available to take him, nor loan him a van. We said our goodbyes and came away with our money. Richard refused to take it from Martin until the painting was with him.

'Nice bloke,' Martin said as we trundled down the dirt track again.

'Hmm.'

'He couldn't keep his eyes off you. It's a pity he lives so far away. Pretty nice place he has there, don't you think?'

He nudged me and then winked. I laughed and said nothing. But it was exactly what I was thinking. Imagine me living in something like that.

'But what would I do in the middle of nowhere?'

'I'm sure you can think of something.'

I slapped his arm playfully. But all the way back to Derby I thought about Richard, and his smile, his eyes and his rugby player body. And figured out how I could orchestrate being there when he delivered the painting.

SIX

The village of Mapleton dates back to 1843. Along its narrow high street, there were all manner of shops. A family run supermarket with a post office. A florist, hairdresser and a small coffee shop. A butcher and delicatessen. An Italian restaurant, a chip shop and a takeaway.

Further along was the one pub set back behind a pond and a green, the road widening on the bend into almost a square. A church and a hall, a community centre and school, all self-contained with lots of passing traffic via the main road.

It was a long way from what Juliette was used to but it was different in its own right. She had wandered up and down the length of it twice now, getting acquainted with its people, the feel of it all.

As she came out of the butcher's, she spotted a woman walking past. 'Sarah?' she said, smiling when she turned. She wasn't sure but she thought she saw a look of panic on her face before a smile appeared. 'Hi, it's Juliette. I've just moved in next door.'

Sarah was a tall thin woman, almost emaciated in her look. Juliette reckoned she was one of those women who could eat anything and get away with it, a swimmer's build. Or maybe netball, an asset to a team as she stretched to score an easy goal.

Her long blonde hair hung loose, in need of a trim, hollow cheek-bones standing out but making her look remarkably pretty. She wore a pale blue maxi dress and flat sandals, her shopping in a tartan bag.

'Oh, yes, hi. Are you settling in okay?' Sarah asked.

'Yes, thanks. It's a bit lonely with my husband commuting to London in the week. It's not for long luckily, and I can still see him at the weekends until then.'

'The best of both worlds,' Sarah replied. 'I've been to London twice. It's very manic.'

'Yes, I miss it and I don't. Its busyness had its advantages and disadvantages.' Juliette grinned. 'I'm heading home now, are you?'

'Yes.'

They walked at a steady pace.

'So what is there to do around here?' Juliette asked. 'Are there any daytime activities, night classes, that type of thing?'

Sarah shook her head. 'It's a sleepy village but it has its moments. There's always something going on at the community centre. You could check that out.'

'Thanks, I will.'

'There's a pub quiz every Thursday night.'

'Ah, that will have to wait until Danny moves here perma-nently. I'm not sure I could force my way in.'

'What do you mean?'

'I'm not a local. Will it take us a while to fit in?'

'I don't think so. I've been here two years and don't get that vibe. Although I do tend to keep myself to myself, with Richard.'

'Are you and him...?'

'Yes,' Sarah replied. 'Oh, there's the book club every fortnight if you're a reader.'

'I am! That sounds right up my street. Do you have any more details?'

'No, sorry. I'm not a member but I bet there'll be a card up somewhere about it. Perhaps try the newsagents, or Karen. She owns the hairdressers, and it was her idea to start the club.'

'Not to worry. I'll find more details when I next go into the village. Gosh, it's so lovely around here. I can't believe the greenery.' Juliette gazed upwards, feeling the warmth of the sun as it popped its head through the trees. Every garden she came to was a riot of colour and aroma of spring. She made a decision to find out what she had in her own and look after it, take an interest in nurturing something from the ground. She laughed inwardly: she'd only been here a week and she was turning into a country bumpkin. She hoped she'd feel the same in a few weeks.

'It is a beautiful place,' Sarah replied. 'I quite like how we're not in each other's pockets. But good neighbours are always looking out for each other as well.'

After a couple of minutes' small talk, they drew up at their front gates. There was barely a metre between them, the hedge that separated their gardens travelling from the main road all the way back.

'If you ever fancy a coffee, do pop round,' Juliette said. 'Quite frankly, it's been great to talk to you. I haven't spoken to a soul since the weekend.'

'Is Danny home soon?'

'Tomorrow evening. I can't wait.'

Sarah's eyes flicked behind Juliette. 'I'd better be going.' With that, she raced along her drive.

'Bye, then,' Juliette said under her breath, wondering why the sudden brush-off. It was only then she noticed Richard waiting at the house, Sarah bustling towards him. When Sarah drew level with him, there were a few words of conversation and Sarah went indoors. Spotting her, Richard's face changed from a scowl to a smile and he gave her a quick wave before following Sarah inside.

Wondering what that was all about, Juliette made her way indoors too. She couldn't wait to get into her shorts and sit on the patio under the umbrella. Oh, the joys of working from home. An outside office whenever the weather dictated.

* * *

Sarah heard Richard behind her as she started to unload the shopping. She kept her back to him purposely.

When she and Richard had got together, they had taken day trips out to nearby landmarks. The Roaches, Buxton Opera House, Matlock, Ilam and Ashbourne. He'd shown her where he'd grown up in nearby Wink Hill, a farm with twenty-five acres. Although he'd helped on the farm, living at home, he'd never wanted to take over full-time. His dad's early demise at forty-seven had given him the impetus to sell up and move.

The first time she'd visited Richard's property, it had wowed her immediately. Set in six acres, with a woodland to its rear, it was a two-storey stone cottage with a converted loft and a further extension with a separate annexe. Far enough away from the road to be secluded but near enough to the village for amenities and a short car drive to nearby towns of Buxton or Leek.

Sarah remembered going into Richard's studio. The more time she spent around him, the more she got to know him.

One morning she went in there with a purpose. It wasn't to see what he was up to. Even so, he showed her around, talking her through some of the pieces he was working on. When their hands touched, it was the catalyst they needed.

It was the first time they had made love. It had been dangerous and exciting as they might be caught out at any moment, but it was heavenly in many ways too. Making love with the scent of her and Richard intermingled with the smell of the chippings. The soft, gentle breeze of summer coming through the open door. The blue sky in the distance, not a cloud in sight. Sweat glistening from their bodies as they moved together in urgency. Fast, furious, intentional.

The second time had been much slower. There had been hardly any work done that day.

Oh, how things had changed since then. Now she wasn't allowed in the studio unless she was bringing him a drink or something to eat that he'd requested to be ready at a certain time. He cited he didn't want to be interrupted when he was in the flow, but she knew it was much more than that.

'Why were you with her?' Richard asked.

'She was in the village and shouted me over.'

'Did you walk back with her?'

'Yes.'

'What did you talk about?'

Sarah turned to him. 'She wanted to know what went on in the village. Clubs to join, socialise – that kind of thing.'

'And what did you say?' He leaned across her, picked an apple up from the bowl and bit into it ferociously.

The intention of his actions didn't go unnoticed with her. A bite of the forbidden fruit. He was such a hypocrite.

'I told her what there was to do, the pub quiz, the book club, volunteering at the community centre.'

'Doesn't she work?'

'Yes, from home.'

Richard gave out a loud dramatic sigh. 'So she's going to be here during the week and then both of them at the weekends?'

'She said she might go to London occasionally but mostly, yes.'

'It's going to make things really hard for us.'

'We'll cope. We have done so far.'

'Easier to do when the property was empty.'

'We'll manage.'

Sarah continued to put the shopping away until Richard got the message.

'I'll be in the studio. Lunch at twelve thirty sharp.'

She nodded. 'I'll bring you a coffee first.'

'That would be lovely. I'd like it in half an hour. Don't make it too strong this time.'

With him out of the room, Sarah put away the rest of the shopping and went upstairs. It was such a lovely day it would be a shame to waste it. Maybe she would sit out in the garden today or go for a walk in the woods. Much better than being cooped up indoors all the time.

SEVEN

Friday had come round rather quickly considering Juliette had spent the week on her own. She took the afternoon off from work and treated herself to a lounge in the bath before heading to pick Danny up.

She was so eager to see him that she'd arrived thirty minutes before the train was due in. So as soon as she spotted him coming out of the station, she waved and ran to him. She had missed everything about him, in particular his familiarity. He'd removed his tie, his collar open, short sleeves revealing tanned arms that she couldn't wait to feel around her again. His hair had been cut and he looked worn out but happy with it.

He dropped his overnight case and took her in his arms, kissing her with a passion she was sure would embarrass onlookers. But she didn't care.

'God, I've missed you so much,' he said as they broke apart and he picked up his case again. 'I can't wait to get you home.'

'Well, if all you want me for is my body... then I'm fine with that.' She giggled as he searched out her hand, and they walked to the car chatting nineteen to the dozen.

It was a twenty-minute drive back home. Juliette smiled: home. It felt like that to her already, but she wondered how long it would take Danny to settle as he flitted back and forth. Still, it wouldn't be for long.

She'd prepared everything for his arrival. She'd shopped locally, grabbing all she needed to make a weekend of his favourite meals. There was wine chilling, beer in the cooler and the barbecue at the ready as the weather was still glorious. But all she really wanted to do was feel the closeness of her husband. She had missed him too.

They pulled into the driveway, Danny bringing in his case. 'I'll take this upstairs,' he said.

'I'll open the wine.'

He reached for her hand once more and pulled her upstairs with him. 'I want you first.' He threw her playfully on the bed and lay on top of her. Brushing the hair from her face, he kissed her gently. 'I have waited for this all week.'

Later, when they were both downstairs again, they chatted while they prepared food. Juliette had forgotten how lovely it was just to be. Living in London, they'd gone out to eat more than they'd prepared food at home. Here it was a pleasure to cook in their country kitchen.

She gazed through the window as she washed the salad. The garden was coming on nicely now. Danny came up behind her, wrapping his arms around her waist and resting his head on her shoulder.

'This is bliss,' he said quietly.

'It is when the weather is so good. The locals tell me it's treacherous in winter.'

'The locals?'

She smiled, wiping her hands on a tea towel before turning towards him.

'And how about you?' Danny added. 'Is it getting to you being here alone?'

'It's only been a week.'

'You know what I mean. At least everything in London is familiar to me.'

'That's why I like being here though.' She sighed. 'It's okay but I'm counting down until you're here for good.'

They sat outside on the patio. It overlooked Sarah and Richard's house slightly and she could see into their garden. But considering they each had acres behind them, it was the only spot. She could see through the kitchen window too. At the moment it was empty.

'I could get used to this,' Danny said as he put down his knife and fork and reached for his glass. 'It's deathly quiet. Is it always like this?'

She nodded.

'And breakfast on Sundays? Is there anywhere good?'

'I've been told there's a farm shop about a mile away that's worth trying. What time is your train back?'

'Ten past eight.'

'So I have you all to myself for' – she checked her watch and worked it out in her head – 'fifty hours.' She leaned closer to kiss him, noticing Richard was in his garden.

'Should I wave or do you think it's too intrusive?'

'What do you mean?'

'Well, if we weren't higher up the hill, we wouldn't see him at all. Maybe he prefers to keep himself to himself.'

'What does he do? Have you found out yet?'

'He paints.'

'Is he good?'

'I checked out his website and it seems he is. Some of his pieces go for the high hundreds.'

'What about his wife – Sarah?'

'She seems quiet but nice. Not sure if it's his wife though. I don't see a ring.'

'She seems a lot younger than him.'

'I'd say a good twenty years.'

He nodded and then stood up. 'No need to know if he'd be bothered about you waving to him. He's just beckoned us over.'

Juliette followed Danny to the edge of the garden where Richard was waiting.

'Hi there,' Danny greeted, looking down on him.

'Hi, have you settled in okay?'

'We're getting there, slowly emptying boxes. I never knew we hoarded so much until it came to packing up. At least we didn't bring it all with us.'

Richard smiled. 'Well, if you need anything, feel free to grab either of us if you see us out in the garden.'

'I will, thanks.' Juliette returned his smile.

'I was wondering if you fancied joining us for a barbecue tomorrow evening. I'm not sure if you have plans but the weather is glorious at the moment so you have to seize your chances.' He laughed. 'Although please feel free to say no if you have something on.'

Danny looked at Juliette and raised his eyebrows. She nodded at him.

'Sure, that would be great,' Danny replied.

'Fabulous.' Richard clapped his hands together. 'About seven?'

'Okay. Shall we bring anything with us?' Juliette asked as the men began to leave.

'Just yourselves.' Richard waved again before disappearing into the house.

'I hope this is a good idea,' Danny said.

'It'll be fine. If we don't get along, we'll have a few uncomfortable hours and we need never do it again.'

'Sounds good to me.' Danny grabbed her hand again. 'I feel like a teenager since I left London. I was counting down the hours before I caught the train. Then when I saw you, I couldn't wait to ravish you. Now I want to explore the garden, but with a view to having you in every corner of it.'

They ran across the lawn and through the gate into the field at the back. Juliette still couldn't believe it was all theirs. Three acres of fields surrounded by hedgerows. There was a brook and a farm further along but here it was extremely private. One day she hoped they would have a smallholding. With another child, or two, to help them to look after their menagerie. Her eyes brimmed with tears. She was so happy right now.

'Come on, Mrs Ansell,' Danny said, pushing her gently up against a tree. 'Get those shorts off.'

'What – here?'

'We're secluded.'

'I know but—'

He silenced her with his lips and as he fiddled with the buttons, she let him. Danny was right, no one could see them here. And it was fun. Just what their marriage needed. Time to make babies without either of them thinking about it.

EIGHT

Sarah had hidden her anxiety when Richard told her what he'd done.

'It's for show,' he told her. 'We welcome them once and they can't ever say we weren't hospitable then.'

'Let's hope the weather holds, so we can stay outside,' she replied.

'Well, we could hardly come inside, could we?'

Sarah scoffed under her breath. Everything was so secretive with Richard. They'd have to be careful, that was for sure.

Later, as they waited for their neighbours to arrive, Richard turned to her. 'You know we're only doing this because we have to? I won't allow anyone to get close to us. Do you understand?'

Sarah nodded, just as the couple from next door came out of their home. They went to greet them at the top of the drive.

Juliette was looking tanned in a strappy maxi dress, her hair in an updo. Although she wore make-up, Sarah could see the glow of happiness shining through because she was with Danny. She couldn't keep her eyes off him, or his off her as they smiled a greeting.

They looked good together, Juliette a little smaller than Danny in height, even with her wedged heels. Danny had dark wavy hair, shorn at the sides. He wore long shorts and a pale blue shirt. His watch was expensive, so were his loafers.

'Welcome to our humble abode.' Richard waved a hand across the garden.

'Not so humble,' Danny said. 'Don't you have six acres?'

'We do, there's a wood we can show you later.' He beckoned them forward. 'Shall we go through to the garden?'

They stepped onto a large lawned area surrounded by shrubbery. In front of the house on a patio, a table was laid out underneath a wooden gazebo, trails of ivy hanging over one side. There were salads and condiments of every sort in bowls spread over it. To the right, a barbecue was lit and hotting up, an array of prepared food sitting beside it in plastic boxes.

'This looks amazing,' Juliette said.

'Come, sit.' Richard smiled at his guests and then snapped his fingers at Sarah. 'Get drinks for everyone.'

'Of course,' Sarah replied. 'What would you both like?'

'Lager will do for me,' Danny said, passing him a carrier bag. 'I know you said not to bring anything, Richard, but I've never been one to arrive anywhere empty-handed.'

'Cheers.' Richard took it from him and gave it to Sarah.

'Do you need any help?' Juliette asked.

'No! It's fine,' Sarah snapped. Then she changed her tone. 'Thanks for asking. I won't be a moment.' In the kitchen, she opened two bottles of lager and poured wine for her and Juliette. She added lemonade to hers: it wouldn't do to get tipsy and let her mouth run away with her. She and Richard had rehearsed all the awkward questions that might come up during conversation and what to say next to steer them away. Even so, it was like treading on razor blades, having to watch every word she said. It was going to be a long evening; she was sure she wouldn't relax.

'How long have you lived and worked in London?' Richard asked when they were all finally seated.

'Born and bred in Islington,' Danny replied.

'I'm from the Midlands originally – Tamworth,' Juliette said. 'Have you both lived around here long?'

'Yes.' Richard lifted an empty bottle in the air. 'More beers,' he demanded, glancing at Sarah.

Sarah got to her feet.

Juliette did too. 'Please let me help.'

'It's fine.' She smiled. 'I won't be a moment.'

Inside the house, she checked to make sure everything was okay before re-joining them. She plonked down bottles in front of Danny and Richard and then produced another bottle of wine from the crook of her arm.

'Here you go.'

There was no thanks from Richard as he reached for his, but there were from Juliette and Danny. Sarah wondered what they were making of the strange couple next door. She could only imagine the conversation that would happen that night once they had left.

Over the next drink, they got to know each other a little. They spoke about their jobs, their lives and what had brought them to Mapleton.

'Have you thought of starting a family yet?' Richard asked.

It was an innocent question but the look of horror that shot from Juliette to Danny clearly showed that something awful had happened.

'I didn't mean to put my foot in it,' Richard backtracked.

Danny raised a hand before covering it with Juliette's. 'We lost our daughter last year. She was four years old.'

'I'm so sorry,' Sarah spoke in unison with Richard.

'She was here one week and gone the next,' Juliette said quietly. 'Meningitis. We're still coming to terms with it.'

'Is that why you've moved here?'

'Partly,' Danny said. 'A lot of it was to do with wanting a simpler life for now.'

'I can't begin to understand what you went through.' Richard looked sheepish.

'It's hard to tell people as it brings back the pain,' Danny replied. 'But now you know.'

Juliette was looking at the table the whole time the men were talking. She glanced up at Sarah, her eyes brimming with tears. Sarah felt them well up in her eyes too.

'Let's get this show on the road.' Richard stood up. 'Time to get the barbie going.'

Sarah watched as Danny gave Juliette a loving look of reassurance and her heart almost broke for them.

A few minutes later, the barbecue was in full swing. Juliette was teasing Richard and Danny as they both wanted to become barbecue man. The maudlin atmosphere had lifted.

After they'd eaten, Richard insisted on showing them around the woods. They walked through the gardens, admiring the mature flowers and rockeries, the tiny bridge to nowhere over the small pond that Richard had created last year.

As the two men walked ahead, Juliette fell into step by Sarah's side.

'I've had a wonderful time,' she said, linking arms with her.

The gesture took Sarah by surprise so she went along with it, knowing it would irritate Richard.

'Yes, it's been a lovely evening,' she said, relishing the feel of her so close. It was ages since she'd had a good conversation with a woman. Tonight they had chatted and she'd got to know a few things about the couple that would work well in her favour in the future.

'How about you and Richard? No children on the horizon for you two?'

'No, not yet.'

They entered the woods and followed a well-trodden pathway. Sarah enjoyed watching Juliette's reaction to it. Seeing it through someone else's eyes was amazing. Sarah had many a nightmare about it.

'Juliette!' Danny shouted to them. 'Come and look at this.'

The men waited while they caught up and came out into a clearing. There was almost a complete dome of branches overhead. It seemed as if they were in an igloo made out of trees. In the middle were a few stumps that could be used as seats, remnants of a fire in the middle of them.

'Wow, this is amazing.' Juliette spread out her arms and twirled around. There was hardly any light coming through and she stumbled. Danny came to her rescue and helped her up again.

'This is our special place, isn't it, Sarah?' Richard came towards her and reached for her hand.

She nodded.

'We often light a fire here and sit with a bottle of wine, don't we?'

'We do.' She found her voice at last.

'How many acres does the wood cover?' Danny asked, looking up at the trees.

'Three. I said I'd clear it but really the garden area is large enough and a wood, well, it's enchanting. I love to come here to be on my own. I get a lot of my ideas here, being at one with nature.'

Sarah could feel his fingers squeezing her hand tightly but she wouldn't complain. It would do no good. She had no doubt that he would have a go at her for something she'd said that evening. But he'd been just as bad with his loose lips.

Still, she wouldn't ever say that.

NINE

Juliette woke the next morning. The smell of bacon wafted into the room from downstairs as she heard it sizzling in the pan. Not wanting to move for fear of the hangover from hell rearing its ugly head, she snuggled down into the pillow for a few minutes. But then, unable to resist the sun shining in through the window and the breakfast aroma, she threw back the duvet and stood up. Her head wasn't too bad – yet.

She padded to the window to take in the view, still amazed that all the land behind them belonged to her and Danny. There were more fields in the distance and a further forest on the periphery before rolling hills behind it. The colours of the flora and fauna almost took her breath away. She wondered if it would feel as magical in the dreary winter months when it was raining and damp. Having said that, she couldn't wait for the first fall of snow. Oh, to run through the garden leaving footprints behind.

She opened a window and breathed in the air. There was nothing to hear except birdsong, an exceptionally loud blackbird full of the joys of the day.

To her right, she could just about see where they had been barbecuing the night before. She thought back to the strange evening. It had been fun and excruciating at the same time. Something she was hoping Danny wouldn't want to repeat too often. Of course she wanted to settle in and make new friends, but she didn't want anyone to be too close so that they made a nuisance of themselves. Coming from London, it would be quite a culture shock.

Making her way downstairs, she tiptoed into the kitchen and wrapped her arms around Danny as he put the finishing touches to the plates. They were both piled high with an English breakfast, coffee and juice set out on the patio. The doors were thrown open to let in the garden.

'Isn't this divine?' she said, giving him another squeeze before moving to grab the plates to take outside.

'It is!' Danny's eyes were shining. 'I haven't felt so relaxed in a good while.'

They went into the garden and ate their breakfast as they chatted about the night before.

'Don't you think it was weird how Richard put Sarah down at every opportunity?' Danny asked, tucking into a sausage.

Juliette's shoulders sagged. 'You noticed too? I thought it was because he was trying to make a good impression at first, but it did get a bit much.'

'At one time, I thought you were going to say something.' Danny laughed. 'You should have seen your face.'

'He was so rude! "Fetch another bottle of wine. Get me some more beer. Bring out the salad dressing." I had to stop myself from saying please, to make a point.'

'And yet when we explained about Emily, he was almost attentive, reaching across the table for her hand. I wonder why they don't have children. I asked Sarah but she said they weren't planning any at the moment.'

'Perhaps he's too old.'

'Yes, I'd love to know how that happened. They...' She paused to find the right words. 'I don't know. They just don't seem to fit very well. They sure are an odd couple.'

'And yet you invited them round next weekend.'

Juliette grimaced. 'Sorry, I'd forgotten that.'

'Well, I don't mind once in a while but I don't want to live in their pockets.'

'Me neither. Sarah seems nice though. Quiet, inoffensive.'

'That's when she could get a word in edgeways.' Danny took a sip of his coffee before continuing. 'Richard did love to talk about his work.'

'He's a creative. It's good to see someone so enthused.'

'I suppose. Although he wouldn't let us see inside his studio. I was hoping to get a look after he'd talked about it so much.'

'Maybe he'll show you at the next barbecue.' Juliette snorted.

'Which means I'll never see it, hopefully.'

They sat in companionable silence, listening to the birds and looking over the garden. It was so peaceful Juliette almost didn't want to ruin it. But she wanted to run something past Danny.

'I was thinking of a memorial for Emily. A corner of the garden perhaps, maybe a bench where we can go and sit to remember her.'

Danny leaned over to squeeze her hand. 'I think that's a great idea,' he said.

'Really? I thought you'd see it as morbid.'

'Not at all. Em is still a big part of us. And we need to have somewhere for her brother or sister to get to know about her. What better way? We can take a look around some garden centres this afternoon, if you like?'

'That would be great.'

'As long as we can stop off at the pub for Sunday lunch.'

'After what we've just eaten? Greedy guts.'

'I'm a growing man.' He patted his stomach, where there was not an ounce of fat. 'Besides, I had a run this morning while you were snoring your head off.'

'I do not snore!'

'How would you know? One of these nights I'm going to record you.'

She stood up, moved to sit on his lap and wrapped an arm around his neck. 'I wish it would feel as good as this forever,' she said. 'I almost forgot the pain for a moment there.'

'Forever is a long time,' Danny admonished. 'Although I'm very tempted to agree with you.'

'I might try and befriend Sarah a little. Would you mind?'

'Of course not.'

Juliette smiled and looked towards next door's house again. Perhaps she could get Sarah to come to the book club with her.

TEN

2015

True to his word, Richard delivered the painting at the weekend. I hung around at Martin's flat when he was due. It wasn't hard as I never liked being at home for any longer than to sleep and eat. I can't remember my dad at all now. Wouldn't know him if he walked straight past me. My mum's a waste of space too.

I don't know what we did to deserve such losers but we had to put up with a lot. Mum was always getting sacked from her job because she'd turn up drunk or wouldn't turn up at all most days. We often went without food, luckily getting free school meals to tide us over, and our house was always in need of a good clean. I never brought anyone round. Even cleaning up all the time wouldn't have made a difference. I tried, for a long time, but then it wasn't worth it.

Mum went to pot when she started snorting coke. I tried to get her away from it but the older she got, the worse she became. I thought it was kids who were supposed to go off the rails, but it was our mum.

So I spent a fair bit of time at Martin's place, to escape my own. When things got too rough, I'd sleep on his sofa. He rented a small flat above a row of shops. That wasn't much either but it was clean and tidy, and it always felt much safer. Especially since Nigel, Mum's latest fella, had moved in.

It took me ages to get ready. I wanted to make the very best impression the second time we met. I rooted out my favourite dress and strappy heels, spruced up my skin with fake tan, painted my nails and treated myself to a good haircut. I was gleaming from top to toe.

Richard's smile told me all I needed to know as he pulled up outside in a pickup truck. He was everything I'd remembered and more.

'Hi.' I waved as he unloaded the canvas. 'Did you find the address okay?'

'Sure, I have satnav.' Richard smiled as he unloaded the canvas.

I cursed inwardly. Of course he'd have satnav in his fancy pickup. I looked at it again, the registration new. I'd break my neck trying to get in and out of that.

Martin was even more pleased now the picture was with him. He handed over the money and Richard pocketed it.

'Thanks for doing this,' Martin said, shaking Richard's hand. 'My mum and dad will love it.'

'Happy to help.' Richard smiled at him. 'Would you like to grab a bite to eat with me before I head back?'

'I'll come,' I said, a little too excitedly.

'Not me,' Martin replied, failing to hide the smirk on his face. 'Things to do.'

'Well, if you're sure.'

'He's sure.' I grinned before he could be persuaded to join us.

We had a pub lunch, a 'getting to know you' chat over good food, and then he drove me back to the flat. I wasn't going to let him know where I lived.

'I'd like to see you again,' he said. 'I know there're miles between us but it's a forty-minute drive and I could pick you up at the weekend. Perhaps take you somewhere nice?'

'I'd like that,' I replied.

'You're not worried by the age gap?'

'How old are you?'

'I'm forty soon.'

'I'm twenty-seven.'

'Really? You don't look that old.'

'Well, I am,' I lied. I was only just twenty but he would never find out until it was too late.

'May I kiss you goodbye?'

I laughed, pulling him towards me as my answer. His lips grazed mine, he stared into my eyes and kissed me properly. Then we swapped phone numbers before he left.

'See you soon,' he shouted, waving as he drove off. I gave out a contented sigh. Today had been a good one.

* * *

The next weekend, he picked me up and, after a pub lunch, we went back to his house. I couldn't help but be nervous. He was twice my age and we were practically in the middle of nowhere. He could do anything to me and no one would ever know. I giggled to myself. Somehow I realised he'd be a true gent. You can tell that about someone, can't you? Whether or not you can trust them. I knew I could trust Richard.

After showing me around, we sat at the table drinking tea. I wanted wine but declined when he offered. It was only fair as he'd have to drive me home afterwards. That was going to take him the best part of an hour and a half.

'Can I ask you something?' I started.

'Sure.'

'How did you manage to buy a place like this? I mean it's huge! Did you marry and divorce a wealthy woman or are you self-made?'

'There was no woman involved, although I am divorced. I was married for seven years – no children. And even though I make a living from my art, my father died and left me a farm. I sold it and bought this place with the proceeds.'

'Oh, I'm sorry.'

'Don't be. It was a long time ago now.'

'How did he die?'

'Suicide. He shot himself.'

'No! That's so sad. How old was he?'

'Forty-seven. It was over twenty years ago now.'

'And you've lived here ever since?'

He nodded.

'I never knew my father. He left before me and my sister started school. He was a loser.'

'Mine wasn't all that nice either.' Richard smiled then. 'Do you have work in the morning?'

'I'm on a late shift. Two until ten.'

'Would you like to stay over?'

'I would.'

There was an eager anticipation for the rest of the day. And when we left the next morning, I realised I'd be coming back. Many times, perhaps even for good at one point. Because Richard Sykes-Morgan was definitely my ticket out of Derby.

ELEVEN

Despite asking, Sarah was reluctant to come to the book club with Juliette, so she set off on her own on Wednesday evening. The weather had been warm again but thunderstorms had arrived that afternoon, so the air was muggy and the sky grey. She stepped around a large puddle as she walked towards the village.

It was a beautiful evening. There was hardly a car that passed her. She wondered if she would get bored of the peace and tranquillity soon, miss the hustle and bustle of London. So for now she'd enjoy it. There was at least one decent coffee shop that she had visited which had passed muster. Their home-made cakes were divine. She planned to treat Danny to some that weekend.

The book club was being held in an upstairs room at the local pub, The Valley Arms. Even though she'd protested, Danny had dragged her there for Sunday lunch. They'd introduced themselves to the landlord, Malcolm, and Juliette had seen a notice about the book club on the wall by the side of the nook. It had saved her having to pop in at the hairdressers.

She went through the bar, smiling at the few people who were in there already. Malcolm spotted her and waved, then pointed to a door to her right. She nodded her thanks and went upstairs. It opened up into a large room with laminate flooring and three windows. A hatch in the wall had the roller shutter down and she assumed it might be a private bar for small functions.

There were five women sitting around two settees in the middle of the room. Most of them were in conversation with each other until she appeared. One of them stood up. She was in her early forties, had a motherly figure, with short blonde hair and immaculate make-up.

'Hello!' She beckoned her over. 'Do come and join us.'

Juliette's smile was shy as she did as she was told. The woman patted the seat next to her and she sat down.

'My name's Karen. I own the hairdressers on the high street.' She pointed in turn to the other women. 'That's Barbara – you might recognise her from the coffee shop.'

Barbara looked the same age as Karen but was small and thin. Dark hair to her blonde.

'I do, hi.'

'That's Rita whose husband owns the garage.' Karen pointed to an elderly lady with purple hair, her dress almost the same colour. She was wearing ballet shoes that seemed a little tight for her feet. Next to her was a teenager in denim dungaree shorts, a red vest and Converse shoes. Her long hair was tied back in a ponytail and she had the most amazing blue eyes.

'This is Freya, our youngest bookworm. Freya is at college, studying to be a journalist. And I assume you know Linda, as she's told us all about you.' Karen pointed to the woman sitting in the armchair.

'Oh?' Juliette raised her eyebrows. 'Hi.'

'Nothing is secret around here.' Linda smiled. 'Don't worry, I've only told them that you moved in recently and that you're on your own during the week.'

'And I saw you with a dishy man at the weekend,' Karen added. 'Your husband, partner?'

'Husband.'

'Lucky you.' Karen stood up. 'Let's get you something to drink. Red or white?'

'Red please. Is there a kitty?'

'Usually, but the first night you're always a guest. Besides, you haven't read the book we're about to discuss. Or have you?' She picked up a paperback. 'This one?'

'I have read it, actually,' Juliette said, thankfully. 'It was last year, but I remember it well. I've seen the film too. Cried like a baby.'

'Oh, me too.' Rita leaned across and touched her arm. 'I just adored Lou. She was such a likeable character. And to put herself through all that was commendable.'

'Through all what?' Karen asked, re-joining them and handing a glass to Juliette. 'Don't tell me you're talking about what she did for him.'

'No, I mean her broken heart.'

For the next fifteen minutes, Juliette listened to the women talk through their likes and dislikes, joining in occasionally. Within a few minutes, she had relaxed. They were a lively bunch.

'The woman next door to Juliette worked in the coffee shop for a few months,' Barbara said. 'Louisa.'

'Who's that?'

'She and Richard were an item. She was his previous partner.'

'Oh, I thought he'd been with Sarah for a long time. When was this?'

'A few years ago now. I assume she'd moved on as I haven't seen her in some time. She was a nice woman, although Richard kept a firm leash on her.' She smirked. 'Or at least he tried. She was a bit of a wild one at times. A hard worker though.'

By the time the book club was over, Juliette was both happy to leave and sad to do so. The night had been a success and, for once, it hadn't been hard to explain about Emily. Since Danny had told Richard and Sarah at the weekend, she'd realised she'd have to start doing the same. It had been painless, even with a lump in her throat. The women had asked to see photos and she'd shown them without tearing up.

* * *

Walking home a little worse for wear after Karen had dragged her into the lounge downstairs for another drink before she left, Juliette laughed to herself at some of the things they'd said. She had fitted in quite well, she thought, and had been invited to a charity coffee morning on Friday. She was going to have a go at making a cake to take along. Perhaps she could persuade Sarah next door to join her for an hour.

As she drew level with the house, she spotted Richard in his driveway and shouted hello to him. He turned in her direction but then put his head down again. Strange, she was sure he'd heard her. Thinking perhaps he didn't want company, she went inside. It was late after all. But there was still time to do one thing. She rang Danny.

'Hey, I'm home. I've had a great evening.'

'Not invited us to any more shindigs, have you?'

She could tell he was teasing her. He'd said as much in the pub at the weekend. After talking to the landlord, who had introduced them to some of the locals, he'd said he quite fancied himself joining in some sporting recreation.

'Well, you have a round of golf to play on Saturday morning and then a horse ride in the afternoon.'

'A horse ride.' She heard him snigger as she slipped off her shoes.

'And sailing on Sunday.'

'Ha ha, very funny.'

'You said you wanted to embrace the country life.'

'I did.' He sighed. 'I can't wait actually. It's so hard transitioning. Maybe I should go off sick while I serve my notice.'

'And come here to do what?'

'I could think of something.' His laugh was dirty. 'Hey, speaking of which, I've been headhunted. A firm in Staffordshire wants to meet with me. I might come down a day earlier next week and arrange to see them on Friday if it suits.'

'That's brilliant news, although I'm sure I'll be helping out in the market voluntarily by then.'

'I'm not sure if you're joking or not.'

'Neither am I,' she admitted. 'I got talked into it by Linda. She's in the next house, way down the lane. It's her field we join on to. She's quite nice.'

'I'm going.' Danny laughed. 'I can't stand all this neighbourly stuff.'

'You wait until you're here full-time. I shall get you roped into everything.'

Juliette missed him so much. It was nice to have him here at the weekends and she couldn't wait to collect him on Friday evening. Until then, his laughter cheered her up in between goodbyes.

Now, she needed some sleep. She switched off the kitchen light and stepped into the hallway, jumping when she saw the front door was wide open. She rushed to shut it, drawing across the lock as well as turning the double bolt. How the hell had she left that open? She could have sworn she'd closed it.

Scolding herself as she went upstairs, she blamed the women she'd spent the night with for letting her get tipsy. Well, she'd had a good night. She giggled. She could hardly blame herself, could she?

TWELVE

Juliette sat up in bed, gasping for breath. Sweat poured from her in the heat of the night. She looked around, disorientated until she realised she'd been having a nightmare. Then she flopped back with exhaustion, tears pouring down her face.

In her dream, she'd seen Emily in the hospital bed. The medical staff were holding her back as they attached tubes and machines to her daughter's tiny body. She'd wanted to reach out to her but the nurse kept wheeling the bed further away from her. No matter how fast she ran, Emily was out of reach.

Although her screams of anguish must have awoken her, it wasn't the first time. It had been a regular occurrence since Emily's death. It had been so unexpected. Then again, Juliette mused, when is sudden death anything but? The night before she fell ill, Emily had been excited to go to school to show off her new backpack. The next morning she'd been feeling ill with flu-like symptoms and a high temperature.

Juliette had kept her off school and Emily had slept for most of the day, under a duvet on the settee where she could keep an eye on her as she worked. But when Emily had gradually worsened, Juliette would never forget lifting up her pyjama top to find red blotches all over her skin. She'd called an ambulance and then she'd got Danny out of a meeting.

There'd been a frantic race to the hospital, meeting Danny outside the doors as the ambulance pulled up. They'd rushed through A&E with Emily lying on a trolley bed, so tiny, so vulnerable. As they'd parked her in a bay, Emily hadn't recognised either of her parents, no matter how many times they said who they were.

The memory of their daughter being in so much pain still haunted them. Meningitis had come on so quickly and was already destroying Emily's organs. She was put on life support for two days before they had to make the painful decision to switch it off. There was nothing left of Emily. She was being kept alive by machines. All their plans went out of the window in a matter of a week.

Juliette had done a lot of research into meningitis afterwards. Of course most parents knew the glass test, but Emily had had no rash until later. They thought she might survive by losing a limb or two and that would have been traumatic but fine. They could have dealt with that because Emily would still be with them. But Emily had dropped into a coma and hadn't come round from it. It had devastated them both, their families too. How could it have happened so quickly?

Juliette had sunk into a deep depression after the funeral, refusing to socialise with anyone. Staying at home, not going out unless absolutely necessary. Most people she knew had children and she realised that half the invitations she'd received before her death had been for Emily. Play dates, birthdays, trips to the cinema or ballpark. It was there she'd spent time talking to the other mums. It could no longer be a part of her life.

Her work suffered but she was able to get a friend to help until she felt more able to cope. Her clients had been understanding if things were a little late, although she made sure she never missed an important deadline for them.

That was when she and Danny started to talk about moving away from the city. At first it had been small talk but gradually their conversations about it had become longer. There were too many memories, too many missed opportunities to goad them. And at least here she could concentrate on her goal to have another child, when the time was right.

She got up and opened the curtains, already knowing the day was looking good by the sun's rays that were bursting through the edges of the window. She glanced outside: not a cloud in the sky. Great for working outside on the terrace.

After a quick shower she made her way downstairs, pausing halfway down. The front door was open. Her shoulders sank as she remembered closing it last night. Had the medication she'd taken been affected by the wine? Why would she come downstairs again, open the door and then go back to bed?

With the shake of her head, she closed the door and went through to the kitchen. But her hand shot to her mouth when she saw one of the French doors open too. Frantically she checked the rooms downstairs but there was nothing out of place. There couldn't have been anyone else inside the house. She prayed there hadn't been. It must have been her.

Whatever had happened, it unnerved her enough to ring and speak to Danny.

'Hello, it's early,' he replied. 'Everything okay?'

'Yes, fine,' she fibbed, unable to tell him now she had the opportunity. Hearing his voice was enough to ground her again. There must be some valid explanation. 'I thought I'd catch you before you go to work. What are you up to today?'

'The usual. Meetings interspersed with tube journeys. It's so hot here.'

'It is here too. I have a few hours of work, which I'm going to do in the garden, and then I'll mow the lawn.'

'I can do that at the weekend.'

'It's fine. I want to try out the new machine.'

There was a long sigh down the line. 'I wish I was there with you.'

'Me too, but it won't be long now.'

'I hope so. Have a good day.'

After disconnecting the call, Juliette sat down with a thump at the kitchen table. Why would she have been out in the garden in the middle of the night? Try as she might, there was no explanation. Unless she had started to sleepwalk all of a sudden?

THIRTEEN

It was half past seven and a glorious evening. Juliette wiped her brow as she walked down the garden back towards the house. The weather had been hot again and she was sad that Danny wasn't here to share it with her. Knowing their luck, it would probably rain by the weekend when he was home again.

There was a noise to her left and she turned her head just in time to see Richard heading into his studio. The wooden building stood proud, the size of four single garages with a roller shutter door at the far end. There was a mezzanine up into the eaves, where Richard did most of his work apparently.

Behind it, she could see a barn, old and dilapidated. She remembered it from their walk the other evening but forgot to ask him what he used it for.

As she stood thinking, Richard knocked on the window and beckoned her to him. She sighed: trust her to get caught out. She went over to the hedge to greet him.

'Hi there. Another grand week we're having, although I'm getting tired of having to water everything twice a day.' He smiled. 'How are you? Everything good next door?'

'Yes, fine thanks. I'm still not used to the silence. It's quite eerie at times.'

'How's Danny?'

'He's looking forward to coming here permanently.' She grinned. 'He's counting down the days.'

'Do you have a date yet?'

'Not yet but it will be no longer than a few months.'

'Excellent. I bet you can't wait.'

Juliette felt herself burning under his gaze as he stared at her.

He turned back to look at the house and then at her. 'I don't suppose you'd like to see my studio while you're here?'

'I'd love to.' Her laughter was inwards this time. Danny would be envious that she'd got in there first. Besides, she was intrigued to see inside.

'Well, come on round and I'll let you in.' He put a finger to his lips. 'Although don't tell Sarah. She's not allowed in here when I'm working.'

'Oh, I don't want to intrude.'

'I'm almost finished for the day. She's gone out for the evening anyway.'

'Anywhere nice?'

'Just for a glass of wine with a few friends.'

Juliette walked around to the garden next door. She wondered who Sarah had gone to see. She hadn't mentioned it, although she didn't have to tell her everything. She hoped she was having a good evening. She deserved to get out more.

Richard was waiting at the studio door. He really was a nice-looking man when he smiled. A tan suited him too. He was ageing well, fitting out his overall just so. Flecks of blue peppered his hair.

'Come on in.' He waved an arm and she stepped inside. Paint and paraphernalia were everywhere she looked. Lots of wooden shelving and cupboards to hide away essentials. There was an easel with a drawing on it, two more that were empty. A stool was next to the one Richard was working on. A large window overlooked the rear garden, as well as towards the woods. The view was incredible.

'What do you paint in?' she asked, hoping her ignorance of his art wouldn't show.

'Mostly oils. I draw in charcoal too. Those are my main passions.'

'You're clearly talented. I-I looked at your website.'

'Did you?'

She nodded, a little embarrassed as she wandered around admiring some of the drawings around the walls. 'Are these commissions you're working on?'

'Yes. I've had a few orders in recently. It's keeping me busy, and the wolf from the door.'

Juliette could never imagine him having money worries, not living in the property he owned.

'Are you artistic?' Richard asked.

'I was particularly fond of making stamps out of potatoes with Emily and blobbing them over a piece of paper. And drawing matchstick people.'

He smiled.

'I have a degree in media and art and wanted to do web design and marketing, but when it came to it, I found I was more of a numbers person, really.'

'Wouldn't do for us all to be the same. You have the most beautiful bone structure.'

'Oh.' Juliette's hand went up to her cheek. 'Thanks.'

Richard paused and then beckoned her towards the stairs. 'Let me show you what I'm working on at the moment.'

She followed him up, gasping as she saw the sunset on the canvas in front of her. 'Richard, that's amazing,' she exclaimed. 'It's like looking out of our bedroom window. I almost feel as if I could walk right into it.'

It was obviously the right answer as Richard beamed.

'Have you always wanted to be an artist?' she queried.

His face darkened for a fraction of a second before he was all charm again. 'Yes, but I never really got the opportunity to paint professionally until my father died.'

'Oh, I'm sorry.' Juliette gave out a sigh.

'Please don't be. We didn't get on that well. He had a farm which was passed on to me. I was working on it until then, but after his death I sold it and bought this place. It was then I decided to try and sell some of my earlier work, and I've never looked back.'

'Gosh, every cloud and all that.'

He smiled. 'Indeed.' From behind him, he pulled out a bottle of whisky. 'Join me?'

'I'd better be getting back soon.' She paused. 'Just a little one.'

He poured her a finger, himself two. They clinked glasses and looked out at the sunset.

'I love it here,' he said.

'I think I'm getting there,' she replied.

'We were worried when we heard the house had been sold. It had been empty for so long and we'd got used to having no neighbours close by.'

'Well, I hope we won't be too noisy for you. Do you and Sarah plan on having children?'

He shook his head. 'I'm not sure that would be a good idea.'

Juliette grimaced, wondering if she'd put her foot in it again.

'Sarah has a mild form of ME. She doesn't like to talk about it but she struggles with day-to-day tasks and she's forever tired. That's why you don't see her out much.'

'That's a shame.'

'I'm hoping she won't be too tired once she gets back this evening. I offered to drive her into the village but she insisted on walking. I know it isn't far for us, but for her, she will probably be in pain tomorrow.'

'Has she tried cognitive behaviour therapy? A friend of mine in London said it practically transformed her life. She'd tried over-the-counter medicine, even antidepressants but she said CBT made her more aware, therefore more in control of the symptoms. Perhaps Sarah could look into it.'

'I'll mention it to her, thanks.'

Juliette glanced at her watch and knocked back the rest of her drink. 'I have to go. Danny is ringing me in a few minutes.'

Richard nodded, taking the empty glass from her. 'It's been nice to have some company this evening, Juliette.'

She smiled and made her way downstairs. She said her good-byes and wandered back to her home, feeling his eyes on her. At the gate, she turned back and Richard was still watching her. He waved to her and she returned it before going inside.

FOURTEEN

The next morning, Juliette decided to tackle emptying some of the remaining boxes still piled up in the garage. Over the course of an hour, she emptied several, scattering contents throughout the house as she went through the different rooms. By the time she finished, there were only a few containers left to pop up in the loft, so she pulled down the ladder and took them up.

After pushing them to the back of the loft space under the eaves, she spotted Emily's box and her heart sank. She'd stored it out of the way purposely but now she'd seen it, she would have to look through its contents. It was full of her keepsakes. She pulled it towards her and sat cross-legged while she dived inside.

It was therapeutic as much as it was upsetting to see her things. Juliette's hand fell on Emily's favourite toy, a cuddly bear with jeans and a T-shirt that Emily had loved to dance around the kitchen with.

Tears stung her eyes as she pressed it to her nose, trying to find the scent of her daughter. But there was nothing there.

She flicked through a pile of books. For as long as she could remember, Emily had been a bookworm, much to her delight. She'd wanted a story read to her most evenings. Sometimes Danny had been home to do the honours, but a lot of the time it was down to her. Often she'd complained she was tired. How she'd love to be able to read to her one more time.

With a heavy heart, she closed the box and went downstairs. It had been put up there for a reason. She wasn't strong enough to look at it yet, but she would be in time.

Out in the garden again, she noticed Sarah standing beside a flower border. She stepped across to greet her, standing above the hedge that separated the gardens.

'Morning,' she said, looking down at Sarah. 'And another good one. I don't know how long this weather snap will last but I'm going to make the most of it. How are you?'

'I'm well, thanks. I've just been planting a few containers.' She held up her hands. 'I hate the feel of soil underneath my nails but I don't like wearing gloves either.'

'I don't know if I dare tackle our garden.' Juliette sighed. 'I'm sure I'd be pulling out flowers and leaving weeds behind.'

'You can learn a lot from books.' Sarah threw a thumb over her shoulder. 'I have a few in the house. Would you like to borrow them?'

Juliette beamed at her. 'That would be great, thank you! I really want to take an interest in it all.'

As Sarah disappeared into the house, Juliette shielded her eyes from the sun and looked across her neighbour's garden. It really was beautifully laid out. She knew Richard tended the lawns as she'd seen him sitting on the lawnmower.

As she stood there, he emerged from his studio. He got to her just as Sarah came out of the house with the books.

'Hi, Juliette. Everything good?'

'Yes, fine thanks,' she told him. 'I was just telling Sarah how I want to help out in my own garden and she offered to lend me some books.'

'Ah, yes, she has to refer to those often, don't you, my love?' Richard rolled his eyes as Sarah drew level. 'She's useless at remembering what to do from one year to the next.'

Sarah smiled at him and handed the books to Juliette without a word.

Juliette had to admire her restraint. She almost wanted to say something in Sarah's defence. Why was Richard so rude to her? Didn't he see what he was doing? It seemed very unlikely. Maybe she could give Sarah a few minutes' respite from him.

'I don't suppose you'd like to come round and point out some plants for me?' She turned to her. 'If you have time, you're welcome to have a coffee too.'

Juliette saw her glance at Richard. Was she after his approval? She saw him nod and Sarah smiled.

'I'd like that,' Sarah replied.

'How about this afternoon? Shall we say around two?'

'Maybe not this week. I have a lot to do.'

'Next week perhaps?' Juliette persisted.

'I'll let you know.'

'Okay.' She knew when she was beat. She held up the books. 'Well, thanks for these. I'll see what I can do with them. I'm sure I can learn a lot.'

* * *

In the kitchen, Juliette poured a glass of fresh orange and sat at the island for a few minutes. What a weird couple Richard and Sarah were. She couldn't get an edge on their relationship. Perhaps she was better not getting involved. But there was something so vulnerable about Sarah.

Afterwards, she rinsed out her glass and was about to put it on the drainer when a child's laughter came through the window. She glanced next door to see a little girl with long blonde hair. She wore a red summer dress and sandals with ankle socks. She was running up and down the garden like a free spirit.

Juliette wondered who she was. Richard and Sarah must have had visitors shortly after she'd spoken with them. She looked again but there was no one there that time. Going round to the front of the house, she couldn't see any cars in next door's drive except their own.

She gasped, hungrily taking in air as tears poured down her face. She was sure she'd seen a child. But she missed Emily so much that just the sight of a child could start her off. During their last weekend in London, they'd had to leave brunch at a coffee shop when a young girl had come in with her mum. She'd been wearing a coat similar to the one she'd bought Emily for her fifth birthday – the one she never got to wear – and it had set her off. She'd run out crying and, although Danny had soothed her, they'd gone straight home.

It was particularly hard to see other mothers with their children, which was why they'd chosen a property that wasn't near a school. She couldn't bear to see children walking past all the time. The school in Mapleton was at the other end of the village.

Grief weary, she climbed the stairs, deciding to lie on the bed for a while. It was cooler and she could cry herself to sleep. Grabbing a blanket for comfort, she covered herself over and closed her eyes. Images of Emily invaded her mind. The sound of her laughter. Her moods and tantrums. Her interest in clothes at such a young age.

Emily always had to have her hair just so. When the time was right, Juliette would let her choose what she wanted to wear. Emily could be a diva but she could make her smile with a single word, or a certain look. And she'd been clever too. She was going to be a star in the world. And now she was a star in the sky.

Juliette would make sure they got the garden memorial ready soon. It would give her something to do. A project to concentrate on. The books she'd borrowed would have to do for now.

Even though she was back at work from next week, she'd get going on it.

FIFTEEN

2015

Over the course of a few months, I began to spend more and more weekends with Richard. It was such a change from my shitty life during the week. His home and his outlook were so mature and I always felt content with him. Almost as if I was safe with him from the start.

After the childhood I'd had, it was great to sleep somewhere without having to be alert for anyone coming into my room. It was fabulous to see fresh food and lots of it instead of making myself toast or a sandwich with what was left in the fridge. Even working full-time, all my money went on food and rent.

Every time we drove back through the gate of White Oaks, I pictured myself returning as his wife, having children and living happily ever after. Well, everyone has to dream, don't they? I could, and I wanted it so much.

I'd never been in such a large house before. It took me a while to get used to the space. There were so many rooms. Then there was a quirky annexe in the garden as well as the studio. There were places in the house that I would certainly change. It could have done with a woman's touch. But maybe I'd get to add my taste to it one day.

Richard never worked when I was with him, which gave us

time to explore the property, the village and ourselves. Occasionally we dined out with a few of his friends but mostly there would be only the two of us. I didn't mind that. I cherished the time we had together as it was only a couple of times a week at that stage.

You could see people from the village glancing our way. I guess that might have been because of the age gap, but no one ever said anything to us about it. Everyone seemed to like Richard. Whenever we went into The Valley Arms, people would come and chat to him. It was a nice establishment too. Nothing like the dives I'd been used to drinking in.

I loved going into his studio. The smell of the paint and imagining him at work was what kept me going through the week until the following weekend. Often he would come to see me during the week, but I never invited him to see my mum or go to her house. I'd always get him to pick me up somewhere else and we'd drive to a nice pub not too far away. He never wanted to meet my family and friends anyway. I guess he wanted me all to himself, and for his home to be for my eyes only.

The day he took me by surprise, we'd been together for four months and were sitting out in the garden. The weather was quite warm but there was a storm brewing. You could feel it coming in, the air becoming oppressive and heavy.

We were walking in the woods as the heavens opened and he dragged me into the middle of it. There was a clearing and to my amazement it was hardly wet at all.

'It's so beautiful here.' I sighed. 'I wish I could stay forever.'

'Then why don't you?'

I turned to him and laughed. 'As if it were that easy.'

'Anything is possible.'

I slapped him playfully on his arm. 'Stop teasing.'

He pulled me into his arms and kissed me. 'I'm not. Stay here with me.'

'You mean move in with you?'

'I mean much more than that.'

He gazed into my eyes and I found myself falling into him. I couldn't help it. The man mesmerised me, like some kind of magician hypnotising his audience.

'Marry me,' he said.

I laughed.

I couldn't help it. Here I was, twenty years old, having confessed to him my real age a while ago, being asked to marry a man who I cared for and live in a home that I'd longed for. It was a dream come true.

I was waiting for the catch.

'I'm being serious,' Richard insisted after I said nothing. And then, in the middle of the woods, while the rain lashed around us, he dropped to one knee. 'Will you marry me?'

'Yes!' I waited for him to stand up again and then flew into his arms.

Richard was my everything. He made me feel secure, he was protective and always a gentleman. I didn't need anyone else. It was just us against the world.

We were wed three months later. There were only the two of us, plus a couple of witnesses. Richard didn't want the whole big affair and neither did I. I was aware of what my family and friends in Derby would think about the age gap and the quickness, so I didn't tell them.

We went away for a week, to Spain. It was romantic and fun. We were consumed by each other and I had never felt so content. I loved him, with all my heart. So what if everything had happened so suddenly? Richard and I were made for each other.

On our wedding day, he told me he'd been looking for someone like me for a long time. Like I mentioned, he was a charmer. And I fell for him, hook, line, and sinker. I was powerless to resist him.

Little did I know what I was letting myself in for. Had I known then what I know now, I would have realised how manipulative and dangerous he was. I wish I could have seen through his scheming, his lies and insecurities. I would have been safe, and far away if so.

SIXTEEN

Juliette was on the way back from the village. She'd been to stock up for Danny's return that evening, although she'd booked them into The Valley Arms for a meal as well. She wanted to introduce him to a few people she'd met over the last week. It would be good for him to have some friends to go out with once he moved here permanently.

It was almost the end of her first few weeks in Mapleton. It amazed her how easily she was adapting to her new life. But she still had an ache in her heart that Emily had never got the chance to spend time here too.

Passing her neighbour's home, she saw Linda in the garden and stopped to chat.

'I couldn't believe that storm last night,' she said. 'The wind made my window rattle. Did it wake you up too?'

'No, I slept right through it.' Juliette laughed. 'I suppose it's being used to living with the noise of a busy city that I tune out up here. Mind, I do wake up occasionally and then find it too quiet to get back to sleep. So swings and roundabouts.'

Linda smiled at her. 'Are you settling in now? It was lovely to see you at the book club.'

'Yes, I've surprised myself by getting out and about. I thought I might not without Danny, but everyone has been so welcoming.'

'How are you getting on with Richard and Sarah?'

'They seem okay.'

'Hmm. You know he's a lot older than her?'

'Yes, but I don't see a problem with—'

'She used to be the nanny.'

'Oh! I had no idea.'

'They had a little girl. She left with Louisa.'

Juliette frowned. 'Does he see his daughter?' Maybe that was the child she'd seen in their garden.

'Not that I know of. When I asked after them, Richard said they'd been having problems for a while, but it's obvious it was more than that.'

'I don't follow.'

'Well, Sarah was the nanny and she's still there.'

'Ah.' Juliette nodded her understanding. 'They never said.'

'I suppose it's not the thing one can bring up in conversation.'

'I suppose not.' Juliette checked her watch with gusto. 'I have to get a move on. I need to collect Danny from the station soon.'

'Ah, love's young dream.' Linda sighed. 'The look on your face when you say his name. I was like that with my Brian. He's been gone three years now, God rest his soul.'

'Oh, sorry to hear that.'

Linda waved away her comment. 'Don't be. He was a cheeky blighter.'

Juliette smiled, seeing the same look in Linda's eyes that she suspected would be in her own. She hoped she felt the same way about Danny when they were old and grey.

She said her goodbyes and let herself into her own house. In the kitchen, she looked out of the window. Next door's garden was empty. She couldn't see Richard or Sarah. And there was certainly no child. But there was some secrecy, she was sure.

* * *

On her way to pick Danny up from the station later that afternoon, Juliette spotted Richard next door. 'Richard, hi!' She waved to get his attention.

She was glad to see he came walking towards her.

'Everything all right?' he asked.

'Oh, yes, fine, thanks. I hope I'm not making too much noise.' It was the first thing she thought of to say. 'You must be used to the house being empty.'

'It's taking a while to adjust to you being in it. Not that we mind, I hasten to add.' He smiled. 'It's been lovely to hear voices coming from the garden.'

'So you don't have many visitors?' she probed, unable to help herself.

'We don't have any at all.'

'That's strange. I saw a little girl in your garden the other day. She was about Emily's age and so she startled me.' She stopped when she saw his face was like thunder. 'Sorry, again. I didn't mean to imply it was your fault.'

'I don't understand what you're talking about.'

'The child. It was a little girl. She wore a red dress, had blonde hair and was skipping around the garden.'

'When was this?'

'Monday. I saw her from my kitchen window.'

'There was no child in our garden on Monday.'

'Oh, I—'

'You're mistaken.' Richard made a point of checking his watch. 'I'd better be off. Lots to do. Catch you later.'

'Yes, okay. See you.'

Juliette stood for a while, watching him until he was out of sight. She frowned. What had that been about? She had seen a child in their garden. There was no need for him to deny it.

* * *

Once at the station, as she waited for Danny's train to arrive, she thought more about what Linda had said. It was interesting how neither Richard nor Sarah had corrected them when they assumed they were married.

'I have some gossip for you,' she said, almost as soon as she and Danny had got in the car to drive home. 'It's about Richard and Sarah. You know we said there was a big age gap between them? Well, Sarah was the nanny.'

'To who?' Danny asked.

Juliette laughed at the expression on his face as he tried to work out the logistics. 'Apparently, Richard had a wife and a young daughter. They left about a year ago and Sarah stayed on.'

'So they were having an affair?'

'More than likely. Else why wouldn't Sarah have left if the child had?'

'Interesting.'

'Even more so is that I saw a little girl in their garden the other day, but when I mentioned it to Richard, he denied it.'

Danny shook his head. 'That's weird.'

'I know. I wonder if his daughter came for a quick visit and he didn't want to tell me. I bet it's a touchy subject.'

'I can imagine.'

'Should we invite them to the pub this evening? It's going to be fun getting to know people.'

'So you can interrogate them?'

'No! Well, yes a little.' She laughed.

Danny did too. 'When we were in London, we didn't know half the neighbours in the street and yet here you are content to get to know ours. I haven't seen you so happy since... well, you know.'

'There's something different about a village. I'm really starting to love it here in Mapleton. It's going to be our perfect home.'

* * *

Sarah was coming downstairs when Richard came into the kitchen. As she joined him, she could tell by the way he threw his keys on the table that something had annoyed him. She wasn't going to ask what, knowing full well he'd tell her about it anyway.

'I bumped into Juliette. She's asking questions already. We need to be more careful.'

Sarah was intrigued then. 'Asking questions about what?'

'She claims she saw a child in the garden.'

'Well, she's wrong about that.'

'She is.' He paused for a moment. 'I want you to invite yourself for that coffee next week. Get some cakes from the village and see what you can find out. Are they here permanently or just to see if they can settle out of London? Perhaps they intend to spend a lot of time in the city rather than here? Anything that will work in our favour.'

'She seems nice to me. I'm sure she'll be no trouble.'

'Know that for certain, do you?' Richard growled. 'They've barely moved in and all of a sudden, you act as if Juliette is a long-lost friend that you share a history with.'

'No, I was saying that—'

'Well, don't. Just mind your own business but find out what you can.'

He left her then and she made a coffee, taking it through to the living room. Of all the rooms in the house, this was Sarah's favourite. Most of the back wall was made up of bi-folding doors that let the garden into the front room when they were open. It was sheer bliss to sit with the breeze blowing on you on hot evenings, either watching the TV or reading a book. An inglenook fireplace stood on the opposite wall. Two brown, soft leather settees facing each other, a pile of cushions thrown on top of them in creams and oranges. She'd had no hand in the decoration, it had been like this since before she'd arrived. And yet, she liked it all.

While Richard was out of the way, Sarah took the opportunity to relax. She slipped off her shoes and rested her feet on the coffee table, gazing out onto the garden as she drank her drink. She wasn't sure she would ever tire of the view, the way it made her feel as she gazed out onto the greenery. Yet she hoped it wasn't all going to be for nothing. Richard had some funny ways of keeping control and she didn't want to push him too much.

She also knew better than to question his sudden interest in Juliette. Was it because he thought she was getting too close? Or did he like her? Juliette was a beautiful woman; Sarah knew his feelings for her were waning but she wasn't sure she wanted to do anything about it. Keeping the peace was what she was interested in, for as long as it took.

Still, if Richard had set his sights on Juliette, it was a little too close to home for her liking. But that wouldn't stop him. He would see it as a challenge. Although she wasn't sure Juliette would fall for his charms, no matter if he did throw himself at her.

Juliette and Danny seemed very much in love. Sarah had been envious since meeting them, their close bond oozing from them. They seemed content in each other's company, not a couple who slobber over each other and make people feel uncomfortable. Just a hand on an arm during conversation, a shared smile between the two of them. It made her realise what she'd been missing.

Was that how it should be? she wondered. There hadn't been many men in Sarah's life to compare with really. She did tire of Richard's constant attention and nit-picking though. After so long with him, she thought she knew his every move, but he would always surprise her, being one step ahead.

It could get lonely at White Oaks but she was determined to stick it out. Living with Richard was now both a nightmare and a challenge.

But she was in this for however long it took.

SEVENTEEN

Juliette was in the kitchen. She'd almost finished for the day after getting all her invoices paid and a few emails out to her clients. The doors were open to the garden and, despite the weather breaking finally, it was still warm if overcast. She reckoned they might have another storm later that evening. It was so muggy.

Emily would have loved this garden. Juliette went over to the area that they had designated for her bench. They'd commissioned an engraved plaque and they'd planted flowers and shrubs around the edge of a stone circle they had paved together. There was a lantern so she could sit there at night too, and she'd ordered a few blankets and cushions to make it cosy. It was going to look lovely once the bench was in place.

Danny had suggested opening a bottle of champagne and raising a toast to the future when everything was finished. It was a nice suggestion, but she'd said no. It seemed too final. Still, at least she'd have somewhere to come when she was missing Emily so much it hurt to breathe.

She thought back to the child she had seen in the garden next door. Emily had worn a red dress last summer. Juliette remembered she'd chosen it herself for her friend Tilly's birthday party. She'd loved it so much that she'd wanted to sleep in it that night.

Worn out and tired, Juliette had compromised and allowed her to wear it the next day too. It was a party dress for special occasions. She had looked silly walking around the supermarket with her as they did the weekly shop, but Emily loved it. She said she felt like a princess.

Which begged the question, was she missing Emily so much she wanted to see a child next door?

She pressed a hand to her eyes as they began to leak again. Emily wouldn't want her to be like this. She had to be brave for her little girl. And as horrible as it seemed, she had to be strong to ensure she became pregnant again.

Mentally, she had her fingers tightly crossed that Danny would get the job he'd been interviewed for. He'd come back from the meeting excited and buoyed up about the future and his prospects. His face had lit up as he'd talked her through it, saying he'd had a tour of the offices and met many of the staff he'd hopefully be working with.

She couldn't believe how neither of them were missing their London lives. Of course, Danny still had his to a degree but he was a different man when she saw him at the weekends. It had been a good move. Now all they needed was a new addition to the family. And maybe a dog too, she laughed to herself.

Her head snapped to the right, alert to the sound of singing. It was coming from next door. Surely that couldn't be a coincidence? She grabbed her phone and tiptoed over the grass towards the hedgerow. She peeped over, hoping to go unnoticed.

There. She could hear it again. But she couldn't see the little girl. Then the noise stopped.

Juliette sat on the lawn for a moment, waiting. For what? She didn't know. Was she so desperate for a child of her own that she would imagine seeing one next door? She wasn't sure.

But then a child ran across the garden. She *hadn't* been seeing things. Quickly, she took a photo, managing to capture the back of the little girl. She checked the image. She had something to show

Danny now. Rather than send it to him, she decided to keep it for when he was back home.

She went to bed thinking about the little girl, and when she got up the next morning, she checked her phone.

There was no image of a child.

She scrolled through, wondering if it had disappeared from her screen but was available in the cloud. But it had gone. She groaned out loud.

Surely she hadn't imagined it? Was she now hallucinating during the day, seeing someone who didn't exist? She thought the photo would prove she wasn't mistaken. Now the lack of it could seem that she very much was.

EIGHTEEN

Juliette had been surprised when Richard shouted her over the next morning and mentioned that Sarah would like to join her for coffee. She was busy with clients but arranged a quick lunch for the two of them.

She made a salad bowl, boiled some new potatoes and put out a tray of cheese and hams to choose from. Fresh bread had been in the cupboard already.

She was looking forward to having some company if truth be told. She'd found it particularly hard to be by herself this week.

'It's lovely to see you,' Juliette said as she sat in her garden with Sarah. 'I start talking to myself from the middle of the week.'

'So it's lonely without Danny?'

'Well.' She sniggered. 'Sometimes it's much more peaceful than if he was here.'

'You seem to be fitting into village life from what I can see.'

'Yes, the book club was fun and I love nipping to the coffee shop with my laptop. What do you do during the day?'

Juliette had dropped it in so subtly but she'd been dying to ask. Perhaps now Sarah would come forward about being the nanny.

'I paint too,' Sarah replied. 'Landscapes mostly. Richard will take them to sell when he does craft shows. They're not much but I get pocket money for them. Saves me from being totally reliant on him.'

'I suppose.' She paused. 'What did you do before you came here?'

'I worked in a factory. When I met Richard, he didn't want me to work and I was happy to leave that place behind.'

'I expect you miss the camaraderie? Some of the places I've worked in we ended up being like family.'

'I wasn't really close to anyone.'

A silence dropped between them and for some reason, Juliette sensed the conversation was over. She decided to jump in with what she wanted to ask her.

'Did Richard tell you about the child I thought I saw in your garden?'

Sarah took a sip from her drink before replying. 'He did mention it. No one has visited us for quite some time now.'

'I know. I'm sorry. I really thought I saw a little girl. And then last night, I thought I heard crying. I was out in the garden and well, the noise travels as it's so quiet, doesn't it? I think I'm going mad at times.' Juliette couldn't bring herself to mention the disappearing photograph.

'Maybe it's the foxes, or a cat?' Sarah offered.

'Maybe.' It was good of her to try and make her feel better, but it wasn't an animal she'd heard.

'It will take a long time to get over your daughter's death, if you ever do,' Sarah added.

There was another pause as Juliette waited for her to speak again. It was a good opportunity for her to say she missed Richard's daughter.

But Sarah didn't say anything. Instead she looked at her watch.

'Would you like a drop of wine?' Juliette asked, not wanting her to leave just yet.

'Oh, no, I—'

'I insist.'

Juliette went to fetch a bottle and came out moments later to find Richard standing next to Sarah.

'Oh, hi. Would you like to join us for a sneaky afternoon drink?' She pressed her index finger and thumb together. 'Just a little one.'

'No, thanks.' His smile was saccharine. 'Work to do, you know. Which is what I came to remind Sarah about. I have some errands to run this afternoon.'

'She'll be fine here with me,' Juliette said as she poured a glass of wine. 'I'll look after her.' She was about to add the wine to another glass when Richard put his hand across it.

'I don't like to leave an empty house,' he said.

Juliette sniggered. 'I'm sure it's capable of looking after itself.'

Sarah wiped at her mouth with her napkin and pushed out her chair. 'I'd best get back,' she said, standing up. 'Richard is right. I do have a lot of work to do.'

Sarah wouldn't meet her eye. Juliette had seen the glances passing between them and decided it wouldn't be wise to interfere.

'We'll only be another half an hour or so, Richard,' she went on regardless. 'I'm sure that's okay with you, isn't it?'

Richard glared at her, then nodded.

'Of course.' He looked at Sarah. 'Please don't be late.'

Once they were alone again, Juliette poured wine into the empty glass. 'A little won't hurt, while he doesn't know about it,' she said, winking at Sarah. 'Cheers.'

As they settled back into small talk, Juliette kept glancing at Sarah. There was something not right about the control Richard exerted on her but who was she to get involved? If that was how they chose to live, then so be it.

Yet it did make her wonder why he'd suggested Sarah came round for coffee. He really blew hot and cold, as if he couldn't figure out whether he should let Sarah out of his sight or not. She'd hate to be in a relationship like that.

So if she could give the woman a little reprieve from his oppression, then surely that couldn't be a bad thing.

NINETEEN

2016

I absolutely loved living in White Oaks with Richard now that we were married. I had a choice of rooms to sit in, a garden to walk around and a village a few minutes away that I could wander round and not feel like a cheapskate. It was nothing like the life I had left behind in Derby, and more to do with the sort of lifestyle I had dreamed about. Somewhere safe, warm, clean, with lots of food and no malice.

I set about looking for a job, but Richard wasn't too enamoured with the idea. At first he gave me money for shopping, and I cleaned the house as much as I could to feel like I was contributing. But one morning when I was in the village, I saw a notice in the coffee shop for a part-time assistant and went inside to find out more.

'Hi, I've come about the job advertised in the window.'

'Ah, right.' The woman behind the counter smiled. 'As you can see, I'm a bit busy now. Can you call, say, at half past four?'

'Sure.' I turned to go as she served another customer but, on impulse, I decided to clear a few tables. The woman was rushed off her feet and it wouldn't take me more than a few minutes.

As I got back to the counter for the first time, my hands full of dishes, I placed them at the end and she beamed at me. The job was done in no time and I popped the final load down. The small queue had been sorted and everyone was sitting down enjoying their beverages.

'Thanks ever so much for that,' the woman said, holding out a hand to me. 'I'm Barbara. I've seen you in here a few times, haven't I?'

'Yes, I only live a few minutes' walk away.'

'Well, now we have time, would you like a coffee and a piece of cake? I'll have to keep my eye on things but there's a lull because you've helped me out.'

We chatted and got to know each other and before I'd eaten the most delicious piece of coffee and walnut cake, she'd offered me a month's trial. I was delighted. I might have been on to a good thing with Richard but I'm not a total scrounger.

* * *

'I have a job!' I told Richard once I was back home. 'At the coffee shop. Fifteen hours a week. I'm—'

'I said you don't need one. I told you I would provide for you.'

'I can't hang around here all day,' I protested. 'You're usually in your studio and it's boring.'

'Then get a hobby.'

'I don't need a hobby. I need a job.'

'Being a skivvy for other people is not exactly a career.'

I wasn't going to be perturbed. 'Well, I don't care what you think, I'm going to do it.'

'Don't expect me to be happy about it.'

'I thought you'd be pleased I was bringing in some money.' I folded my arms like a petulant child.

'Fifteen hours with a piddly rate of pay per hour is hardly contributing to anything.' Richard swept his hand around the room. 'Besides, there's plenty to do in the house.'

'I don't mind cleaning up but I'm not a housekeeper.'

'It's a huge property and needs looking after.'

'Well, I'll fit that in too.' I gave him one of my little-girl-lost looks. 'Please don't be mad.' I hugged him. 'I don't want to argue over something so trivial.'

He was like a brick as I tried to get some warmth from him.

'Please yourself.' He pushed me away. 'But I don't want you gossiping about anything, do you hear?'

I paused. 'What are you really scared of? That people will talk about us?'

'Not at all. I doubt anyone would be interested.'

'Exactly.' I smiled at him then. He would get used to the idea in time.

Over the next month, I went to work in the coffee shop for three hours per day, over the busiest lunch period. I soon got to know lots of people and would regale Richard with tales of who was doing what and with whom. Pretty soon, I knew nearly everything that was going on in the village and felt I had a group of friends besides Richard.

I never told him that I was questioned about our relationship so many times. I never told anyone more than we were married. There was really nothing to tell back then.

But that part-time job was the start of things if I think about it now. Richard hadn't liked me taking control. Pretty soon, he was arguing with me about anything I did, big or small. I tried so hard to do things right for him, and before he moaned at me, but he was always one step ahead.

I hadn't expected things to change so much once we were married, but Richard began to show his true colours quite soon after. It took me by surprise how much he'd lured me in, like a fly into a spider's web, and made me his property.

And then when I started to feel ill, I hadn't realised how involved he was with that either.

TWENTY

Danny was washing his car when he heard someone shout his name. He turned to see Richard at the bottom of the drive and walked down to greet him.

'How are you doing?' Richard asked. 'Commuting life suiting you?'

'Actually, yes, it is.' Danny nodded. 'Coming up here every weekend gives me time to switch off from work. I don't think I've ever done that before.'

Richard nodded. He ran a hand through his hair. 'Could I talk to you about something?'

'Sure.'

'It's a bit sensitive but I thought you should know. Juliette asked me about a child she'd seen in our garden the other day. She said she saw a little girl with blonde hair, wearing a red dress. The thing is, Danny, there hasn't been a child in our garden for a good while.'

'Oh! That's strange.'

'This may sound silly, but I took this photo.' Richard passed his phone to Danny.

Danny looked at the screen. There was a red T-shirt on the washing line, the yellow buds of a magnolia tree in the background.

'I just wonder if it was this she saw and...' Richard paused.

'She mistook it for a child because she wanted to,' Danny finished the sentence for him.

'Yes. I've thought about it all week, whether to tell you or not.'

'I'm glad that you have.' He handed back his phone. 'Juliette hasn't mentioned anything to me about it.'

'Perhaps she's realised and doesn't want to say.'

'Perhaps so.' Danny felt deceitful lying about Juliette.

'I can imagine as a mother she took the death of her child hard,' Richard went on. 'Both of you, really.'

Danny said nothing. Richard was right. It hadn't just affected Juliette. But he supposed as a mother she had more of a bond with their daughter.

'We're just setting up a seating area in the garden where we can sit and remember her,' he said. 'Emily was a busy child, always up to something. She would have loved all this space to play in. I miss her too.'

'Danny? Oh, hi, Richard.'

Danny turned to see Juliette in the doorway. She waved but stayed where she was.

'I'd better see what she wants.' Danny threw his thumb over his shoulder. 'Speak soon, yeah?'

'Yeah.' Richard nodded. 'Hope everything is okay about what we discussed.'

'It's fine. Thanks for telling me.'

* * *

Inside the house, Danny found Juliette hanging up a pair of curtains at the window. 'Could you hold the bottom of these while I thread them through the poll, please? They're so heavy, my arms are aching.'

'Here, let me hang them for you.'

'My hero.' She rolled her eyes before grinning, stepping down from the ladder. 'What did Richard want?'

He'd thought he wouldn't say anything about it straight away, but he couldn't help himself. 'He mentioned the child you allegedly saw in the garden.'

'There was no alleged,' Juliette said. 'I saw a little girl.'

'That's the thing, Jules. He showed me a photo of a red T-shirt hanging on the line. He says you were mistaken.'

Juliette gasped. 'And you believe him?'

'Well, I... don't you think it's weird that he's denying it?'

'What *I* find strange is you're saying you don't believe me over someone you've met a handful of times.'

'It's not that. It's – what if there wasn't a child and your tablets are making you see things? Are there any side effects?'

'I don't have any, and you know that.'

'But you've been under a lot of stress lately and it just explains things. Perhaps you'd be best getting it checked out. Have you registered at the local surgery yet?'

'No.' Juliette folded her arms.

'Perhaps you could get an appointment in London and come to stay with me for a week?'

'I have work to do.'

'It's portable.'

She shook her head.

He sighed. 'Next week then?'

'I'm telling you I saw a child. Why won't you believe me?' Juliette burst into tears.

Danny dropped to the floor with one stride and pulled her into his arms. 'I'm sorry,' he said. 'I thought perhaps you were overdoing things and that you were thinking of Emily.'

'I'm always thinking of Emily,' she sobbed.

'I know. Me too.' He waited for her tears to subside, thinking what a shit he'd been. But he was worried about her. He had seen the photo. There was no child next door. She must have been mistaken. There could be no other explanation.

* * *

'What did you find out?' Sarah asked Richard when he came into the house.

'Nothing. I planted an idea in his head that Juliette was imagining a child in our garden. Danny's worried her grief is overtaking her.'

'That's cruel.'

'It is.' Richard smirked.

'So you're trying to get Juliette to suspect that something is going on?' she asked.

'Of course not. I just want her to think she's seeing things. Then if she hears anything untoward, she'll dismiss it and we'll be home and dry. There is a method in my madness, you know.'

'Madness being the optimum word,' she muttered.

'What was that?' He glared at her.

'Nothing.'

He grabbed her roughly by the chin, squeezing hard. 'Watch that mouth of yours.'

They stood in silence, as if he was daring her to speak out again. She wouldn't give him the satisfaction of that, nor seeing how much it hurt.

Finally, he let her go.

'What are you cooking for supper?' he asked, the moment seemingly over.

'I thought a nice steak, new potatoes and I have some fresh veg from the garden.'

'Great. I'll leave you to it. Make sure everything is done for six p.m. I'll be working until then. Don't disturb me. And make sure nothing else does, either.'

Sarah nodded curtly, blowing out her breath as he left the room. She relaxed again when he'd gone. He created such an oppressive atmosphere at times. Never had she been so glad he had the studio to work in, to give her some peace during the days.

TWENTY-ONE

With Danny coming up every weekend, Juliette had given herself a project to either find somewhere to visit locally, or else book in an evening or lunch at a different place. This weekend they were going to The Traveller's Rest, Stanley.

Inside the pub, they were shown into the restaurant area and seated at a table near the window.

'According to the menu, they do a cracking pie night every Monday, so the first one that you're here, I'll book in for that,' Juliette said as she studied what to have that night. 'It's very popular.'

'Sounds good to me.' Danny reached for her hand. 'There's a bank holiday coming up. Perhaps then?'

'I'm counting the days.'

'For the pie?'

'Obviously.' Juliette giggled. 'I'm so pleased it's all gone well for you. Are you nervous about starting with a new firm?'

'I think it's you who should be worried, seeing as I'll be working from home two days a week. Won't I cramp your style?'

'I'm sure I can manage. Besides, once we're both here, our bills and outgoings will be less, so maybe I won't have to work every day of the week.' Already she'd taken to leaving Friday afternoons free and her weekends were kept clear for when Danny was around, so the life-work balance had shifted in the right direction for them.

'What are you having?' She looked up from the menu. 'I think I'm going to try the chicken.'

'I'm going to have... steak.' He snapped it shut.

'So predictable.'

They placed their orders and wine was poured. Danny had a lemonade too.

'Have you thought any more about...' Juliette stopped, her eyes widening with disbelief.

'What is it?'

'It's Richard, from next door. And he's with another woman.'

Danny turned his head.

'Don't look!' she whispered loudly.

'What am I supposed to do? Face you and not move all evening?' He shook his head. 'Besides, it might be completely innocent.'

Juliette put a hand to her face. 'I don't know why I'm blushing. I'm not doing anything I shouldn't be.'

'What's the woman like?'

'Mid-twenties, tall, blonde hair. Very attractive.'

'He must be a charmer, getting them so young.'

'If I didn't know you, I'd say you were envious.'

'Naw, but I am going to have a quick look.' He did so just as Richard leaned over to kiss the woman across the table.

'I told you!' Juliette said. 'That's definitely not business.'

The waitress came across with their orders and bustled around them as they got ready to eat.

'What's he doing now?' Danny asked.

'I wish I'd let you sit facing the room,' she said. 'I'm right in his eyeline and I can't stop looking.'

'Well, I suppose it's none of our business what he gets up to. It's not as if it's doing us any harm.'

'But what about Sarah? I've a good mind to make it obvious we can see him, watch his face when he knows he's been caught.'

'It's nothing to do with us,' Danny repeated. 'Let's eat.'

Juliette gave Richard one last glance before shaking her head. 'I hope he hasn't seen us, actually. That would make things very awkward. Oh, they're standing up. Looks like they're going.'

'Has he spotted you now?'

'I don't think so.' She sat still while she watched the couple disappear and then she gave out a huge sigh of relief. 'They've gone.'

'Good. Now we can concentrate on us.'

'Yes, tell me about the new job.'

* * *

Sarah had been on her own since seven thirty that evening. It was nearly eleven and she was wondering what Richard had been up to. He'd said he was going to The Valley Arms, but she wasn't entirely sure that was true. Obviously she couldn't follow him, but she did wonder if he was out with another woman again.

It wasn't as if she didn't know there were others. It was more how blatant he was about it. Sometimes he even took women out around the village. It was as if he wanted to show everyone that he'd still got it. Why he'd want to do that was beyond her. But still, it did give her a little peace every once in a while. Until her anger got the better of her.

He'd disappear most evenings now, leaving her alone. She missed the affection they used to share. When they'd first got together everything had been good. Richard had been attentive and loving. How different things were now.

The first time she had suspected he'd been with someone else was when he bought new clothes and a different brand from his usual aftershave. He'd had a haircut too. She'd questioned him about it but he'd denied it was anything more than he fancied a change. A couple of days later, she'd been in the village and had seen him flirting with a young woman. They were in the car park. He was running a hand along her arm, the way he used to do with her. The woman had laughed at something he'd said and mirrored his actions. Anyone from a distance could see that they were most likely fucking.

He'd denied anything was going on when she'd questioned him and had thought better of asking him anything again once she'd had the wrath of a backhander. It had still stung though that she wasn't enough for him any more. Especially after what she had done for him.

Finally, she heard Richard's car pull into the drive. She didn't get up to greet him, waiting for him to show his face in the living room. He always did, trying to rile her into showing some emotion. Other than a few comments she'd throw at him, she'd never given him the satisfaction.

'I wasn't expecting you to be up,' he said, flopping down into the armchair with a stupid grin on his face.

'Where have you been?'

'Out and about.'

'On your own?'

'Yes, of course.'

He caught her rolling her eyes and laughed.

'You're seeing someone else, aren't you?'

'It's none of your business. You have a roof over your head. It doesn't mean that you own me.'

She sniffed. 'I can smell her perfume.'

'Give it a rest. What I get up to outside of the house is nothing to do with you.'

'Maybe I should do the same.'

Richard sighed. 'You're very good at getting what you want, aren't you?'

'What do you mean?'

'If you want me to fuck you, then I will.'

She left the room but he followed her into the kitchen. He was predictable as he pulled her into his arms, kissing her so forcefully she knew her lips would feel bruised afterwards. His hands reached for her T-shirt and pulled it out of her jeans.

She responded in the way she knew he liked, getting him excited so that he would be quick. Like they mostly did now, he bent her over the table and took her from behind. She wondered if he ever imagined she was someone else. She often closed her eyes and dreamed of Henry Cavill. Imagining Richard was another man almost took away the forceful nature of his actions.

The sex was functional, and over and done with quickly. It was the one thing she hated but endured. She used to love it, was after it all the time at first. But now, as the feeling she was going to be replaced had become stronger over the past few weeks, her fighting spirit was building. She needed to start thinking of her future, their future. Things couldn't go on this way indefinitely.

Sarah would always let Richard think he had the upper hand. Even if it meant shutting herself off to what he was doing while she was biding her time.

TWENTY-TWO

Juliette dropped onto the settee with a grateful sigh. She reached for her glass of wine and took a sip. Today had been a good day and she decided to celebrate on her own.

She had secured three clients that morning, on a monthly retainer. Retainers gave her the peace of mind that money would be coming in on a regular basis, at least for the foreseeable future. Working for yourself was most people's dream but the reality was a lot harder than it seemed. Often in her line of work it was feast or famine when it came to earning money. She saved a lot in preparation but it sometimes meant she didn't treat herself enough as she was wary of spending too much.

Juliette was getting used to the house now. Most things had been unpacked and put in their place, only the odd box hanging around in the garage. They'd yet to decorate it to their taste but for now she was fine as most of the walls had been replastered and painted magnolia. Before the house became theirs, the electrics had been renewed too. Juliette was glad she hadn't had to live through the mess of that.

It was nice to see familiar belongings in the living room that instantly made it feel like home. Two navy three-seaters, a coffee table in between. A yellow throw was over the one they hardly used, scatter cushions on them both.

The standard lamp in the corner had been a present from Danny's parents. The canary yellow curtains they'd brought with them from their previous house had surprisingly fitted the large bay window at the front of the room, which itself threw sunlight across the room in the late afternoon.

She gazed at the collection of photos on the back wall. Each one was of Emily on her birthdays. Juliette saw the smiles of delight on her daughter's face on the fourth one. The look of glee as she was ready to blow out the candles on her caterpillar cake. She was such a beautiful child. Never in her wildest dreams did Juliette think she wouldn't get to see her fifth year out. Before she started to feel too low, she decided to see if Danny was around for a chat.

After catching up with him on the phone, she was watching a rerun of *Midsomer Murders* when she heard a sound that made her jump. It was as if something, or someone had banged on a window. She froze, listening for it to happen again. When it didn't, she sighed with relief. Perhaps it was next door, nothing to worry about.

When she heard it again, she sat up sharply. It was the one thing she disliked about living alone. An overactive imagination with every bang, creak or shout. When Danny had first gone back to London, it had taken her an age to get used to the sighs of the house as it settled each night. The noise from the traffic on the road was distant now, but back in the city it seemed to invade her mind and come into her bedroom. Her senses had been on high alert and she'd often walked around during the night as she'd been unable to settle.

Hoping it was the neighbourhood cat who'd come to see if she'd left out any scraps, she got to her feet. Holding her head high to feel more confident than she felt, she went through to the kitchen, the source of the sound. She left off the light, seeing straight out into the garden into the dark. The security light at the bottom of the garden had been set off. She peered out but could see nothing. Perhaps it was the cat after all.

But as she turned away, she caught a shadow. *Was* someone out there? She covered her mouth, afraid to scream out. Even though she knew she shouldn't scare herself, she stared out of the window again. Almost willing a shadow to move, or a figure to re-emerge. But nothing happened.

Had she seen someone?

If she had, whoever it might have been would be well gone now, she assumed, probably breaking into someone else's property, whereas she would most likely be awake all night, listening to the same familiar noises over and over, waiting for a sign that something more sinister was going on.

She wanted to ring Danny again but knew it would worry him. What if she'd just seen a shadow? So she went to bed, closing the curtains with a quick look outside to see that all was well.

In the morning, as she went downstairs, she spotted an envelope on the mat in the hallway. She picked it up to see it was addressed to no one. Inside was a typed note:

Be careful who you trust.

Juliette frowned. What was that all about? Her blood went cold as she searched out her phone and headed into the kitchen. On the side of the fridge was a magnet that she'd picked up with details of the local police number.

As she waited to be connected, she wondered if she was being silly bothering them, but equally if it made her feel better, it was the right thing to do, even if it did turn out to be her imagination playing tricks on her again. Better to be safe than sorry.

Someone had delivered that note.

TWENTY-THREE
2016

I was only at the coffee shop for four months before I started being ill. After three mornings in a row of nausea upon waking, I wondered if I could be pregnant. I decided not to say anything to Richard until I found out for myself.

I went into Leek, our nearest town, to buy a test. I didn't want to buy one from the local chemist in Mapleton as the gossip drums would start to bang. That was the trouble with living and working in a village. People knew each other's business. I wanted to be the first person to tell Richard if it was positive. I didn't even want anyone to hint at it to him. So it was better to be certain first before rumours were spread willy-nilly.

In the car on the drive back, I dreamed of how it would be if I was pregnant. Me, a mum! Honestly, I couldn't keep the smile from my face. It was excellent timing. I was young and healthy. Richard and I had spent a few months together since we were married, getting to know each other, and I was sure this would bring us closer together somehow. Richard was a fuddy-duddy, set in his ways. Perhaps a child would mellow him.

We'd spoken about children once he'd proposed to me. Of course, he'd said he wanted them but had wondered if he'd left it too late. When I complimented him on his young outlook, he seemed satisfied. He said we should start trying straight away as he dragged me off to bed.

Waiting for the minute to see the outcome of the test was excruciating. For some reason, my thoughts turned to my sister. I still struggled to understand why she wouldn't engage with me after I'd left Derby. It was a shame, I missed her, but since I'd lost my phone, I couldn't remember her number to try any more. I certainly wasn't going to turn up unannounced at home. She had my details and she knew where I was if she needed me. Maybe she was grown up enough now to look after herself.

The test was positive. I raced downstairs to tell Richard.

'I'm pregnant,' I shouted and rushed into his arms. But his body was stiff and although his arms went around me, I could tell he wasn't happy. I looked up at him, his shoulders dropping along with his face.

I was hurt by his reaction. 'I thought you wanted to start a family as soon as possible.'

'You're right.' He nodded as if trying to convince himself. 'I did say that. It's just a shock, that's all.'

'You're not pleased?'

'Of course I am.' He gave me a hug. 'It was unexpected. I'm delighted.'

It was from that moment, although I didn't know it then, that things started to change. Falling pregnant was the best and the worst thing that happened to me. I began to fall more under his control, becoming ever dependent on him. Of course, he did it under the guise of caring for me. Making me feel loved as he did things for me. Later he would say I was useless at everything, playing on my emotions.

Richard wanted a son, so when Daisy came along he began to lose interest. To me, Daisy was perfect, beautiful, and I was so happy. But Richard barely looked her way at first. He wouldn't pick her up unless he was showing her off to someone, or pretending he was a doting father when a midwife or nurse called to see us. But gradually Daisy won him over and, after a few weeks, she had him wrapped around her little finger. He was besotted with her.

And then he insisted we try for another baby straight away. I kept telling him I wasn't ready. I wanted to give my body time to recover, and also to be with Daisy as I learned how to be a mother to her.

As punishment, he stopped sleeping with me. Looking back, I think it was an excuse really.

My life was fine for a while. Daisy took up a lot of my time during those early months. I loved bonding with her too. She was my everything. I wanted her to have the life that I never had as a child. Growing up in a beautiful home with loving parents. It was all I'd ever wanted and I was determined that she would be a happy, balanced little girl.

Of course, that was long before my migraines started and I began to feel sick all the time.

TWENTY-FOUR

As Juliette left the house that morning, she was glad that she'd called the police. Perhaps a visit from an officer would ease her mind if they said someone had been caught prowling nearby, so that it couldn't be her imagination playing tricks on her. Mind, she knew she'd be lucky to get an officer to visit over such a small matter.

So she was pleased when she'd been told a police community support officer would call to see her. First she had to nip into Leek that morning. She needed some stationery and had a parcel to post. It wouldn't take much longer than an hour.

Richard was in his front garden when she went out to her car. Thankfully, she hadn't seen him since the weekend. She wondered if he'd been avoiding her, so that his clandestine dinner would remain secret.

'Hi, Juliette,' he said as he spotted her. 'How are things?'

'Oh, they're fine, thanks.' She paused. 'Although I think I saw someone in the garden last night.'

'Really? What time?'

'About half past nine. It could have been my imagination but I thought I'd check with the local police to see if there's been any reports of prowlers, or the likes.'

'I hope you weren't too worried. You know if you ever feel in danger, you must come round to us. Either of us would be happy to help.'

'That's very kind of you.' She smiled. 'Thanks.' She was about to get into her car when he spoke again.

'I've been meaning to talk to you all week. It was about when you and Danny saw me on Saturday evening.'

'Oh.' Juliette opened the door, wanting to get away as quickly as possible. 'It's none of my business,' she parroted what Danny had said to her.

'I know and I thank you for being discreet. Sarah and I have an open relationship but best to keep it quiet.'

She nodded. 'Of course.'

'It doesn't happen too regularly,' he added. 'I only see Amy a couple of times a month. I'm sure you can see that Sarah and I struggle as a couple and let's just say the intimacy isn't there as much nowadays.'

'I really don't feel comfortable discussing this with you, Richard,' she said, getting into the car. 'Whatever you and Sarah do is no business of mine, nor of Danny's. I'm happy for you, if you're happy.'

'Sure. I didn't mean to embarrass you.'

'I know.' Her smile was false. 'I have to go.'

She closed the door and left him standing there. What a creep! All that crap about having an open relationship was a load of baloney to her. She was a one-man woman, couldn't see the point of affairs. If you were that unhappy with someone, leave them. There were plenty more potential partners out there.

But there was equally something sinister about Richard's actions. Why would he want to discuss this with her rather than Danny? After all, he was quick to speak to him when he accused her of imagining a child in their back garden.

* * *

The local police community support officer visited Juliette as planned. She was a friendly woman, in her mid-forties, who looked around the property and gave her some advice for security. It was to do with installing CCTV and more outside lights. Juliette didn't want to live in a fortress; another one of the reasons why they were moving out of London was to feel safer. There was no point doing this and recreating a prison. Besides, if there had been someone, it was most probably a thief scavenging through the garden sheds for what they could find, rather than someone with a gun waiting to shoot her at the first sign of trouble. Though neither was a good thing. She'd definitely tell Danny to install more outside lighting.

After a hectic afternoon of catching up on work, Juliette made dinner and took it in the conservatory. It was too wet to sit outside, warmer weather had been promised for the weekend.

It was when she was gazing out of the window as she tucked into her food that she first saw it. She paused, fork halfway to her mouth. There was something on Emily's bench.

As she drew closer, she broke out in goosebumps, pulling her thin cardigan around her. Closer still, and she covered her mouth with her hand as she gave out a gasp. It was Emily's teddy bear, the one she had put up in the loft.

She reached for it, almost scared to touch it, to see if it was real or if it was a figment of her imagination. Emily had been vivid in her dreams the night before. Was this her way of letting her know?

She shook the silly thoughts from her head and picked up the bear. Sitting on the bench, she looked at it. Her parents had bought the toy for Emily, shortly after she was born. It was one of the things she had latched on to, been unwilling to let go as she grew older. Juliette had been hoping she could give it to her grandchild in the future. That had been dashed good and proper.

There could be no mistaking this was Emily's toy. What was going on?

Had she got it down herself and come to sit with it on Emily's bench? It must be that. There could be no other explanation. Someone couldn't have come into their home, found the toy in the loft and brought it back down without anyone noticing. It wasn't impossible but highly improbable.

One thing was certain, she wasn't sharing this episode with Danny. He'd think she was going mad after the child next door incident.

Perhaps it was time to go back to the doctor's after all? Maybe it was best if she came off all the medication now she was here. She would be able to cope better. The move had proved to be good for her, and she had promised Danny she would get checked out. Yes, she'd make an appointment, book a train and go back with Danny on Sunday evening. She could manoeuvre her work round to suit. A break away might do her good too.

* * *

Later that evening, coming back from a walk across the field behind their house, Juliette glanced up at the house. She was still staggered by its beauty, the orange of the sky around it as the sun set on another glorious day.

She sat on Emily's bench while she finished her wine. It really did help that Emily hadn't been to the house now. There was nowhere Juliette could see her sitting, no room where she should have been sleeping.

A movement next door caught her eye and she sat up straight in a flash. The blind had gone up at a window where it was always down and she'd spotted a face. It didn't belong to Sarah, she was certain. A little girl with blonde hair. The same child she had seen before.

She couldn't be imagining that, could she?

She ran indoors to get her phone, but by the time she got back, the child was gone. But there *was* a child. And she wanted to know why it was a secret.

And why she was being hidden.

Next door, she heard the back door open. Keeping quiet, she watched as Sarah walked to the bottom of her garden and disappeared into the woods. Buoyed up with the wine, Juliette decided to follow her. Further down, there was a small gap in the hedge that she could squeeze through.

At the entrance to the woods, she paused for a moment before going inside. She followed the path, ignoring the feeling of the darkness creeping in, and praying she wouldn't get lost. Then she stopped. Sarah was up ahead at the clearing. She was standing in the middle of it, looking down at the ground and talking to herself.

'I miss you so much,' she said.

Juliette stayed still. Confused, she decided now was not the time to speak to her and turned to go back.

A branch cracked under her feet and she froze. When she chanced a look over her shoulder, Sarah was no longer in the clearing. Knowing she was trespassing, she headed back along the path and out of the woods as quickly as she could, hoping she wasn't spotted.

TWENTY-FIVE

2017

Having to look after the home and Daisy when she was born became too much. I wasn't sure what was happening to me, if I was honest. I had never felt so exhausted. It was as if a heavy weight was pressing on me, making me ache, sleep longer and generally be unaware of my surroundings. Some days I struggled to get out of bed at all.

Because of how I was feeling, I slipped into a depression and Richard didn't like that. He would chide me about being unable to function properly, annoyed that he'd had to care for Daisy. He'd take her to his studio a lot of the time while I slept. I know it wasn't ideal but I was unable to do anything about it. My head felt so woolly at times with the tablets prescribed by the doctor that I couldn't even protest. If I had anyone close to talk to, I would have told them I was a failure. Richard told me that too, constantly. That I was no good at anything.

Sometimes I would look at Daisy and fear for her life. It was good that Richard was there to look after us both or else I don't know what would have happened.

Two months later, I still felt like a walking zombie, unable to shake off the brain fuzz and the feeling of impending doom. In the end, he agreed to take me to see the doctor.

I was nervous when I sat in the surgery. Richard was holding Daisy, looking very much the doting dad to whoever smiled at him. He had the illusion down to a tee.

'Mrs Sykes-Morgan.'

I stood up to go into the consultation room. Richard followed suit and I looked at him in desperation.

'I'll be fine on my own,' I said.

'Nonsense. I'm coming with you.' He picked up Daisy's carry-all and flipped it over his shoulder. 'Get a move on.'

Doctor Alliott was in his mid-forties, slim, with a crisp white shirt, sleeves rolled up.

'What seems to be the problem?' he asked me, a smile on a round face.

He hadn't known me long and I tried to explain as best I could how I was feeling exhausted, suffering headaches and nausea constantly.

But Richard began to talk over me.

'She's been a little bit down in the dumps, doctor, that's all.'

'How long have you been feeling this way?' Doctor Alliott spoke directly to me.

'Far too long,' Richard replied. 'Daisy is eight months old now.'

Doctor Alliott stared at me for a little longer than necessary. I think he wanted to make me understand that he could see right through Richard.

'Are all these questions necessary?' Richard went on.

'Do you think you could wait outside for a moment while I talk to your wife, please?'

'Well, I don't know.' Richard looked at Doctor Alliott but, after a moment, he backed down and left in a huff.

'Are you okay?' Doctor Alliott asked me. 'I can give you medication for your condition. It seems from your symptoms that you have postnatal depression. Unless there is anything else you'd like to add?'

I shook my head quickly. If Richard was listening outside the door, I'd be in for it later.

Doctor Alliott waited a moment for me to speak, but when he realised I wasn't going to say anything, he gave me a faint smile and wrote out a prescription.

'Take one of these every day and come back to see me in a month. I can judge your progress then and decide whether to up the dosage or lower it. I hope you get on okay. And any time you need to talk, just make an appointment. Yes?'

I nodded and got to my feet.

Outside Richard was sitting in the waiting area. 'Everything okay?' he asked.

I nodded and took Daisy from him. It had been such a relief to talk to someone else about what was going on, even if Richard had been there for the most part, putting words into my mouth. Doctor Alliott told me I wasn't a failure, that the birth of Daisy had affected me and that I would bounce back with the tablets he'd prescribed.

But I didn't.

I became much worse. I hadn't realised at the time how much of a shadow of myself I had become. Richard was so clever about undermining me. At first I had no idea he was doing it, and then, when I realised, he'd make me doubt myself. He ground me down until I didn't know what to believe.

Why hadn't I realised how manipulative he was?

TWENTY-SIX

While the weather was dry after a recent downpour, Juliette was pruning flowers. She'd been studying the different species in the books that Sarah had loaned to her and was becoming a dab hand in the garden. Personally, it had given her so much satisfaction as well as something to do.

The garden was looking so colourful now. Because of its maturity, plants were appearing everywhere she looked and it was becoming a riot of luscious greens interspersed with red, orange, yellow and cream. Several rhododendron bushes were bursting with buds ready to open. A weeping willow stood in the centre of the lawn, easily the best feature of the garden.

Wiping her brow, she looked up as someone shouted her name. She could see Sarah and Richard at the adjoining hedge. It had been a few days since she'd seen either of them. She walked over to join them.

'How's the gardening going?' Richard asked as she drew level.

'So-so, it's quite therapeutic. I've been tidying up some borders.'

'Would you join us for a glass of lemonade?' Sarah enquired.

'Sure.' Juliette kept a smirk to herself. It felt like she was in an Enid Blyton novel.

She walked around to next door and joined them in the rear garden. They sat down and Sarah poured three drinks and passed one to her and then Richard.

'Are you looking forward to the bank holiday?' Richard asked.

'Yes, I think Danny has something planned.'

'Oh?'

'It's a surprise. He's taking me somewhere local though, so he says.'

'Intriguing.'

Juliette lifted her face to the sun coming through the trees. It had been a warm but muggy day.

'I bet we're not going to get many more evenings like these.' Richard sighed. 'It's been a great summer. And how... how are you after the other day?'

'Sorry, I'm not with you?'

'In the woods.'

Juliette frowned, unsure what Richard was referring to. She looked at Sarah for further reference. Had Sarah seen her and told Richard, making something else up completely? A sense of dread crept through her.

Sarah baulked. 'You really don't remember?'

'Remember what?'

'You were in our woods the other morning,' Richard told her.

Juliette paused. 'I don't think so.'

'We wondered whether to tell you or not, but you gave us a fright and—'

'What exactly happened?' She wanted to know.

'It was six o'clock,' Richard replied. 'I was at the kitchen window and I saw you. You were walking towards the woods. I raced out after you. It's a maze in there if you go off the path.'

Juliette couldn't speak as Richard continued.

'I found you in the clearing. You were crying.'

'I – no. Are you sure?'

'We both saw you, didn't we?' He turned to Sarah who nodded.

'Was I in there long?'

'About fifteen minutes. You had nothing on your feet. Do you sleepwalk?'

'Not that I know of, unless it's something recent.' Juliette wasn't going to mention the doors she'd left open during the night, among other things.

'Our apologies for throwing this at you,' Sarah said. 'But we thought you'd want to know.'

'Yes, thanks for telling me.' Juliette could feel her skin reddening by the second. 'Although I'd prefer it if you didn't mention this to Danny, if you don't mind?'

'Not at all.' Richard nodded. 'Let's keep it between us.'

'Obviously, I'm clearly mortified about it. I'm on medication. I had no idea it was affecting me so much until recently. I came off it last week though, so hopefully this will be a one-off incident!' Her voice went up an octave higher than she would have liked. 'Is there anything else you need to tell me?'

'We've seen you crying on several occasions, sitting on the bench you bought, but that's to be expected.' Sarah nodded, a half-smile on her lips.

It was all making sense now. The bench, the garden, it must have triggered something. Thank goodness Danny was coming home for good soon. She knocked back the last of the drink and put the glass down on the table. 'I'd better be off before I shame myself any further.'

'I'm so sorry to bring it up,' Richard said.

'It's fine. But hopefully it won't happen again.'

'Well, I'm here if you want to chat.' Sarah stood up sharpish, her eyes averted from Richard's. 'I'd better get inside. It's nearing lunchtime.'

'Of course.' Now wasn't the time to question Sarah about Richard. Now was the time to sort herself out.

* * *

Back in her home, Juliette went upstairs to her bedroom. She sat on the edge of the bed, tears pouring down her face. What was wrong with her? First the teddy bear had turned up and now she'd been walking around in her pyjamas, grieving for Emily? She couldn't recall either of these things.

Perhaps her doctor would shed some light on it. She was due to speak to her in the morning after her recent visit. Juliette didn't want to be put on any more tablets, not now she was trying for a baby.

* * *

'I think it's all getting a bit too much for Juliette when she's alone,' Sarah said to Richard.

Richard shrugged at the idea. 'I think she's doing fine.'

'She's grieving. It's not entirely fair on her.'

'And you're telling me that because I care?'

Sarah said no more. It was pointless. Despite her playing along with his actions, Richard wouldn't listen to her. That was the problem with him. Once he got his claws into something he thought was a good idea, giving him a better outcome, he wouldn't give in. Juliette would be in for a long ride if he found out he couldn't manipulate her too.

And there wasn't anything Sarah could do to stop that happening.

TWENTY-SEVEN

After a final few days spent with Danny in London, Juliette had been glad to come back to Mapleton. They'd dined in their favourite restaurants and drank wine in their usual haunts. She'd caught up with friends and seen a few ex-colleagues for a meal. Danny had taken two afternoons off and, for once, they'd done the touristy thing.

They'd visited Borough Market, walked along the South Bank to the London Eye, stopped for a drink in a bar off Haymarket and mooched around Covent Garden. Yet on the train back to Stoke, she'd felt an enormous sense of excitement. It had been delightful. It was meant to be that they would stay here now. And with Danny getting the job, he'd be here for good in six weeks.

Juliette had surprised herself by thinking about home all the time. Home in the Midlands. She had settled into Mapleton a lot quicker than she had anticipated, and she couldn't wait to sleep in her bed, when the night was so quiet and the atmosphere peaceful and calm. She couldn't believe how quickly she had grown to love the house and its surroundings.

It was now Thursday morning and she felt awful from the minute she awoke. She roused herself enough to eat a little breakfast and seemed better for it. Then she busied herself doing some work until it was time for the call from her doctor.

Kate Sharlow was a woman in her forties. She, Danny and Emily had been her patients for quite some time. She'd been a huge comfort to Juliette when Emily had been taken ill. It was her quick actions that meant even though Emily hadn't survived, she didn't suffer as much as she could have done.

After they'd said their greetings, Kate got right to business. 'It was lovely to see you during our last appointment,' she said. 'More so because I hope you've been checking out the schools in your new area catchment too. You'll be needing one in the future.' Kate paused. 'Congratulations, Juliette, you're pregnant.'

Juliette's mouth dropped open for a moment before turning into the largest smile she'd had in months.

'Really? Ohmigod, that's fantastic news! How far gone am I?'

'Eight weeks.'

'I had no idea it would be that long. Although it might explain a few things.' Juliette had told Kate what had been happening recently. She missed off the part where her neighbour alleged that she'd been found in their woods with her pyjamas on.

'It's possible they could be linked to the pregnancy, but I can't be one hundred per cent certain,' Kate told her. 'However, all the other tests I ran on you have come back fine, so if you're perhaps a little stressed, maybe that brought it on.'

'I don't feel stressed.'

'Says the woman who moved house a few weeks ago. And you had a lot to deal with last year.'

Juliette nodded. 'I suppose.'

They chatted some more about what she needed to do next. Resting was one of the most important things, especially until she was further along. There was nothing strenuous that she was doing, so it could be okay.

She lay a hand on her stomach and smiled. 'Hello, little one. I'm hoping to welcome you to our world pretty soon. Let me tell you that you will be loved so much. So get big and healthy in there.

And I'll eat for two, obviously, which gives me an excuse to celebrate with ice cream.'

As she rummaged in the freezer for a carton, she imagined Danny's reaction when she told him. She wanted to pick up the phone right now and call him, but he'd be home tomorrow and she thought it might be nicer to do it in person. She'd cook something special and give him a hint. Perhaps get a card with a cryptic message.

This was the new beginning they needed. She gazed at the photo of Emily that sat proud on her work desk. 'I'll never forget you, my little miss. I hope you'll be happy to see your little brother or sister.'

The words she spoke aloud made her cry. Hormones. They'd be all over the place. No wonder she had been feeling weird. That explained everything, thank goodness.

* * *

Juliette could hardly stop herself from bouncing as she drove Danny back from the station. She was bursting to tell him her news but she had to wait a few minutes longer. At last they were home.

'Are we in or out this evening?' Danny asked her as he followed her through to the kitchen.

'I thought we could eat in.' She reached for a beer for him from the fridge. 'I've been a little tired this week.'

'You work too hard,' he said. 'You're not drinking?'

She shook her head. 'Sit down, I have something for you.'

He pulled a stool out and sat at the breakfast bar, his hands reaching for the TV remote. She slapped them away playfully and gave him a box wrapped in a white ribbon.

'What's this?' he asked, a smile of curiosity on his face.

She said nothing as he undid the bow and took the lid off. Inside, wrapped in tissue paper was a pair of baby bootees.

He looked up at her, then down at it again, before gasping. 'Does this mean?'

She nodded, welling up when she saw his eyes glistening. 'I'm pregnant.'

He almost fell off the stool in his haste to hug her. She clung to him as he cried out in happiness.

'I'm eight weeks gone.'

'We'd better get a holiday or two in beforehand then.' He laughed. 'I can't believe it.' Then he sighed. 'Is it wrong we feel so happy after losing Emily?'

'No. We lost a large part of what made us when she died. Bringing another life into the world will be good. She wouldn't want us to be stuck in no-man's land, not getting over the grief of losing her. I think I'll always refer to her in the present. We will always have two children.'

'Or three maybe, if we're quick.'

'Speak for yourself! You don't have to bear them.'

'No, but I am the one that starts everything off.' He laughed and hugged her again, kissing the top of her head. 'I am so happy.'

'Me too.'

'It's going to be hard keeping it quiet for another month.'

'I know. But it can be our little secret until then. Just you, me and the bump.'

He pressed his hand to her stomach. 'Hello, little one. I'm going to be your dad.'

'Oh, don't get all soppy on me or else you'll have me crying too. Let's get started on the food.'

'Ever getting your priorities right, I see.'

'I'm eating for two now, whether you like it or not.'

'Oh, I like it,' he replied. 'I like it a lot.'

TWENTY-EIGHT

Juliette had been feeling nauseous for most of the morning, so once she'd had a bite to eat at lunchtime, she planned to get her head into some work. Since she'd found out she was pregnant, she'd been worrying about the business and how she was going to manage it with a baby alongside it. She needed to have a think about how much time she wanted to take for maternity leave. Work at the moment took up about thirty hours. Once Danny was home, she reckoned she could fit that around having a child, after having a few months off.

Working for yourself wasn't like having a conventional job. Although she wouldn't be entitled to maternity pay, thirty hours a week fitted around seven days was just over four hours a day. She could do that when the child was asleep, or with Danny in an evening if push came to shove. Besides, she could always get an assistant if necessary. Perhaps she could do that for three months around the birth anyway. If she could get someone to help virtually, that would lessen the burden. She would look into that. She didn't want to lose her clients, nor did she want to become a full-time mum. She enjoyed her work too much.

She smiled, thinking of next summer when Bump would be with them. Everything would be so rosy. Then she snorted. Having a baby wasn't all sweetness and light. It was hard work, even if rewarding. But the thought of ten tiny fingers, ten small toes and a button nose made her shiver in anticipation.

Juliette hoped her age wouldn't go against her. It was a nice idea, like Danny had suggested, that maybe they could have one child, perhaps even two more, but right now she'd be happy with a healthy one.

At the kitchen window, she spotted Sarah out in her garden. There was no sign of Richard. She checked the drive to see his car wasn't there. It was unusual to see Sarah out when Richard had left. She went over to the hedge.

'Hi, Sarah.' She waved as the woman looked in her direction.

Sarah waved back.

'How are you?' she added when Sarah didn't move.

Finally Sarah got up and came towards her. 'I'm fine. How are you?'

Buoyed with her news, she decided it would be fine to tell her. 'Can you keep a secret?'

'What is it?'

'I'm not really supposed to tell anyone yet, so don't mention anything to Danny. I found out a few days ago that I'm pregnant.'

'Oh, wow,' Sarah cried. 'Congratulations.'

'Thanks. I can't quite believe it.'

'When are you due?'

'Next spring. I'm eight weeks gone.' Juliette beamed at her. 'Danny and I are super pleased. And I know people might think that we're replacing Emily but it will never be like that.'

'Of course not. I'm sure no one would be that silly.'

'I know. I think about her every day. And every day, it gets a little less painful to realise that she's gone. But still, it's a way of looking forward to the future again.'

'Well, I'm thrilled for you.' Sarah nodded, then wiped at her cheek.

'Hey.' Juliette noticed her tears. 'I'm sorry. I know talking about pregnancies can upset people. Me and my big mouth. I hope I haven't offended you.'

'It's not that.' Sarah gnawed on her bottom lip. 'I don't know how long I can keep doing this.'

'Doing what?'

'It's so deceitful.'

'What is?'

Sarah stood there for a moment, her face telling a tale of anguish. 'I-I haven't been honest with you.' She looked up at Juliette. 'You remember the child you thought you saw in the garden?'

'How could I forget? I feel so stupid now and I—'

'No, it wasn't your imagination. She's real.'

TWENTY-NINE

Juliette froze. 'I don't understand.'

'Her name is Daisy.'

'What?'

'She's Richard's child from his previous marriage. He goes out most nights and he locks me in the room with her.'

'I don't believe he'd—whatever for?'

'He controls everything I do.' Sarah glanced down the drive as if she was terrified that he would return any minute. 'I've thought of telling you lots of times but I didn't know if you'd believe me.'

'So instead you make me think I'm seeing and hearing things? That's pretty low.'

'I'm sorry. I have no choice but to go along with him. Richard – he scares me. He can be really cruel. I had to take a chance now he's gone out, to talk to you. I wasn't going to mention anything but I-I can't go on living like this. Under his control. It's not right. Yet I don't know what to do.'

'Why do you stay?' Juliette wanted to know.

'Because I'm frightened of what he'll do to me if I leave – and Daisy. I stayed with him after his wife left because he wanted me to look after his daughter.'

'Do you know why she went?'

Sarah shook her head, but Juliette sensed she was lying.

'Don't you think it's strange she hasn't been in contact for over a year, not even to see how Daisy is doing?' Sarah added. 'Who would leave their child like that? I certainly wouldn't and I don't think Louisa would either.'

'Wait a minute, are you saying you think something has happened to her?'

Sarah looked down for a moment. 'He says if I tell anyone of my suspicions then he'll hurt her.'

'Is Daisy here with you now?'

'Yes, we keep her hidden.'

'What?' Juliette's eyes widened.

Sarah gulped. 'Richard doesn't want her to be seen in case people start asking questions about Louisa.'

Juliette thought back to talking to Linda and hearing that Richard's wife and daughter had left. Was it possible he had harmed Louisa and then hadn't known what to do about Daisy? If Daisy was still around, there would be questions asked and explanations needed.

She looked at Sarah, who was still in tears. 'You know more, don't you?'

Sarah paused but then shook her head.

'What did he say about her leaving?'

'He said she'd gone suddenly, and that I was to look after Daisy while he thought about what to do next.'

A sensation of falling came over her. Juliette put her hand out to rebalance herself and luckily the motion subsided. But the feeling of nausea stayed with her. What was happening here?

'You have to go to the police,' she said. 'You can't keep—'

'No,' Sarah cried. 'It's too dangerous. But you could help me. We could find Louisa and if we can't, *then* we involve the police. We have to have proof.'

'Of what, exactly?'

'I-I don't know but I think Louisa is missing and I don't want anything to happen to Daisy, or me.'

Juliette shook her head in disbelief. 'So Richard keeps you against your will?'

'He says I can leave any time I want but that I'll never see Daisy again.'

'Well, I suppose as she isn't your child, you won't get custody.'

'I can't leave her with him,' Sarah cried.

'You think he'd harm her too?'

'I'm not sure. But I can't chance finding out. So I stay. I won't have that on my conscience.'

'Are you okay though?' Juliette couldn't begin to imagine how scared Sarah would be feeling. 'You're not in immediate danger?'

'I don't think so. Richard can be volatile but you've seen me, I play along so he thinks it's all under control.'

'You've been doing that for a year?'

Sarah nodded. 'Please don't think ill of me. You don't know what he's capable of.'

Juliette paused, thinking what to do next. 'Do you know where he's gone today? What time he'll be back?'

'He's out to collect some supplies for the business. He's usually away for a few hours, once a fortnight.'

Despite not getting her head around what was happening, she had to ask. 'I need you to do something for me while I think what we can do next. I want to see Daisy.'

'You can't.' Sarah shook her head fervently. 'What happens if he comes home early?'

'You can keep a lookout. If we leave the kitchen door open, I can run out that way and get back into my own garden somehow. I promise I'll only be a few minutes at the most but I have to see her. I need to believe she exists. I've been told for the past few weeks that I was imagining things.'

Sarah had the decency to blush. She lowered her eyes momentarily, but then she looked at Juliette again, fear visible this time.

'What if Daisy says something to Richard?' she said quietly.

But Juliette was determined. 'I'm coming round.'

'No! Forget I said anything.'

'But—'

'Please!'

'I have to see her. Don't you see? To make sure she is real – for me.'

Juliette stood her ground until Sarah relented.

'Okay.' She nodded. 'But you must be quick.'

Juliette raced round next door and followed Sarah upstairs. Sarah went into the front bedroom first, glancing through the window to check the driveway was still empty and then with one final look at Juliette, she opened the door to a room at the back of the house.

'Daisy, say hello to the lady.'

Juliette stepped into the room. The walls were covered in unicorns, on the bedding and curtains too. The sash window let in a little light. As it only overlooked the rear garden, venetian blinds ensured privacy while still letting in light.

The little girl was sitting at a child's desk, a colouring book open at a page that was half coloured in. She had the biggest, bluest eyes and pigtails. Her clothes were clean and the room was spotless.

'Hello, lady,' Daisy said.

Juliette couldn't find her voice at first. Then she gave a little wave. 'Hi, Daisy. What are you colouring in?'

'It's a picture of a unicorn.' Daisy held it up for her to see.

'That's very pretty.' Juliette admired the riot of colours underneath the drawing. 'You're very clever to do that.'

Daisy smiled. 'Would you like it? I can do another one?'

'Oh, I—'

'Are you hungry?' Sarah interrupted. 'I'm going to make lunch soon.'

'It's fish fingers day!' Daisy clapped her hands, the picture forgotten in her excitement.

'It is.' Sarah smiled and then moved to the door. 'I won't be a moment. Say goodbye to the lady.'

'Bye.' Daisy turned back to her colouring.

Once downstairs, with no sight of Richard, Juliette turned to Sarah.

'Are you sure you're both safe? I'm worried about you and I think you should leave.'

'I can't. Richard will smooth talk anyone who interferes and then I get punished for it,' she said. 'I have to get the evidence.' Sarah looked up at her. 'I want to go, but I can't leave Daisy. Besides, I'd have to flee the country so he couldn't find me and he's taken my passport. And Daisy isn't my daughter so I don't have one for her.'

Juliette had to admit that the child seemed content and in no particular danger. She didn't appear to be coming to any harm, so for now she would bide her time.

She would give Sarah a fortnight, until Richard went out for the day again, to search out the information she needed to find Louisa and then she could decide when to go to the police.

And until then she wasn't telling a soul, not even Danny.

THIRTY

That stupid bitch.

That's the thing with living in a small village. Everyone knows everyone's business.

But in actual fact, most people don't see what goes on right under their noses as they're too busy trying to compete with each other.

For a whole year, we've kept our secret safe. And then someone moves in next door and all our planning goes to pot.

It's quite tiresome playing the nice neighbour. It's terribly wearing to be civil all the time, even when I'm playing tricks on Juliette. You see, she's the weakest link in the puzzle and if I can convince her that she's seeing and hearing things, then it's a bit like playing wolf, isn't it? No one will believe her if she does see or hear more than she should.

Of course, I've got to be careful that the police aren't brought into all of this. If they start poking their nose in where it's not wanted, it will make things very awkward.

This can still work. We just need to plan more meticulously.

And, really, having Juliette next door might just work out in our favour.

PART TWO
TWO YEARS AGO

THIRTY-ONE

Louisa had exhausted herself cooking Richard a Sunday dinner. He insisted on all the trimmings and that they were home-made. She'd baked an apple pie too, even though she'd felt giddy on her legs several times. It was as if she couldn't stand the heat in the kitchen. She hoped he'd enjoy it as much as it had taken out of her.

But as he sat down at the table across from her, not even a smile or a thank you for the effort, she wondered why she even bothered to think otherwise.

'You look rough,' he said between mouthfuls of food.

Tears pricked her eyes. 'I didn't get much sleep last night.'

'I know. You kept me awake with your tossing and turning.'

'I'm sorry.'

'I've been thinking. We should hire a nanny.'

'A nanny?' She put down her cutlery. 'Are you saying that I'm not a good mother?'

'I just feel that you need some extra support with Daisy when things get on top of you.'

'But I'm okay now. I feel much better.' She pushed herself up from the chair. 'Look, I'm up and about and I'm walking more. I went for a stroll around the garden this morning. Daisy loved it and—'

'I'm going to put an advertisement out locally, see if anyone comes forward.'

'I don't *need* help.'

'If you think back to how you've been lately, you'll see that you do. You might be feeling better at the moment but what about next week and the week after? We can't be having poor Daisy cooped up forever. She needs to get out with people.'

'You *are* saying I'm a bad mother.'

Richard paused, his fists clenched.

Louisa visibly shrank and said nothing else. Richard was saying what *he* thought was the truth, not what was happening. She *had* been fine for a while now. But she didn't dare to disagree with him for fear of retaliation.

'I'll get someone you can rely on,' he told her before walking out of the room.

And just like that the conversation was over. Louisa felt as if she was being replaced. It wasn't a nice feeling.

Over the next few weeks, Richard kept on at her, pressuring her into thinking it was for her own good. In the end, she persuaded herself that she would have more time to do things she enjoyed. Perhaps she could go back to work part-time in the coffee shop. Or maybe she could help out with his business.

Suddenly there was an even bigger light at the end of the tunnel. If she got better, she could leave and take Daisy with her. Louisa had long known their marriage had become a sham. People had stopped coming to see her because Richard was always putting them off. He was controlling her. She didn't know who she was any more. And she hated it.

So to humour him, she let him think she was willing.

But then her headaches started to worsen. She became confined to bed as she spent a lot of her days in a darkened room. The pain was debilitating. She had Daisy to think about, so she agreed to pass the main care over to another person, entrusting them to look after her daughter.

Of course Louisa had no say in who the nanny would be. She

expected Richard to employ an old fuddy-duddy who would dress her down and say she wasn't looking after Daisy properly. Luckily for her, whoever it was would be sleeping in the annexe. She wouldn't like someone under her roof. She wouldn't put it past Richard not to spy on them.

'Do you think a visit from Sarah might do you good?' Richard asked as she was dishing out supper.

Louisa froze momentarily. 'My sister?' She frowned. 'You know I haven't seen her in years.'

'She might want to see her niece.'

'She doesn't even know about Daisy.'

'So it would be good for you to catch up.'

Louisa thought about it for a moment. The last time she and Sarah had spoken was when they'd had that awful row, and she hadn't seen her since. 'It's been too long.' She shook her head sadly.

'What's time when you can reconnect again?'

Louisa sat down, wondering if he was playing a trick on her. If she said she wanted to see Sarah, would he then say it was impossible? Laugh at her for getting her hopes up? Over the years she had wondered how Sarah was, but she'd pushed it to the back of her mind the longer the silence between them had gone on.

Before she could respond, he picked up a bowl of potatoes and spooned some more onto his plate. 'Let's invite her to stay for a few days, a week perhaps.'

'I suppose I could write to her, see if she's still living with Mum. I doubt *she* will have moved out of the dump she made us call home.'

'Do you have a mobile number for her?'

'I have an old address book. If she's on the same number, I can—'

'Get me the book and leave it with me.'

Louisa nodded, knowing better than to argue the point. It really did seem as if he felt it was a good idea. And maybe if she could get her sister on side, she might have a chance of getting away with Daisy, to somewhere Richard wouldn't find her. It was certainly worth thinking about.

THIRTY-TWO

Sarah tried to stop her mouth from dropping to the floor as the taxi pulled up outside White Oaks.

'Nice gaff,' the driver said as he turned to her. 'Do you live here?'

'No, my sister does. I'm just visiting.' She spoke so calmly but the envy inside ran deep already. There she was in Derby sharing a doss hole with two other girls and Louisa was living like this? It didn't seem right.

It had been strange to receive a message from Richard. She hadn't spoken to her older sister for so long, not since Louisa had landed on her feet and bagged herself a rich man. It was something the sisters used to joke about when they were teens. Something to stop them from reflecting too much on how poor their lives were.

When Louisa had met Richard, she'd changed almost overnight. She became obsessed with him, wanting to move in with him straight away. Everyone could see she was only after his money.

From the first time Sarah had met him, Richard had charmed her too. But he was so old. Almost twenty-five years older, a big age gap when you're fifteen. Now Sarah was twenty, it didn't seem quite so big.

Glancing at the property as she got out of the vehicle, she could see its attraction. The house was enormous, detached, set back from the road and it was so quiet. Sarah almost held her breath waiting for... what, she didn't know. A screech of a brake. A beep of a horn. Music blasting from somewhere. Lights, camera, action. Here it was so tranquil she almost felt rested as soon as she walked up the drive.

As she got to the door, it opened and there was her sister. The awkward moment she'd envisioned wasn't there as Louisa threw out her arms. Sarah dropped her overnight bag to the ground and hugged her.

Louisa was a lot thinner than the last time Sarah had seen her. Her blonde hair was dirtier now, long and lank, lacking any kind of style. The bags under her eyes were dark, almost making her eyes look hollow.

'I knew you'd come,' Louisa said.

Sarah kept her thoughts to herself, wanting to ask why the silence and then contact all of a sudden.

'You didn't think I might have changed my phone number?' she asked. 'Or moved?'

'There were always those possibilities, but I knew Mum would still be there.'

It stung that Sarah had been right where Louisa thought she would be. In other words, her sister knew she wouldn't have gone further than her hometown. No ambition, nothing to write home about.

'She could have been dead for all you care,' she couldn't help but snap.

'Oh, Sarah, I'm so sorry. We should never have stayed out of touch for so long.'

'It is good to see you,' Sarah said, genuinely meaning it even though she felt aggrieved.

'I look hideous,' Louisa said. 'It's the medication. The doctor keeps messing around with it. Anyway, come on in.'

Sarah picked up her bag and followed her indoors, into a large farmhouse-style kitchen. The whole of the flat she was sharing wasn't much bigger than this room. It was full of mismatched units, a large pine table at its centre. The fridge was covered in magnets of all shapes and sizes, a few alphabet letters spelling 'hello'. Then she spotted the view through the window.

'Is that your garden?'

'Yes. The wood at the back is ours as well. We have six acres – four bedrooms too.'

'Wow,' she muttered.

'I've put you in the guest room at the back. How long are you staying?'

'Just for a few days. I can't take any longer off work. I said it was for compassionate leave.'

'Well, it is, I suppose! Although I'm not dead yet.'

Sarah sat down at the table as Louisa busied herself filling the kettle. Her eyes were still flitting everywhere spotting the up-to-date gadgets. No wonder Louisa had been quick to marry Richard. It was a different world than the one she had left behind.

Everyone she knew thought it had been too quick, but Louisa didn't seem to care. It was as if he consumed her. And from the minute she'd left, there had been excuse after excuse so that she wouldn't visit. After they'd had the mother of all rows, Sarah had given up, assuming Louisa didn't want to know her now she was all posh. Apart from a few text messages, she hadn't heard from her again. Until now.

'Richard is in his studio,' Louisa said as she turned back to her. 'He'll be in there for a while yet. Let me show you your room while we wait for the water to boil.'

Sarah followed her upstairs to the first floor. There were rooms to her right and left.

Louisa pointed at one of them. 'This is where you'll sleep,' she said, pressing a finger to her lips. 'I need you to be quiet though. There's someone I want you to see but she might still be asleep and if she is, I'd rather not wake her.'

'Okay,' Sarah replied.

Louisa pushed open the door. Inside, the room had a double bed, a row of wardrobes and a large window overlooking the back garden and woods. It was decorated in lilacs and greys and looked like something out of a magazine.

'This is lovely,' Sarah said, putting her bag down again.

'It's the furthest away I could put you,' Louisa explained. 'We do have an annexe but I wanted you in the house.' She beckoned her out into the hallway again to another door across the landing. With a smile at Sarah, she opened the door quietly.

Sarah glanced inside. The curtains were closed, the room benefitting from the effects of losing the hot sun. There in the corner of the room was a small bed, a child asleep under the covers.

'This is Daisy.'

Sarah's eyes glistened with tears. It had been a shock to find out she was an auntie. Then again, how would she know if Louisa hadn't been in touch to tell her? She stared at the sleeping child, seeing a mass of blonde curls and long eyelashes. Pain shot through her as she remembered what she'd lost.

'She's beautiful,' she whispered, wanting to reach out and touch her.

'She's a handful. Runs me ragged, hence the need for help.'

Sarah stayed poker-faced. 'What do you mean?'

'Richard is insisting I get a nanny. I'm barely mobile some days and he wants Daisy to have a normal life.'

Sarah didn't want to give too much away but she had to say something to be polite. 'What's wrong with you?' she asked.

'The doctors haven't said yet, but it's looking like ME.'

'Oh!' She paused. 'Is that hereditary?'

'I'm not sure. I'll check for you.' Louisa nudged her playfully. 'Look at you. You're gorgeous and so full of life. You don't need to worry.'

Sarah smiled. 'So you can't take Daisy out at all?'

'It's too tiring. And I get these debilitating headaches that knock me out of life for days at a time. It's heartbreaking to see Daisy indoors so much.'

'Have you had many people apply?'

'Richard said there are a few but he hasn't started interviewing yet.' Louisa backed out of the room. 'Let's go and have some tea while she's asleep. She'll be out of that bed as soon as her eyes open.'

As they went downstairs again, Sarah took everything in. She had never been in such a large house. It was beautifully decorated, tasteful, rich. How had Louisa come to be living here? It made going back to Derby even more horrid to think about. Perhaps there was something she could do about that if she played her cards right.

'It's good to see you again, after so long,' Louisa said, giving her an impromptu hug. 'It was mainly my fault for being so stubborn. And then I was so busy helping Richard out, and then having Daisy. On top of that, I had postnatal depression.'

'It's okay,' Sarah replied, although it was far from it. It was all feasible, she supposed, but was more likely an excuse. Louisa probably hadn't wanted to see her. Which begged the question, because Louisa obviously didn't know anything about it: why was Richard offering Sarah the nanny job?

THIRTY-THREE

Sarah wasn't quite prepared for the rush of hormones that flooded her body when she set eyes on Richard again. She'd known he was good-looking in a mature kind of way, but he seemed to have aged even better. He carried no excess weight on his medium frame, he was tanned and wearing denim shorts to above the knee. His work boots and a white T-shirt gave him the air of a little boy, but his features were all about the older man.

To an outsider, Sarah was a more vibrant version of her sister. Her blonde hair was dyed to make it brighter, her hair styled in a long-layered bob with a blunt fringe. She was the same height and build as Louisa, but she didn't walk as if she had the weight of the world on her shoulders.

She saw Richard's eyes light up, then flicker from top to toe and back again until they landed on her own. Feeling herself blushing under his stare, she looked away for a moment.

'Richard, Sarah's here,' Louisa stated the obvious. 'Come and join us for a drink.'

'Nothing for me,' Richard said, not taking his eyes from Sarah's. 'I'm just finishing off a canvas but thought I'd come and say hello.'

'Hi,' Sarah said. 'I bet you don't remember me.'

'How could I forget someone as beautiful as her sister?'

'Stop it, you,' Louisa tittered.

Sarah baulked. What was up with her sister? She was acting like a lovestruck puppy.

Richard ignored Louisa and sat across from Sarah. 'How're things with you?' he asked.

'Good, thanks.'

Richard smiled at her. 'Well, treat this house as your home while you're here. Louisa will cook something nice for this evening. What would you like?'

'I'm not fussy.'

'I can make your favourite, lasagne,' Louisa said.

Sarah didn't have the heart to say it hadn't been that since she was in high school. It showed how little they knew about each other now.

'Please don't go to any trouble,' she replied.

'Nonsense. Louisa lounges around most days,' Richard said. 'It will do her good to be on her feet for a while.'

Sarah watched as Louisa lowered her eyes momentarily, her skin reddening. Still, it was good to see someone sensing her sister's ploy to be a kept woman.

The door behind her opened and in rushed the little girl she'd seen asleep earlier.

'Hello, poppet,' Louisa cried as she climbed onto her knee.

Daisy's hair was sticking up at the back where she had lain on it. She had large brown eyes and a small nose and lips. Her pyjamas were pink, covered in tiny white stars.

'Daisy, this is your auntie, Sarah. Say hello.'

''Lo.' Daisy waved a hand and smiled.

Sarah closed her eyes momentarily to the pain of her loss. She certainly didn't feel pity for her sister. She remembered quite clearly how she'd dumped her in favour of her new life.

Louisa reached across and gave her hand a squeeze. 'It's going to be great catching up with you,' she said.

Sarah smiled but said nothing.

'How's Derby been for the past few years?' Richard asked.

'Okay, I suppose,' Sarah replied.

'No fella waiting for you to return?'

She scoffed. 'As if. I'm happy being single, thank you very much.'

'Do I detect a woman scorned?'

Sarah narrowed her eyes but the way Richard was trying to keep a straight face made her realise he was joking with her.

'Let's just say I haven't found the right man yet.'

'From what I can recall, there weren't too many to choose from.' Louisa chuckled.

'Slept with all of them, have you?' Richard snapped. 'Before you came to live with me?'

'Of course not!' Louisa shook her head. 'I meant there were—'

'Not many who were suitable marriage material,' Sarah butted in, coming to Louisa's rescue. 'Not even for a long-term relationship actually.'

'That's good to hear. For a moment, I thought you were suggesting Louisa was the estate bike that everyone had rode.'

As Louisa fought back tears at Richard's remark, Sarah wondered why he was being so spiteful. Had she walked in during an argument between them? Because if not, there was something quite odd about their relationship.

Maybe coming here could work out to her advantage after all.

THIRTY-FOUR

2015

Sarah had her head in a magazine when Louisa came into their bedroom. She was reading up on how to create a flick with mascara and a black eyeliner, hoping to master it soon. One of the lads at school was showing a little interest in her and she wanted to make the most of what she'd got.

Usually she'd speak to her older sister about make-up – well, about anything really – but just lately Louisa didn't have any time for her. Not since she'd met some bloke who lived in the country.

So when Louisa told her the news, Sarah wasn't prepared for it.

'I have something to tell you,' Louisa said as she pulled down a large suitcase from the top of the wardrobe and placed it on her bed. 'I'm moving in with Richard.'

'What? But you've only known him for five minutes!' Sarah protested.

'It's four months, actually,' Louisa replied, unzipping the case. 'You'll know when you get to my age that love is a wonderful thing and can claim you in a matter of minutes. I knew from the moment I saw Richard that I wanted to be with him.'

'Oh, please.' Sarah made a vomiting motion. 'There's no such thing as love at first sight.'

'How would you know? You've never been in love.'

'I know but... I just think it's a bit drastic to move in with him and be so far away. Do you have to go?' Her voice became whiny. 'I can't cope here without you.'

'Yes you can.' Louisa stopped what she was doing and sat down next to Sarah. 'You'll be finishing school in a few months and it's time to take care of yourself. And besides, I'm only moving forty miles away. You can come and see me any time you like.'

'Yeah, right.' Sarah huffed. 'How am I going to get to you?'

'On the bus, or by train and I'll pick you up at the other end.'

Sarah said nothing as Louisa resumed her packing.

'You should be staying here,' she insisted. 'I need you.'

'You have to get used to being on your own sooner or later.'

'But not yet! I can't survive with only Mum around. She doesn't care about me. All she wants to know is where her next drink is coming from. You shouldn't want to leave me with her.'

'Life isn't fair, kiddo.' Louisa folded a jumper up and put it in the suitcase. 'I've had no fun yet and I'm twenty.'

'I don't want you to go!'

'Give it a break, Sarah.' Louisa sighed, her shoulders drooping. 'It can't always be about you.'

Sarah had the decency to look sheepish. Louisa was right. It *wasn't* all about her. But it was hard at her age to look towards the future without her sister close by. Why couldn't she have settled down with one of the men around the estate? That would have been okay as she could have visited whenever she wanted to.

If truth be told, she was scared of being on her own. Louisa was always giving her the odd fiver here and there and if she didn't have anyone to turn to, how would she cope? She was used to being in the house alone for long periods of time, fending for herself. She was fifteen after all. But she wasn't sure she could manage without Louisa around all the time. She was her rock, her go-to person whenever she had a problem. She had friends to chat with but no one was like Louisa.

'I'll miss you,' she said, standing up to hug her tightly.

'I'll miss you too.' Louisa hugged her back. 'But you can text me any time you like, to save your phone credit.'

Sarah sighed, sitting down again. She pulled her knees up to her chin and grasped her legs. Maybe it was time she grew up and stopped being dependent. She was aiming to go to college in September, make something of her life so *she* could leave the shitty estate she lived on too. There were no decent jobs to be had around here. She didn't want to end up like Louisa, working in the biscuit factory on a conveyor belt.

Once she had left school, she would have the world at her feet. She was going places, she was certain. But first she would have to learn how to survive without her big sister.

THIRTY-FIVE

Although nervous about seeing Sarah again after so long, Louisa had been excited too. As it was Richard's idea to contact her, she hadn't been sure it would happen. She'd thought he was playing with her emotions. He often did that, promised her something and then didn't follow through. But his thoughts about it giving her a boost, as she'd been feeling so low lately, were nice to hear and it made a welcome change.

As soon as Louisa had seen Sarah, it was as if their time apart melted away. She hadn't realised until then how much she had missed her. They had been so close when they were growing up. Although there was an age gap between them, they'd been through a lot together and it had made them stronger. If it weren't for that stupid argument they'd had when she'd last visited Derby, when Sarah kept saying she'd abandoned her, things might have been so different.

But they had both inherited their mother's stubborn streak and after harsh words had been said, neither of them had wanted to wave the white flag of surrender. The silence had continued until it felt too long to get in touch anyway. And every time she was thinking of going to Derby to talk to her, Richard would have something he needed to do, or he'd treat her to a day out. She presumed he wanted time with her whenever he could fit it around his work. His painting was so important to him so she didn't blame him then.

Louisa recalled a time when she and Sarah were inseparable as children, even more so when Dad left and they were stuck with looking after Mum, rather than the other way around. She wasn't a caring mum. All she was interested in was where her next drink would come from. Sometimes Louisa thought she forgot she had two children.

They fended for themselves mostly, even though lots of times they went hungry. They'd get home from school to no food in the house and a note to say Mum would be back later. They never knew where she would be, or who with, more to the point. Her one true love in life was alcohol.

Louisa had followed her once or twice and would see her with other men. She started drinking herself for a few months, when she felt she couldn't cope with the responsibility of looking out for her and her sister all the time. After using vodka to block out her horrible life, she understood why Mum drank so much. Alcohol gave her an edge and numbed the feeling of hopelessness. But she soon realised that she didn't want to be reliant on it.

Mum brought home lots of men, strangers who she assumed used her for sex. Luckily nothing ever happened with her and Sarah, although there was a time when Sarah started to drink too. She would have been about fifteen. Louisa was still at home at that point, still the parent to her. But she was staying at her friend, Martin's, flat too, to get away from the house. It wasn't a nice place to be.

Had she known she and Sarah would lose touch when she left for Mapleton, and that her life would end up how it was, she might have thought twice about leaving. But she was young and in love. Naive to a fault.

* * *

That same night, Sarah lay in bed unable to sleep. It was so quiet she couldn't settle, which seemed ridiculous really. But she was used to much more noise than the occasional hoot of an owl. She wondered if it had taken Louisa long to settle when she had first moved to Mapleton. Sarah couldn't wait to explore the village, to see what it had to offer a twenty-year-old city girl.

Seeing Louisa today, you wouldn't have thought they hadn't been in touch for so long. Looks wise, Louisa had changed a little but she seemed to be the caring sibling that Sarah remembered. So why hadn't she kept in touch with her, or her friends? Sarah could understand her not contacting Mum because they didn't get on, but to leave her little sister all that time?

She would ask her about that when the time was right. First she wanted to settle in, get her feet under the table, so to speak.

THIRTY-SIX

2016

The school-leavers' disco wasn't the place where Sarah expected to get together with her first love. She had known Jessie Davidson since she was twelve and only now, both sixteen, during the final week of their last term, he gave her the come on.

She'd eyed him from afar for a long time, always thinking he was out of her league as he'd been going out with Shannon Trent since time began. But it was as if walking out of the school gates for the last time had given him the need to chat to her.

Louisa had never liked Jessie. 'He's an idiot,' she'd often say when she caught Sarah fawning over him on Facebook. 'He got Shannon pregnant and yet he can't keep his hands to himself even now they have a son.'

'They're not together now,' Sarah had told her. Yet still Louisa went on about his lack of qualities.

But Louisa wasn't here now to tell her what to do. Since she'd left Derby, Sarah had barely spoken to her. For the first week or so, there had been lots of phone calls to see if she was okay but then the calls became fewer and further between. Every time Sarah asked if she could come and see her, Louisa was too busy going here, there and everywhere with Richard. It was as if she'd forgotten her roots the minute she left the house.

The school hall had been decked out with balloons and the paper chain streamers that came out every year. 'Good Luck' and 'Congratulations' banners were strewn across the stage where the local DJ had blagged a spot for the night. The music wasn't exactly modern but it was fun to dance to.

She spotted Jessie smiling at her across the dance floor, giving her the attention she craved. Deciding to go with the flow, she smiled back. He looked smart in jeans, Timberland boots, the sleeves of his checked shirt rolled up to reveal tattoos on each forearm. His dark brown hair was short and spiked and looked as if it had taken him a while to get just right.

While the girls jigged in circles and the boys watched from the edge of the room, Jessie beckoned her over.

'You glad this is our last week?' he shouted in her ear.

'What?' she shouted back, not catching a word of what he'd said. He reached for her hand and they went out into the corridor away from the noise, where he repeated his question.

'Definitely,' she said, sad when he let go of her.

'Me too.' Jessie nodded. 'I've got a job lined up for next Monday, working at Saville Bros, the builder's merchant on the high street. Do you know it?'

'Yes, cool. I have the summer off before college in September.'

'What are you studying?'

'Just getting A levels for now, I think. I don't have a clue what to do yet.'

'Me neither. I might try and get a job as a car mechanic. This will tide me over until then.'

They smiled at each other, almost shyly, considering how long they'd known each other. It didn't bother Sarah that he had a son with Shannon. Chances were it wasn't his anyway, because Shannon had a rep as a sleep-around. Sarah wouldn't have put it past her to pretend Jessie was the father.

'Wanna go out?' he said, reaching for her hand. 'You and me, one night?'

She nodded. 'Yeah, maybe.'

They grinned at each other again and then he kissed her. Even at her tender age, she wasn't a virgin. She had given herself to one of the fifth years when she was fifteen, keeping it from Louisa when she'd thought she was pregnant before, thankfully, starting her period two days later. It would have been just her luck to be caught out first time and even though it was a one-off with the boy, she hadn't wanted to do it with anyone else again since. She'd also got herself on the pill pretty sharpish for precaution.

Jessie had walked Sarah home that evening.

'Is no one in?' he asked when the house was in darkness.

She shrugged. 'My mum will probably be flaked out. I haven't seen her since this morning and she was in her bed then. She likes the sauce too much.'

'Ah.'

He looked at her, penetrating eyes of the deepest blue, and she was sure she fell in love on the spot.

There was a pause.

'I like you, Sarah, a lot, and I know I have a reputation for being a troublemaker, but I can't wait to take you out on a date.'

It was so weird to feel safe with Jessie, not be wary of a male for once. She prayed this was the start of something special. Someone she could turn to, perhaps who she might marry one day and have kids of her own.

She laughed as she got carried away with her thoughts.

'What's up?' he said, smiling at her.

'Nothing. I'm just happy, that's all.'

Later that evening when she was tucked up in bed, and her face hurt from smiling so much, she typed out a message to Louisa.

Remember when you told me I would know about love at first sight? Well, it's not true in my case but I am a little in love already.

Then she deleted it. She knew her sister wouldn't be too happy if she found out about Jessie.

THIRTY-SEVEN

Sarah had been at White Oaks for three days now. She'd been sitting in the garden with Louisa and Daisy when Richard came out of the studio.

'I've finished early today. Thought I might cook my Indian special. What do you think, Louisa?'

'What a treat!' Louisa smiled, turning to Sarah. 'Richard makes the most divine curry.'

Richard pulled out a chair and sat down with them. 'Get me a beer,' he said to Louisa.

Louisa stood up quickly, then hung on to the table.

'Are you okay?' Sarah sat forward.

'I'm fine.' Louisa waved a hand in front of her face. 'It's hot. I felt a little dizzy, that's all.'

As she rushed off, Sarah glanced at Richard.

'She's always like that if you ask her to do anything,' he muttered.

Louisa was back in a flash. But later that evening, as the aromas of the pending meal spread through the house, Louisa began to flake out. Before it was ready, she'd fallen asleep on the settee.

Sarah felt guilty prodding her awake. 'Dinner will be ready in five minutes,' she told her.

Louisa sat up, seeming disorientated as she looked around the room. 'I'm not sure I'm up to it,' she admitted.

'Why don't you go to bed for a little while?' She held out her hand. 'Would you like me to help you?'

Louisa shook her head. 'Richard will be annoyed if—'

'You leave him to me. If he says anything, I'll defend you. He needs to realise that you're poorly.'

Louisa's weak smile was so full of gratitude that Sarah almost felt sorry for her. And, although it was strange to see her sister so docile, Sarah didn't mind in the slightest. It gave her time to put into place more plans. Tonight could be her getting to know Richard evening. Or more to the point, he would be getting to know her too.

Sarah went back into the kitchen, closing the door quietly behind her. Daisy had gone to bed half an hour ago so it was just the two of them.

'Well, that's both the kids down for the night,' she joked about Louisa. 'I doubt we'll hear a peep out of either of them until the morning. Does Louisa often go to bed so early?'

'Most nights.' Richard sighed.

'It must be really lonely for you.'

'It is at times, but I bury myself in my work and forget. She's very good with Daisy when she can be.'

'But there's you to consider too.' Sarah wanted to add that Louisa couldn't give him what he needed as a partner if she was tired all the time.

'Oh, I'm fine.' Richard held up two bottles of wine. 'Red or white?'

'Red please.'

'Can I ask you something?' Richard asked once they were seated with their food.

'Sure.' Sarah ripped off a chunk of naan bread and dipped it into the creamy mixture. 'This is delicious, by the way.'

'Thanks. It's always puzzled me why you and Louisa lost touch. You seemed so close growing up.'

'If you must know, we had an argument. I was young when she fell in love with you. She came to see me one weekend and I didn't want her to leave. One thing led to another and before we knew it, we were slinging mud at each other. I stormed off; Louisa returned to you.' She shrugged. 'Looking back it was silly but neither of us would make the first move to get in touch. But having no parents to fall back on, Louisa was all I had and it hurt that she left me.'

'I thought your mum and dad were still alive.'

'They are. I don't have a clue where Dad is, and Mum is still the bitter alcoholic she was. She barely moves from the house now.'

'And as you resent them for abandoning you as a child, you thought the same of Louisa?'

'Something like that.'

Richard paused to take a sip of wine.

'I can understand where you're coming from. My mum died of cancer when I was seven, and my father turned to drink too. Except he was violent with it.'

'To you?'

He nodded and she smiled in empathy.

'He hid a lot of things from me but he'd often have women over and ill-treat them. He had several relationships, some lasting a few weeks, some a few months until he turned them off with his mannerisms. Let's just say he wasn't a happy drunk.'

Sarah watched as Richard's eyes turned darker. It was as if he was going back in time to a place where he didn't feel safe. Where there was no love, no one to rely on. She could understand that.

She reached across the table and gave his hand a squeeze. 'It never gets any easier, does it? I don't think I'll ever feel that I belong anywhere. God help any man who wants to marry me. I'm going to be a nightmare to live with.'

'Maybe you should have married someone like me.' His eyes trained on hers. 'It's strange but Louisa doesn't seem as affected as you are.'

'That's because she wasn't left behind to fend for herself.' Her words were almost caustic as she spit them out.

'I'm sorry. You seem to have been in a lot of pain as a child.'

'I had no one to trust except her. She looked after me, made sure I had food to eat. That I had clothes to wear. Took care of me when I was sick. That's what our mum should have done but I guess I took things out on Louisa for leaving. I'm not proud of that fact now, not when I see how poorly she is.'

'I was shocked to realise you didn't know about Daisy. That must have hurt.'

'It did.' Sarah sighed. 'She's such a beautiful child.'

'She's quiet though.'

'Perhaps she should be mixing with other children more. How often does she go to nursery? Or to mums and toddlers groups?'

'She doesn't.'

'You mean she sees no one but you and Louisa?'

He nodded.

'That's not good for her.'

'It would be too much for Louisa to take her out. She hasn't left the house for over a year, no matter how I've tried to coerce her. Her doctor gives her another round of medication every time she has an appointment. I swear it's all those tablets she pops that make her this way.'

Sarah took a sip of wine before speaking again. 'Have you mentioned this to him?'

'Many times but he says she'll come out of her depression when she's ready. It can last for years. He also says that she may be bipolar and the delivery of the baby was only circumstantial to her diagnosis.'

'In other words, he doesn't have a clue what's wrong with her.'

'I assume not. There's been no official diagnosis of ME. Louisa tells people she has it as it gives her the label to use.'

'She's certainly changed since she left Derby.' She stared at Richard. 'I wasn't sure I'd hear from her again so your message took me by surprise.'

'I wasn't sure if you would come or not. You have a right to be upset with her.'

'She's also my family. If I can forgive her, then I can move on.'

It was Richard's turn to stare. 'It's a shame you don't live nearer. You're great company.'

'Cheers.'

He poured more wine and they clinked glasses. 'Would you consider the nanny post? I think you'd make a great job of it.'

She paused for drama. 'I'm thinking about it,' she replied.

'Good.'

As he turned to gaze out of the window, Sarah wished she could crawl into his head and see what he was thinking. Did he really love Louisa or was he putting up with her because of Daisy? It was time to do more digging as the week went on.

THIRTY-EIGHT

Louisa sat up in bed, sleep forgotten in an instant. Screams were coming from Daisy's room. She pulled back the duvet and slipped her feet into her slippers.

'What's the matter?' Richard said from her side.

'Daisy is crying. She must have had a scary dream.'

'I can't hear anything.'

'She sounds really distressed. I won't be long.'

Richard switched on the lamp then. 'Louisa, it's two a.m. Come back to bed.'

Louisa stopped for a moment, wondering why he was being so sharp. Daisy was still crying. She couldn't leave her to it.

'I won't be a moment.'

She heard him sigh as she left the room. But as she padded along the landing, the noise stopped. She popped her head around Daisy's door. It was ajar, her nightlight still glowing.

'Mummy's here, Daisy,' Louisa whispered as she crossed the room to her daughter. Yet as she got to the bed, she realised she was fast asleep. She'd expected Daisy to be sitting up after crying out like that, wanting the arms of her mum to soothe her. But no, she was dead to the world.

She stooped by the side of the bed, watching as her daughter's chest rose and fell. Perhaps she'd been calling out in her sleep. Louisa had definitely heard her, despite what Richard had said.

After a couple of minutes, she went back to her own bedroom.

'Well?' Richard asked.

'She's fine. She must have been crying in her sleep.'

'I never heard a thing. You're imagining it again.'

'I heard her as plain as anything.'

'Yeah, yeah. Hurry up and switch the light off.'

Louisa did as she was told but lay awake in the dark. She knew she was listening out for Daisy. Sure enough, the moment she dropped off to sleep, Daisy started crying again. She sighed and pulled back the covers.

'Where are you going now?' Richard snapped.

'Daisy is upset. Can't you hear her?'

'I have an important meeting in the morning and waking me up every hour is going to ruin my concentration.'

'But I can hear her!' Daisy's cries were getting louder by the second. 'I'm going to her.'

Richard muttered under his breath as she raced into Daisy's room. But again she was asleep. She couldn't understand it. Daisy very rarely cried during her sleep and twice in one night was unheard of. She went back to her bedroom, confused and disorientated.

'I hope you're not going to get up again,' Richard growled. 'Because if you do, don't bother coming back to bed. Find a chair to sleep in.'

Louisa said nothing. It wouldn't be worth the hassle she would receive. Richard was terrible if he'd been kept awake. She'd had the wrath of him on many occasions. Again, she lay in silence, waiting for a tiny peep out of Daisy, ready to jump up again.

Thankfully, she was quiet for the rest of the night. But the next morning Richard was in a foul mood.

'What was going on last night?' he questioned as soon as he woke up.

'You mean with Daisy? I have no idea but I bet she'll be fine today, not even realising she's interrupted us.'

'Don't try and put the blame on Daisy. She was fine and wasn't screaming out. Hearing things isn't doing any of us any favours.'

'But I heard her.'

'I didn't.'

'I'm not making it up. She was...'

'She was asleep when you went into her room, both times.'

'Yes, but—'

'You can't be in our room tonight. I need my rest.'

'I know that and—'

He sighed. 'Maybe you need to take a sleeping pill, to help you get through the night.'

'No,' she protested. 'They make me feel like a zombie.'

'They give *me* a good night's rest.'

'Well, perhaps I should go back to the doctors to get something milder.'

'Perhaps you'll do as you're told for once and take the ones you have already.'

His cold stare was enough to make her want to escape the room. In his hand, he held the plastic bottle containing the pills. 'Take one tonight and see what happens.'

She took the bottle from him, knowing she wasn't going to do anything of the sort. She would feign sleep if she had to, and hope that Daisy didn't scream out too.

While Richard had a shower, Louisa went to start breakfast. But as she took a few steps downstairs, she noticed that the front door was wide open.

She rushed to close it, going through to the kitchen to see if Sarah was up too. But there was no one there. A quick check around the property ensured everything was still secure.

What was going on? Dare she mention it to Richard in case he accused her of leaving it open? She couldn't remember coming downstairs last night. No, she was certain she hadn't.

'Morning,' Sarah said as she came into the kitchen a few minutes later.

'Morning, did you sleep well?'

'I did. There's something about country living. I'm sleeping deeper than ever. It's so relaxing.'

'I'm sorry about Daisy's crying though.' Louisa gave a sad smile. 'I think she's having nightmares.'

'The poor thing. But don't worry. I didn't hear anything so she was no trouble to me.'

'I'm surprised. She was screaming so loud at one point.'

'Oh dear. I hope you managed to comfort her.'

'Yes, she was fine.' Louisa decided not to mention that Daisy had been asleep both times she had gone to her. 'And you didn't come downstairs for anything during the night?' she mentioned casually.

Sarah shook her head. 'No, why?'

'Oh, no reason.' Louisa wondered whether to say anything to Richard about the front door being open. He'd likely not believe her anyway; most probably she'd get the blame.

'It was great to get up knowing that I haven't got to go to that bloody factory,' Sarah said. 'You were so lucky to get away, Lou.'

Louisa smiled half-heartedly. Lucky? To live here, yes.

To live under these circumstances? She begged to differ.

THIRTY-NINE

When it was time to leave, Sarah had no intention of going back to Derby. It hadn't been a hard decision to see whether Richard's offer was workable. Her life there was so boring. There was nothing to look forward to, nothing to work towards. And really, why should *she* have to slave for someone else when Louisa lived in such luxury?

Having spent time with Louisa and Daisy, Sarah was getting to know how much Louisa was capable of doing and, even more, what she wasn't able to do. It surprised her how often Louisa would have to lie down with a headache, or back pain, or even being plain old tired. Some mornings that week, she hadn't got up until midday.

Daisy was a pleasant child, considering. It seemed to Sarah that she was used to spending time alone. She would sit and colour in with crayons on the floor of Louisa's bedroom. She would look at books for ages in the living room, singing quietly as she turned the pages. When the weather was sunny, she would sit as good as gold with her in the garden.

Today, Sarah was in the kitchen as Daisy had gone down for a nap with Louisa. Richard was heading towards the house when he spotted her in the kitchen window. She waved and went to greet him at the door.

'Hi,' she said.

'Hey, on your own again?'

'Yes, Louisa and Daisy are taking a nap. Do you fancy a coffee?'

'Please.'

She filled the kettle with water and turned back to him.

'I'm glad you came to stay for a while,' Richard spoke. 'It's been a nice change having someone else to talk to.'

'Well, you're welcome to slip out this evening if you have somewhere to go. I'm here for both of them. Take the offer while you can.'

'Thanks. I might just do that. I've cancelled so many prior engagements that I often don't get invited to anything happening locally now.'

Sarah paused, wondering how to bring up the subject of her staying. 'Do you ever yearn for the old Louisa?'

'Yes, but she won't ever be coming back.'

'Well, it's certainly clear to me why you need help. She can't manage with Daisy, and you shouldn't have to be running around after her when you have work to do. I'd like to help.'

Richard's face lit up. 'You'll take the nanny job?'

She nodded. 'If you think I'd be suitable.'

'Of course! Daisy loves you already, and I know Louisa can be quite demanding at times but there's room in the annexe for someone to live onsite. You can stay in there.'

'That's settled then.' She grinned at him.

'What about the job you have now? Do you have to give notice?'

'I pack biscuits into boxes six days a week.' She rolled her eyes. 'I doubt they'll even miss me but I suppose I'll have to give them a week before I leave.'

'And you wouldn't be bored here, out in the sticks? It's so quiet compared to Derby, totally different from city living if you're used to going out on the town a lot.'

'It's not so bad!' she insisted. 'It beats living on our estate.'

Richard smiled, his eyes resting on hers for a fraction longer than necessary. Then he leaned over and ran a finger over the back of her hand. 'I think this will work out fine. I'd pay you well and you'd have free board and lodgings. You'd be near to your sister too.'

'Of course.' Sarah grinned, keeping quiet about that not being the only reason she wanted to stay.

'I'll set up the annexe for you. It won't take long. Would you like to see it?'

'Sure.' Sarah followed him across the garden and waited as he unlocked the door. He held it open for her and she stepped inside.

'It'll be a bit dusty but I'll get Louisa to give it a clean for you.'

Sarah glanced around, trying not to grin like a Cheshire cat. The room opened up into a living room with a kitchen at the far end of it. It was all rustic, not to her taste at all, but somehow it felt cosy and homely.

'This is the shower room.' Richard opened a door to her left. 'And this is the bedroom.'

'It's perfect,' she told him, trying not to show too much enthusiasm. To live here would be like a dream come true. No more getting up early, suffering backache after standing for eight-hour shifts. No more cadging overtime to make her money go further. No reminders of what could have been, and what went wrong.

'Great. I'll get it sorted for you.'

He smiled at her, gazing long enough to make her shiver inwardly.

'I'm glad you like our arrangement,' he added.

Once they'd had coffee, Sarah watched Richard as he went back to his studio. She laughed slyly. That had been easier than she'd thought. It would be plain sailing to make herself indispensable. She was going to be here for good. Never mind what Louisa thought of her little sister taking over.

Louisa, however, was excited that she was staying.

'It will be so much fun with you around,' she exclaimed. 'We'll be able to go out together when I'm not so tired.'

'I'm going to be staying in the annexe,' Sarah told her. 'I love it. It's really quirky.'

'It will be home from home.' Louisa snorted. 'Actually it will be much better than the home you're used to.'

Sarah smiled but it didn't reach her eyes. She wasn't about to reveal yet why she hated her sister so much. She had that card to play later. For now, she was here to stay.

And that was all that mattered.

FORTY

2017

Sarah could remember chatting to Louisa about young love never running smooth. And oh how she now knew. When she and Jessie started dating, they'd been full of plans for the future. Now a year later, and after five months at college, she'd found out she was pregnant.

She didn't know what to think about the news. With Jessie at work, there was only her mum at home and she wasn't going to confide in her. She knew she wouldn't be fussed as she didn't care what happened to anyone but herself.

Yet her mum could read her better than she thought.

'What's wrong with you?' she said as Sarah flopped onto the settee.

'Nothing.'

'Anyone would think you'd had some bad news.'

Sarah stayed quiet, hoping she could watch the TV in peace. But her mum went on.

'There's nothing worse than being pregnant at your age like I was, so there is that you have to be grateful for, whatever is the matter with you.'

'Would it be so bad if I was?' she queried.

'What?'

'Pregnant.'

'Oh for crying out loud, please tell me you're not.'

Sarah's cheeks reddened as she stared at the TV.

'Have you taken a test?'

'Yes.'

'And?'

'It's positive.'

'You stupid, stupid girl. I thought you were on the pill.'

'I am.'

'So you must have forgotten to take it? Typical.'

'Why is it always my fault?' Sarah cried.

'You're the one who opened your legs willingly.' Her mum paused. 'He didn't force himself on you? Because that would be a very different matter.'

'No, Mum. He didn't.'

'Thanks for small mercies. Mind, you'll have to move out once you've had it. I'm too old for all that nappy changing malarkey. And I'm not looking after it while you're at college. You'll have to quit.'

'But I need to get an education so I can get a better job now,' she protested.

'You should have thought of that beforehand. I'm not made of money either. Babies are expensive, you know.'

'Jessie will take care of that. He's working now and—'

'—already has one child to pay out for. There could be more, knowing him.'

'Mum!' Sarah cried. 'He's not that bad.'

'Not while he's clean. But the minute he gets drugged up again, he'll dump you as quick as he can say have an abortion.'

'I am not getting rid of it.' Sarah choked back tears. 'You can't make me.'

'Like I said, don't expect me to babysit for you. I've provided you with a roof over your head for long enough now. You're on your own if you go through with it.'

Sarah ran out of the room and upstairs, throwing herself onto the bed. As she cried, she pummelled the mattress. Why was everything going wrong for her?

She called Louisa but the phone rang out, unanswered as usual. She threw it down, frustration boiling up alongside hurt. It was as if her sister had forgotten she existed. No wonder she wanted something of her own to love, to nurture, to cherish. Someone who would love her back unconditionally.

It wasn't ideal that she'd got pregnant but she couldn't get rid of it. She'd made her bed and she would lie in it. Where, she didn't know. But it wouldn't be here. This house had never been a home, nor would it ever be.

She thought back to the night before Louisa had left. Mum had come in drunk, there had been another row as usual and she had slinked off to bed. The two sisters had sat up until the early hours, talking about life and plans and their futures. Sarah hadn't realised then that she wouldn't see Louisa for so long. She missed her sister so much. Couldn't stand the new fella her mum had shacked up with this time.

But Sarah was seventeen now, an adult in her own right. An adult soon to be a mother. She needed to have a word with Jessie to see what she should do next.

* * *

Jessie wasn't keen at all. 'We're so young,' he argued. 'We should have some fun first before we settle down. Go on a few holidays, get some money saved.'

'So it's okay for you to have Shannon's baby and not mine?' She'd stormed off in a huff but he'd followed her.

'Of course not! But—'

She slapped his hand away as he came towards her. She hadn't expected him to be unhappy. Of course they were young, but Shannon had barely been fifteen when she'd had his son.

'Don't you want to have a baby with me?' she asked.

'Of course I do.' Jessie nodded. 'Just not yet.'

'You don't love me!'

'I do!'

'No you don't. You'll leave me, just like my sister did. Well, at least I know where I stand because I'm having our baby,' she said defiantly. 'It's your choice to stay with me or not.'

'I'm not going to leave you.' Jessie reached for her again. 'It isn't ideal timing but we'll make it work.'

'Really?' Her smile was shy.

'Really. It'll be fine.'

'Then you need to get used to the idea that you're going to be a dad again.'

'It will do wonders for my street cred,' he joked.

She slapped him playfully and he drew her into his arms. It was where she belonged, where she felt safe.

Jessie was her world. Their baby would be the best thing to happen to them. They would become a family, the one thing she wished for more than anything.

FORTY-ONE

Sarah returned to Derby briefly. It was agony working her last week at the factory but at least she had time to say goodbye to all her friends. Half of them couldn't understand why she would leave to live in the middle of nowhere. The rest saw the lure of the house in the country and a cushy job.

Her mum wasn't very pleased she was leaving.

'How the hell am I going to pay the rent now that you won't be bringing in any money?' she sniped when Sarah told her.

'You'll have to get a job, Mum,' Sarah taunted. 'Like normal people do. It might do you good to get off your arse and out of the house.'

'Oi, less of your cheek.'

'Well, I've supported you far more than you did me when I was young.'

'I've done my best for you girls and look how you repay me. I can't believe you're leaving to stay with Louisa.'

'I wish I'd left here a long time ago,' Sarah muttered.

'Why, you cheeky cow. Just because you're going to live with your sister who thinks she's Lady Muck, you can't talk to me how you like.'

'She's ill, Mum. I'm going to look after her.' For some reason,

Sarah had chosen not to mention to her mum that she was a grand-mother. She didn't want her demanding to see Daisy, traumatising both her and Louisa with a visit.

'I'm ill too. Who's going to look after me?'

'I'm sure some other fool will be around the corner.'

She'd left the air turning blue, her mother cursing her, as she'd got into the taxi and headed for the train station. Stuff her, she mused. There was no way she was missing out on the opportunity to get away from this dump.

As they turned out of the street she'd lived in since she was born, Sarah settled into the seat and smiled. Her life here was well and truly over.

Once back in Mapleton, Sarah settled herself into the annexe. Looking after Daisy was a doddle compared to the boring role she had left behind. She had many opportunities to play in the garden with her when Louisa was ill. When she was alone, she made time to drag Richard out of his studio for a drink, or at least a five-minute break. Over a few weeks, she got to know him really well. And soon she could tell that he was getting attracted to her. It wouldn't take much to change them from friends to lovers.

* * *

On the night she knew it would happen, she put Daisy to bed and checked on Louisa. Her sister was out for the count after her last round of medication and Sarah knew she wouldn't wake until the morning. Which was just as well for what she had planned.

She went downstairs, grabbed a bottle of wine and two glasses and headed out to the studio. The heat was still stifling, even though the sun had gone in an hour ago. The day had been sticky, but she'd showered and smelled delicious, even if she said so herself.

The wine lodged under her arm, she knocked on the door and went inside. Louisa had told her that Richard didn't like being disturbed when he was working. Perhaps he said that to keep her away from him. She was such a whinger when she was tired, moping around as if she was dying.

Richard looked up as she came in, treating her to a lazy grin.

'To what do I owe this pleasure?' he asked.

'It's late. You've been working all day. I have wine to drink and I don't want to do that alone. Louisa and Daisy are asleep so it's just us two.'

'Sounds good to me.'

She filled the glasses and handed one to him. Then she took a stroll around his studio admiring his work. Suddenly, she spotted a small canvas and gasped.

'You weren't supposed to see that,' he said.

The image was of Sarah. She was sitting on the garden wall, the wind in her hair as she looked up at the sun. She seemed content, happy with life and Richard had caught her expertly.

'When did you do this?' she asked.

'A couple of days ago. It didn't take me long.'

'It's amazing. You are so talented.'

'I like working magic with my hands.'

Taking that as her cue, she walked towards him, running a finger along his thigh as she drew level. She put down her wine glass and took his from him. Then she kept his hand in hers, turning it over as she examined it. A shot of desire pulsed through her body as she imagined what he could do with it.

He was still looking at her as she moved closer. Their lips met and she pressed herself against him, enjoying the feeling of them together. She never gave a thought to her sister as she removed his T-shirt and ran a hand over his chest.

She slipped the straps of her dress from her shoulder and pulled it down. She was naked beneath it and she heard an intake of breath as he took in her body. Then she was pawing at his jeans as he ran his hands over her, before they dropped onto the settee at the back of the room.

As they made love, Sarah glanced over Richard's shoulder towards the house. Part of her wished Louisa could see them as they joined together for the first time. It wouldn't be the last, but she'd have enjoyed seeing her sister's face as she realised what was going on underneath her nose.

She moaned at Richard's touch, turning her face towards him. All she had to do now was concentrate on him. He was her meal ticket to a better life. She had a job here, and if she played it right, she would soon have the man as well.

Then she could get Louisa out of the picture and have the house too.

FORTY-TWO

Over the next few weeks, Sarah got into a firm routine with Louisa and Daisy. It was fun to be around the little girl, and even though she had to put up with her sister's constant moaning, she was equally pleased she got to spend time with Richard too. The factory job picking out crushed or broken biscuits on a conveyor belt became a distant memory. It was also much better than living at home with her mother, never knowing what mood she'd be in, if she was even in when she got home.

It beat everything about her old life and the longer she was at White Oaks, the more she felt it was her rightful place to be.

She and Richard were having sex a few times each week now. So far, Louisa hadn't suspected a thing and it had been fun getting to know an older man. Sometimes, he was much more capable of giving a woman pleasure than any man she had been with before.

It was mid-afternoon. Richard was out fetching supplies, something he did every fortnight, so she'd had to be around to watch Louisa and Daisy while he was gone. Shortly after he'd left, he'd sent her a saucy message, saying something along the lines of what he would be doing to her on his return.

With Daisy down for a nap and Louisa yet to surface from her bed, she was at a loss for something to do. Louisa had been complaining all morning about her back aching. No wonder when she didn't move for days on end. To her mind, Louisa was her own worst enemy.

Sarah knew there were many people with hidden disabilities but it seemed clear to her that Louisa played on her illness. She'd often catch her dancing around the kitchen when she thought she was alone and then limping afterwards, saying she'd done too much trying to be normal. It really angered her to see how weak Louisa was, how much she used her illness to gain sympathy from Richard. She really was a wet lettuce.

Still, things were warming up between Sarah and Richard, and she wasn't sure how long it would be before their relationship would come out in the open. See how much Louisa liked going back to Derby with her tail between her legs. Louisa would take Daisy with her too – she'd miss her but she was glad of that. Then there would be only the two of them, living here in her idea of an idyllic home. Time to start their own family then.

The sun was high in the sky and it was pleasantly warm. Sarah lay on a lounger in the garden, but after a while it became too hot. She got up and strolled around the garden. Stopping at the studio, she peered through the window to see what Richard was working on, only to see the blinds were down. She moved to the side and retrieved a spare key hidden under the second plant pot along. Louisa had told her about it the other day.

Unlocking the door, she stepped inside. A thrill rushed through her as she nosed around. Richard didn't really like anyone coming into his studio, and he certainly wouldn't take kindly to her being there without him.

She wondered what he was working on. He often said he was doing landscapes but more recently he'd moved on to portraits and they were selling extremely well. There were also small paintings dotted here and there, the bread and butter ones as Richard called them.

Upstairs on the mezzanine, she spotted an easel with what looked to be a large canvas underneath it. She went upstairs to seek it out.

Pulling back a sheet revealed the image of a young white woman. Her long red hair was piled on her head, a few loose strands hanging sexily down towards her neck. She wore a strappy dress with a full skirt and was standing barefoot, smiling as if she were looking at a photographer. Her hands were reaching out as if she was ushering whoever looked her way into the canvas itself. It was provocative yet fun; casual yet intense.

The door went behind her and she turned sharply. It was Richard.

'What are you doing in here?' he asked as he took off his jacket.

Sarah shrugged. 'I wanted to see what you were working on.'

'And have you?'

She pointed to the canvas. 'Why are you painting another woman?'

'Because I have a client who likes her. He's had three portraits so far. I've made a fortune from them.'

'Does she model for you?'

'Of course not or you would have seen her. I get sent photos of her and paint from those.'

'But—'

With a few strides, he was at her side, silencing her with his mouth. She didn't hesitate to pull him into her arms. It heightened her sexuality as it was dangerous. They never made love during the day. It was always when Daisy and Louisa had gone to bed.

He lifted up her skirt and pushed himself into her. 'You ask too many questions,' he said before covering her neck with butterfly kisses. 'You don't need to be jealous of another woman.'

'I'm not!' She tried to push him away but he held on to her.

His eyes bore into hers as he ground his hips on her. She pulled him in closer, closer, longing for that feeling of orgasmic pleasure as he rocked her body along with his own.

God, the man consumed her. She daydreamed about him

constantly. She ached when he wasn't with her. She longed for his touch, the pleasure she would give him and the ecstasy she would receive.

Even when she thought she had the upper hand, at times like this she wasn't so certain.

FORTY-THREE

'What time will dinner be ready?' Richard asked Louisa as he joined her in the kitchen.

'Ten minutes at the most.' She breathed in the freshly showered scent of him as he walked behind her to the fridge. 'You smell nice.'

'Red or white?' He ignored her compliment.

'None for me, thanks. I have a splitting headache.'

'When have you ever not?' he muttered.

Louisa turned away. She didn't want to argue again. It seemed all they did nowadays. It was clear to see he didn't want to be around her any more.

'Sarah will join me for a glass, I'm sure. In fact, she can come over for something to eat. I'll text her to see if she wants to come over.'

Louisa tried not to let her shoulders sag. 'Could we have dinner alone? It would be nice for a change.'

'You don't begrudge your sister, surely?' His tone defied her to disagree.

She shook her head. 'Of course not. I—'

'Good. Text her then.'

Louisa did as she was told. A message of thanks came in from Sarah a few seconds later.

'She'll be across in a few minutes,' she told him.

'Just ready for you to dish the food out.' Richard's smile was sly. 'You will be capable of that?'

Louisa nodded. She raced around the kitchen to get everything ready. Beef stew had been on the stove for most of the day, leaving a delicious aroma around the house that once eaten would become overwhelming.

As she cut into a slice of crusty bread, she jumped as Richard curled his hand around her wrist. His firm grip made her drop the knife. He picked it up and held it next to her face.

'I don't like that bread. I told you not to buy it again.'

'I-I can't recall that.'

'You never remember anything, you useless lump of lard.'

Tears welled in her eyes as he stared at her. She knew his game. He was trying to demean her so that she would go to her room. Then he could have dinner with Sarah, the dinner *she* had cooked for them, while she went hungry.

'I have white bread too,' she offered weakly.

'Useless, that's all you are.' He looked at the pan of stew, then back at her. Her demeanour changed as she realised his intention, only hoping she could move in time to escape the scalding liquid.

Richard laughed. 'You think I'd waste good food on you?' He shook his head. 'Dish it out.'

Louisa did as she was told, trying to stop her hands from shaking as she ladled the stew into three bowls for them all. She placed two of them on the table and turned to get the third. But as she picked it up, Richard blocked her. The bowl slipped out of her hand and onto the floor.

'You clumsy cow.' He stepped back as the stew went everywhere.

'I'm sorry,' Louisa cried, a bag of nerves by this time. She knelt to pick up the bowl that had smashed into three pieces.

Richard bent down beside her. 'If I were you, I'd take a piece of that crockery with you. It's nice and sharp. Would be good for slit-ting a wrist, don't you think?'

She lowered her eyes. How could he be so cruel?

'Anyone home?' The door opened and Sarah stepped into the room.

Richard stood up quickly. 'Sarah, just in time.' He pointed to the table. 'Beef stew. It looks and smells delicious.'

'What's happened?' Sarah glanced at Louisa.

'Oh, she had a funny turn when she was bringing the bowl over to the table. I think she should go for a lie-down once she clears it up.'

'Let me help.' Sarah stooped down.

Louisa shook her head. 'I'm fine. It won't take a minute. Then I'll be out of your way.'

'If you're sure.'

Louisa could hear the hurt in Sarah's voice because she'd rebuked her. She held back tears she would cry only in private. Her sister was always so kind but Richard was too powerful for her to stand up for herself. And even if she did, it never went well. She had a few scars to prove that.

No, she wasn't staying where she wasn't welcome. After she'd cleaned up the stew, she would leave them in peace. It was better that way. She'd rather go hungry than risk the wrath of Richard once they were alone later during the evening.

Because everything would always be her fault, no matter what.

* * *

When Louisa had left the room, Sarah smiled at Richard as they ate their meal together. It was a good job she'd come over straight away. Through the window, she had seen what had happened. Although she couldn't hear the conversation, she knew it hadn't gone well for Louisa. Richard could be so cruel at times. She almost felt sorry for her sister... almost.

Still, Louisa needed to understand what it was like to feel hurt.

Just like she had when she'd been abandoned and left to fend for herself. She laughed, recalling the look of rejection on her sister's face.

'Something amusing you?' Richard asked, smiling back at her.

'No, I'm just happy.'

'It certainly suits you being here.'

'It does.' She threw him a lustful look. 'And I intend to keep it that way. This stew is delicious, isn't it?'

'It is. It seemed a shame to waste it.'

'You're such a bad boy,' she teased.

'I'll show you just how much later on. Right here on the table, if you like.'

Sarah giggled as he reached across and laced his fingers with her own. She wondered if Louisa was out of the way and not listening behind the door. Because she would be so upset if she was.

Sarah didn't care one iota. She was happy with the way things were going with Richard. Well, who wouldn't be?

FORTY-FOUR

2018

Sarah woke up to the sound of the alarm going off. Her daughter, Poppy, who was nine months old, stirred in her cot at the bottom of the bed.

Jessie was asleep beside her. She tried to nudge him awake to no avail. He'd been out the night before and had a skinful. Not that that was anything unusual. Since having Poppy he'd been going out with his mates more and more, often returning drunk. Even more worrying she thought he might be taking drugs again.

She'd noticed a difference in him since Poppy had arrived. He seemed to be losing weight and his mood swings had become quite violent at times. Twice she'd had to stop him from hitting out when he'd raised his hand in the air.

She lay in bed for a few minutes, relishing the time before she had to get up and start another crappy day. It was Jessie's turn to have Poppy today while she went to work. She'd bagged a double shift at the biscuit factory where she swore she would never work.

'Jessie, wake up.' She shook his shoulder and he gave a groan.

'What?' he snapped.

'I have to get ready for work and you need to look after Poppy today. Jessie!'

'It's Saturday.'

'I have overtime. You can't say we don't need the money. Wake up!'

'Give it a rest, will you.'

'You have to, you promised.'

He turned away from her.

Sarah sighed and pulled back the covers. 'I'll get her breakfast.' She went over to the cot. Poppy was playing with her feet, the brightest of smiles appearing when she spotted her mum.

'Good morning, my angel.' She picked her up, kissing the top of her head. 'Let's get you sorted and then we can have breakfast before I have to leave.' She glanced at Jessie who had gone back to sleep. She wanted to be childish and pull off the duvet. Ever since he'd started hanging round with Hudson, his new work colleague at the garage, Jessie had changed. Hudson was single and his parents were loaded, so he didn't understand what Jessie was going through. They barely had enough money to pay for things, which was why they were living with Jessie's mum in the double bedroom at the back of the house.

Once she and Poppy were ready to face the day, Sarah went downstairs.

Paulette, Jessie's mum, was in the kitchen. Like Jessie, she was tall with olive skin. She was wearing pink pyjamas, almost matching the colour of her short hair. Her face showed years of smoking twenty cigarettes a day, even though she had given up a while ago.

Paulette held out her arms for Poppy and Sarah handed her over. She got on well with Paulette, thankfully. It was hard when Ethan came over too. Paulette loved having two grandchildren, but Sarah always felt wary of Ethan's mum, Shannon. She would always ask for money from Jessie, even though she knew he had none spare. Often she'd seen her flirting with him and wondered if they were an item again. But then he'd wink at her and the doubts would go away, for that moment anyway.

'Where's Jessie?' Paulette asked.

'He's still in bed. I have to go to work soon. I hope he gets up. He needs to look after Poppy.'

'I can help. I love spending time with this one.'

'I know you do and I'm really grateful but I wish Jessie would do more, rather than leaving it to us all the time.'

'He's just like his dad. Daryl was a crap father too. He left everything to me until we got divorced. Did I ever tell you why?'

Sarah nodded, hoping she wouldn't tell her again that she caught him with his trousers down, his bare arse going up and down as he pushed himself into her best friend. She made a big show of checking her watch.

'I'd better shout Jessie again.'

'Don't worry.' Paulette blew raspberries on Poppy's tummy much to her delight. 'I'll look after her until he surfaces.'

'Are you sure?'

'Of course.' She smiled. 'You're a good mother, Sarah. And you're providing for her too. You're doing a great job. Now, off you go, before you're late.'

On the bus to the factory, Sarah thanked her lucky stars for Paulette. She thought back to what her own mother had said to her when she'd told her she was pregnant. She hadn't seen her for three months now. Unless she called round with Poppy, Mum never wanted to know. She never rang to see how she was. It was the same with Louisa. Out of sight, out of mind. She was a nobody to her family, and yet she didn't understand why.

Sarah had never felt so lonely. Most of her friends were out enjoying themselves, not lumbered with children. Okay, some of them had got pregnant early on but there were lots more that were working and their money wasn't going on family stuff. They were buying clothes and shoes and handbags, going out in the evenings to enjoy themselves. Doing normal things that teenagers did.

Even her best friend, Hannah, had dropped off now. When Poppy was first born, Hannah had been there for her. She'd helped her with the feeds, kept her company when she was tired and Poppy wasn't sleeping well. She'd even taken Poppy out on occasions to give her a break.

But that had stopped when the novelty wore off. When Poppy began to do more than sleep, became more demanding. Sarah had to cancel no end of nights out and soon the invites dried up. The last she'd seen of Hannah was when she'd bumped into her in town and she'd said she was off to meet Jade for coffee. She'd asked her to come along too, but with Poppy in tow, who would want that? And it had been clear from Hannah's face that it had been small talk rather than a proper invite.

Still, Sarah had Poppy to think about now and that was all that mattered to her. She was thinking of going back to college that autumn, perhaps to catch up on the course she'd been halfway through. There was a creche and she was hoping to drop Poppy off there when she had lectures and classes. Sarah wasn't one for settling. She wanted to do the best for her, and Poppy, come what may.

FORTY-FIVE

It hadn't taken long before Louisa noticed what was going on with Sarah and Richard. She could see it in Sarah's eyes, the way she glanced at him. She could spot it in his mannerisms, the way he looked at Sarah. They were sleeping together, and neither of them seemed to be bothered that she might find out.

It stung that her sister would do that to her. Yet Louisa realised she wasn't capable of giving Richard what he needed any more. Louisa could barely look after herself, let alone Richard and Daisy. Her life was a total mess. *She* was a mess too. She was no worse than Mum, dependent on drugs rather than alcohol.

She recalled how she'd been when she first arrived at White Oaks. Living here back then was like a dream come true. She'd adored it. She'd loved Richard too for a time, but it seemed she'd become a burden to him. More often than not, she wondered if he'd had enough of her.

And if Sarah *was* sleeping with him, her sister certainly hadn't seen his wild side yet. He'd obviously kept his temper under control. Not like he did with her.

She hadn't wanted to say anything until she had more evidence. But it would break her if she had to see them laughing and joking again. And then yesterday when she'd been looking out on the garden, she was sure she had seen them *together*.

So the question had been on her mind for quite some time before she said anything to Sarah. They were in the kitchen at the time, just the two of them.

'Are you and Richard having an affair?' she blurted out.

Sarah turned to her sharply. 'No! Whatever gave you that idea?'

Louisa buckled at her sister's expression. She seemed genuinely shocked at the question. Had she got it wrong? Was she imagining things were going on between Richard and Sarah because she assumed it might be happening?

'I just thought you were getting close, that's all.'

'I enjoy his company as much as yours and I like having a laugh with him. We share the same sense of humour. But honestly, I'd never do that to you.' Tears welled in Sarah's eyes. 'Not to any woman, actually. I'm surprised you'd even think that.'

'He's been with other women, I'm sure of it.' Louisa's tone was less authoritative now.

'Well, I can assure you, he hasn't been with me.'

'I'm sorry.'

'How can you think anything like that? It's hurtful and spiteful too, to ask me. Have you spoken to Richard about it?'

'No.'

'And do you intend to?'

Louisa shook her head. She wouldn't dare mention anything to him.

'But you'll have a go at me and make me feel like shit. It's just like the old days, Louisa. As long as you're okay, screw everyone else. I've a good mind to go back to Derby and see how you'd cope without me.'

'Please don't do that,' Louisa exclaimed. 'I'm sorry. I was over-thinking and—'

'Too right you were. I stay here for one reason and one reason only. To make sure you and Daisy are okay.' Sarah pointed at her.

'Some days you barely say two words to your daughter. Imagine how much danger she would be in without someone to watch over her when you have your turns.'

Louisa couldn't meet Sarah's eye, seeing how hurt she was. But despite her sister's reaction, she wasn't fooled. She could imagine them both laughing at her.

When Sarah flounced out of the room, the tears Louisa had been holding back fell freely. Sarah had denied there was anything going on but she wasn't stupid, no matter how much they assumed she was.

It was time she helped herself, sorted out why she was feeling so awful all the time. If she couldn't get to the surgery with either Richard's or Sarah's help, she'd get the doctor to come out to her if possible.

She made a call but she had no luck at the surgery. Unless it was an emergency, a doctor couldn't do home visits. She'd have to talk to Richard. She'd do it today.

'Richard, could I have a minute?' she said as soon as he came upstairs after he'd finished in the studio that evening.

'I hope this isn't about going to the doctors again.' He reached for fresh clothes and turned his back to her.

'Yes, it is. It can't be right that I'm tired all the time. I can barely get out of bed some days and I want—'

'There's nothing else he can give you.'

'Please, Richard, listen to me for once! I'm the one who has to—'

He raced over to within a few inches of her face, grabbing her by the wrist. 'I am *sick* of this, Louisa. I am tired of you moaning about everything. I brought Sarah to you so that you would feel better, giving you time to rest, but still you nag. It stops right now, do you hear?'

Fearing he would strike her if she continued, she bowed her head and nodded.

'Good. Not another word.'

Once he'd left the room, Louisa flopped down onto the bed and broke down. Being married to Richard was like being in prison. This was what her life would be confined to. Bed rest, not leaving the home because she was too weak. Not being able to interact with her daughter because she was so tired. She'd seen Daisy in the garden earlier with Sarah. Her sister could do the things that she couldn't. It wasn't fair.

If only she was well enough to do more for herself. If only she was stronger, she could tackle him and leave.

If only. If only. If only.

FORTY-SIX

Sarah was in the annexe, waiting for Richard to come across from the studio. She'd been looking forward to it all day. It didn't bother her that she was being deceitful right under her sister's eyes. As long as she had a good time on her mission, who cared.

At half past seven, Richard appeared.

'I need a shower if I'm stopping,' he said, sniffing at his armpits as she pulled him near. 'I whiff a bit.'

'Want me to join you?' She took a quick look back towards the house but Louisa was nowhere to be seen.

Richard shook his head. 'But you can wait for me in bed.'

While he was under the water, Sarah removed her clothes and got out a bottle of whisky and two tumblers. She wanted to encourage Richard to stay longer and whisky was always a good option for that. But then there was a knock at the door. Grabbing a towel to cover her nakedness, she went to open it. It could only be Louisa. Her face was creased up in distress.

'Hi, Lou. What's up?'

'Is Richard here?' Louisa asked, glancing down at her towel for a moment.

'No, he said he was going out this evening.'

'Did he?'

'Yes. This morning, over breakfast. He said he was meeting one of the farmers – what was his name? Oh, it will come to me in a minute. They were going to The Valley Arms.'

'I can't...' Louisa frowned, looking back at the house for a moment. 'I can't remember. Did he say what time he'd be back?'

'I don't think so. Are you okay? You look really peaky.'

'No, no. I'm fine.'

Sarah could see she looked nothing of the sort but didn't want to push her concern. 'Do you want me to get dressed and come over to the house with you?' she offered, hoping Louisa would decline.

Louisa shook her head. 'You have a night by yourself for a change. I'll be fine.'

'If you're sure.'

Louisa was already walking away.

'Night,' Sarah shouted after her.

'Night.'

Sarah closed the door with a grin. She flung the towel onto the settee and ran to the bedroom, jumping on the bed next to Richard who was waiting for her.

'She has no idea you're here,' she told him, running a hand down his chest.

'She has no idea of anything really. In the morning, you could tell her and she wouldn't remember you'd denied it. She's so forgetful.'

An hour later, they'd made love twice and were lying in bed, legs entwined and whisky downed.

'For an old man, you sure know how to keep a girl happy.' Sarah stretched out like a kitten, almost purring.

Richard slapped her bottom. 'Cheeky bitch,' he growled.

'Temper, temper. Do you have a dark side I haven't seen yet?'

'You don't know the half of it.'

She turned towards him, running a hand over his chest. 'Pray, tell me more.'

'I can't.'

'You have secrets from Louisa?' She feigned mock horror.

'I have secrets from everyone.'

'Let's play true or false.'

'I'm a grown man. I don't play games.'

'It's only a bit of fun. You tell me the darkest thing you've ever done and I have to guess whether it's true or a lie.'

He sighed. 'You go first.'

Sarah paused for a moment. 'I killed someone,' she said.

His eyes widened as he turned towards her. 'You're joking, of course.'

'My mum had this man. He'd been messing around with her and thought he could do the same with me. I was only fifteen at the time. The pervert saw me on the landing as he came out of the bathroom, tried to grope me and as I pushed him away, he fell down the stairs. I still remember the crack of his head on the floor as he got to the bottom. He didn't get up again.'

'What happened to him?'

'Mum saw me standing at the top of the stairs, a look of shock on my face, and she guessed what had happened. She went ballistic with me because she had to call an ambulance.

'She told *me* not to say anything. She told the *police* he'd fallen down the stairs and I was asleep in bed. She was so angry for days because I'd brought trouble to her door. But he was a vile bastard. An evil predator, and he wasn't putting his hands over me.'

Richard drew her into his arms as she tried to push away the memories, the fear of wondering what the man was going to do to her. The push that saved it happening again.

'Remind me not to show you *my* dark side,' Richard teased.

'Do you think that's true or false?'

'I'm not sure.'

'Gotcha! I did push the bastard down the stairs but he didn't die. He was concussed and broke his leg. So, what about you?'

Richard went silent and for a moment she wondered whether he'd join in or not. But then he spoke.

'You know I told you my father shot himself? Well, he didn't. I killed him.'

It was Sarah's turn to look wide-eyed.

'One afternoon, he came in drunk and started laying into me. I'd taken beatings off him before but on that day, I'd had enough. While he was in a stupor, he was slouching in the armchair, his legs stretched out in front of him. I got the shotgun and shot him, making it seem as if he had done it. Then I called the police as if I'd just found him.'

'Didn't they suspect you?'

'I was questioned but there were no witnesses to say otherwise. No evidence to say it was me. We both used the rifle to shoot foxes and rabbits. We also both had access to the gun cabinet and cartridges.'

Sarah stayed quiet for a while, wondering about his story. 'Why do I have a feeling that what you've just told me is the truth?' she asked eventually. 'Does Louisa know?'

'No.'

'I think you'd be wise not telling her either. You know how neurotic she can be at times.' She paused. 'Don't you ever wish you could get rid of her? Send her back to Derby perhaps and live your life without her.'

'With you, you mean?'

'Well.' She grinned. 'Maybe.'

'I didn't think you'd ever say that. I thought you had your sister's best interests at heart.'

'I only ever put myself first now.'

Richard rolled over until he was covering her. He kissed her deeply. 'I think I may have met my match with you.'

'Good, because you'd be wise to remember that. I'm not as weak as my sister.'

'And I'm not stupid enough to tell you I killed my father when I didn't.'

He stared at her and for a moment she thought she saw a shimmer of anger. But it was matched with her determination. She was cleverer than she was making out, purposely.

And he wasn't clever enough to realise.

FORTY-SEVEN

2018

When Sarah got in from work that evening, Paulette was sitting with Poppy on her knee.

'Where's Jessie?' Sarah asked her.

'He went out an hour ago. Said he was meeting Hudson.'

Sarah's features darkened. 'He promised to stay in with me tonight. He also said he'd look after Poppy.'

'One out of two isn't bad,' Paulette humoured.

'Don't tell me he's been here all day, because I know that's probably not true.'

Paulette blushed, giving it away. 'He looked after her this morning and then I said as I was in, he might as well go out.'

Sarah sighed as she took Poppy from her. 'I want him to be more involved with Poppy. He's not like he is with Ethan.'

'Boys will be boys.'

'That's not how it works.'

'I'm sorry, I didn't mean to joke. But you know Jessie, he's one of the lads.'

Sarah wondered whether to discuss her concerns with Paulette. It was difficult because he was Jessie's mother. But she was also Poppy's grandmother and if she was fearful for her child, perhaps she'd be better speaking out about it. She decided to bite the bullet.

'Paulette, do you think Jessie has changed recently?'

Paulette looked up with a quizzical look. 'In what way?'

Sarah dropped Poppy into a highchair. 'He seems to be angry all the time.'

'Has he done something to you?' Paulette gasped. 'He hasn't hit you?'

'No, and he'd better not. I'd wallop him back if he did and we'd be gone the next day.'

Paulette nodded her approval. 'That's good to know, though. His father used to clout me all the time. I was hoping it wouldn't be passed down to Jessie as he grew up around it.'

Sarah gave out a huge sigh. 'I just wish he'd take more responsibility with Poppy.'

'I'm sure the men in this family don't want to do that about anything, and that has nothing to do with me.' She stood up. 'I'll make us a cuppa.'

Sarah ran a hand over her daughter's forehead, pushing away her hair as she prepared to feed her. Jessie's huge brown eyes stared back at her, the shape of his nose. Poppy had Jessie's colouring too. She was the spit of her father, a constant reminder of him.

Why didn't Jessie want to spend time with them? Why did he always want to be with that stupid Hudson more?

Her phone beeped as a message came in. She read it and sighed. It was from Jessie.

I have a shift at the pub tonight so I won't be home until late. Jx

Sarah huffed. She was all alone again. Okay, Paulette would be in, but that wasn't the same as spending time with your partner.

She couldn't help but think that Jessie was tiring of her. They seemed to be getting on but she felt like they were an old married couple before their time, and they weren't even married. She was eighteen years old with a nine-month-old daughter and a part-time man. What was all that about? Why couldn't she have some good luck in her life?

And every time he stayed out late, thoughts ran through her mind about other girls. On the odd occasions they did go out on a date, she'd watched them willingly throw themselves at him when he'd gone to the bar to fetch a drink. He was such a flirt too, always laughing and egging them on. Then when she got upset about it, he'd call her a nag.

So was he really working tonight or was he with someone else? She squeezed her eyes tightly shut to rid herself of the images she was conjuring up. Still, she didn't bother to reply to his message.

* * *

When he staggered into their bedroom at half past one, Sarah smelt the booze from across the room.

'You're late,' she snapped.

'There was a lock up when my shift finished.' Jessie burped loudly.

'Be quiet!' she whispered. 'You'll wake Poppy up.'

'Sorry.' Jessie flopped face down on the bed. 'I'm wasted.'

'When are you ever not?'

'Don't start. I haven't got the energy to argue,' he muttered and turned his face away from her.

She switched off the lamp and lay back fuming. Why couldn't she have found herself a decent boyfriend? One who would treasure her and Poppy? Or why...

She stopped herself mid-thought. This wasn't Poppy's fault. She'd brought her into this world. But Sarah wished she'd waited now, had Poppy in a few years' time. When it would have been easier to cope. When she would have seen more than this crappy estate. When she would have felt ready to be a mother.

A few minutes later, she wanted to cover Jessie's face with a pillow as he snored beside her while she struggled to get back to sleep. He hadn't even bothered to remove his clothes. What a loser.

Poppy snuffled in her sleep and she listened to see if she was going to wake. Thankfully, she never stirred.

Rearing a child would be hard, her mother had said. That was okay really. It was having to do everything by herself when she was part of a couple that riled her. She needed to have a good talk to Jessie.

But then she realised how much Paulette did for her and for Poppy and knew she was trapped. Perhaps things would get better when Poppy was older. She prayed they would.

FORTY-EIGHT

Louisa had recently woken from a nap. She'd gone to sleep with a blinding headache, hoping to rid herself of it, but it was still there. She sighed in frustration. Is this all she had to look forward to in life now? More debilitating pain and exhaustion?

A few minutes later, she dragged herself up from the bed and popped in to see Daisy. She was still asleep, all curled up like a kitten, so she left her there and went downstairs.

In the kitchen, Richard and Sarah were sitting at the table. They both glanced at her but it was Richard who spoke first.

'What's going on?' she asked, sensing something was wrong.

'We need a word with you,' Richard said.

Her brow furrowed. 'What about?'

Richard pointed at an empty chair.

After a pause, Louisa sat across from them, hands in her lap. She wondered if this was it. The moment where they confessed they were in love and wanted her and Daisy to leave. A feeling of relief flooded through her at the thought she would be able to get away. Sure, her sister had betrayed her and her husband was a bastard, but she would have the chance to start again, somewhere fresh with Daisy and get the treatment she needed to be well again and...

'Louisa,' Richard broke into her thoughts. 'We want to know how you are... after last night.'

She threw him a look. 'Sorry, I'm not with you.'

'I said she wouldn't remember anything.' Sarah shook her head sadly.

'What do you mean?' Louisa looked at Sarah for further reference. 'What's going on?'

'You were in the woods,' Richard enlightened her.

'No, I wasn't.' Louisa paused. 'Was I?'

Sarah reached a hand across the table and gave Louisa's a gentle squeeze. 'I wondered whether to tell you or not, but you gave us a fright and—'

'*Us?* What exactly happened?'

'I was getting ready for bed when I saw you through the window,' Richard said. 'I raced out after you. I found you in the clearing. You were kneeling down, crying uncontrollably.'

'I – no. I would remember.' Louisa looked aghast as she ran a hand through her hair. 'Are you sure?'

Sarah nodded.

'Was I in there long?'

'About ten minutes,' Richard replied. 'I went to you eventually, and guided you back out. You were wearing pyjamas and had nothing on your feet.'

'But that's absurd. I don't recall a thing.'

'We're worried about you.'

Louisa looked at them both in turn, hoping they would explain things to her.

'When you didn't mention it, we thought you were embarrassed,' Sarah went on. 'We didn't think you wouldn't remember.'

'I don't. Is that wrong?'

'I'm not sure,' Richard said.

'I should have gone to the doctors. Perhaps now you'll let me.'

'No one is saying you can't go, Louisa.' Richard sighed, as if he was speaking to a petulant child. 'It's just that there is nothing else they can do for you. You're on the strongest medication for your condition. And if you start mixing it with other things, imagine the side effects.'

'You're not a doctor,' she said.

Richard sighed. 'Fine, I'll make an appointment for you if you want him to go through the same things he discussed with you on the last visit.'

'That was six months ago!'

'And you've changed since then, personally I feel for the worst. You don't want to leave Daisy while you get some help, which is probably what will—'

'Stay away from Daisy,' Louisa growled.

'We have to think of her safety.'

'I know what you're up to.' She pointed to them both. 'You're trying to say I'm mentally ill, unable to cope with her so you can get rid of me.'

'It's not like that at all,' Sarah cried.

'Calm down, Louisa.' Richard looked at Sarah. 'See, this is what I mean. She's unstable.'

'I am not unstable!' Louisa screamed. The silence that followed made her realise that they could be right.

'Well, we're both here if you want to chat about anything.' Sarah stood up, urging Richard to do the same. 'I'd better go and check on Daisy.'

'She's fine!' Louisa snapped. 'She's gone down for a nap.'

Richard sighed. 'No one's trying to get at you, Louisa.'

Her shoulders sagged as she gave in. 'I'm sorry. I know you mean well. I just don't understand.'

'Why don't you go and have another lie down?' Sarah suggested. 'I'll make you a cup of tea and bring it up to you. Don't worry about Daisy. I'll take care of her too.'

Louisa could only nod. She left the room in a daze and headed upstairs. What was happening to her? Was she losing her mind? Or were they ganging up on her? Did she have two people to worry about now, instead of the one?

* * *

Sarah waited for the kettle to boil, glancing out of the kitchen window. She had never seen Louisa so agitated and it was slightly concerning. She turned back in time to see Richard sprinkling something into the mug she'd put out for Louisa.

'What's that?' she questioned.

'I'm giving her something to help her sleep.'

'But it's lunchtime.'

Richard's smile was snide. 'So it is.'

Sarah paused, her mind working over his words. 'Is this a regular occurrence?'

'I like to keep her under control. Without the medication, she's feisty and I don't like how she acts.'

'So instead you use drugs to calm her down? How long have you been doing that?'

'If I told you, I'd have to kill you.'

His tone was comical but Sarah wondered how much of a threat was hidden in his words. Richard had a darker undertone than she'd first imagined.

'Seriously, why don't you tell her to leave?' she said. 'You don't love her any more, do you?'

'I've never loved her. She's too clingy.'

'So why did you marry her?'

'Because I wanted someone to look after me.'

'You could have paid for a housekeeper.'

'Why should I when I have Louisa to do it for free?'

'You're such a bastard.'

He smiled at her again.

'You're weird. You marry my sister, you get her pregnant so she is kinda chained to you. Then when she starts complaining because she wants more from you, you drug her to keep her dependent on you. You're manipulating her mind. I'm not sure I like that.'

Richard was quiet for a moment. 'So what do you suggest I do instead?'

'I think you should let her go back to Derby. I could persuade her.'

He smirked. 'So you want to be the housekeeper and nanny now?'

'Absolutely not. Daisy would go with Louisa. You could still see her on a regular basis.' She leaned closer to him. 'I want you, and all of you. I think we should start planning to ensure it happens. Maybe we should up Louisa's dosage,' she suggested, holding Richard's eye as he stared at her. 'A little more would work in our favour, don't you think?'

FORTY-NINE

2018

Sarah climbed on board the bus and shuffled to the furthest seat she could find at the back. She sat next to a woman she saw regularly, giving her a half-smile as she made herself comfortable. Then she removed her hood, careful not to drip rain everywhere. It had been pouring down for most of the day and she'd left her umbrella at home. Not that it would have mattered, the wind blowing the icy drops at her regardless.

The windows were steamed up, making it seem as if she was on a magical mystery tour. If only. She actually felt as if she was on the road to nowhere. The bus stank of damp clothes and smelly people. She'd just finished an eight-hour shift and her back was aching.

Tears brimmed in her eyes as she realised even though she didn't want to be at work, she didn't want to go home to Jessie either. They'd had another huge row the night before. She'd been complaining about still living with his mum. Of course she got on with Paulette, and she was a godsend where Poppy was concerned. But Sarah wanted Jessie to help her look for a place of their own. She wouldn't mind if it was a flat. Just as long as they could live there as a family. Decorate it how they wanted. Have their own furniture, their own TV. Their own front door. Perhaps a tiny garden.

Jessie had said it was too early to think of that. He said he needed to save some money. Sarah had accused him of spending more than he saved and the argument had escalated. It had ended up with Paulette coming upstairs to stop them shouting at each other.

Paulette had been brought into it then because Jessie told her his home wasn't good enough for Sarah. She hated how Paulette sided with Jessie when she was hurt. Why was it so hard for them to accept that she wanted better than her present arrangements? It had nothing to do with his mother.

If it weren't for Poppy, Sarah realised, they would have split up a long time ago. She was saving money to leave him anyway, and for now there was nowhere for them to go. But she'd had enough of trying to live love's young dream.

Her thoughts turned to her sister, as they always did when she was low. When things were going well, she blocked Louisa from her mind, the pain of being rejected as raw as the last text she sent that had gone unanswered.

When things were bad, as they were now, she thought about her a lot. What was she up to? Was she still with Richard? Did she have children of her own?

More to the point, was she happy? She couldn't help but miss her. They'd been so close growing up. She still couldn't understand why they hadn't been able to mend their differences after their argument. Families fell out all the time, some not speaking for years like her and Louisa. But most of them apologised and moved on. She wished she'd had a chance to say she was sorry now. Not that she would have admitted that at the time.

It had shaped her life too. Now she was afraid to get close to anyone in case they left as well. It was the reason she'd been so keen to stay with Jessie once she'd found out she was pregnant. She'd wanted to get away from home, be a grown up. Have someone to love her unconditionally. At least she had that with Poppy. Jessie, not so much.

Still, she reckoned, if he wanted to stay with his mum, she could be out of his life within the next few months, sooner perhaps. This morning, she'd been talking to a woman at work who would have a room to rent in her house once her daughter left for university in September. She'd said she'd be fine bringing Poppy to stay too. It would be her saving grace, something to get her through days like today. When she felt hopeless, that there was nothing to look forward to.

She closed her eyes, recalling how Jessie had shouted in her face that morning, pointing his finger, saying she was a nag. She was the breadwinner. How could he say that to her?

Once home, she removed her coat and hung it over a chair in the kitchen to dry out. She could hear the TV on in the living room and went in to find Jessie flat out on the settee. With a sigh, she shook him awake.

'Where's Poppy? Did you put her down to sleep?' she asked.

'She's upstairs in the bathroom.'

'What?' She glared at him, unable to believe what he was saying. 'You left her alone?'

'Don't worry, she's in the baby bath.'

'But you were asleep!'

Jessie looked at his watch and sat up quickly.

The look on his face told her all she needed to know.

Sarah took the stairs two at a time, dashing into the bathroom. She would never forget the image she was faced with for as long as she lived. Poppy was face down in the bath. Although there was no water in it, she lay unmoving, blood from her head pooled under it.

'Poppy!' She picked her up quickly and wrapped her in a towel.

'Fuck, is she okay?' Jessie came behind her, standing in the doorway with his hands in his hair. 'I swear I didn't mean to fall asleep.'

'How long was she on her own?'

'I don't know!'

'You do!'

'About half an hour. I—what do you think happened?'

'She must have stood up, or sat forward, and slipped from the baby bath. She's hit her head on the side of the bath. I don't know how long she's been unconscious.'

'Is she okay?'

'You should have been watching her! Get me my phone.' Sarah broke down as she reached for her daughter. 'Poppy? Poppy, can you hear me? Mummy's here. Everything will be okay now.'

FIFTY

Sarah waved Richard off on his fortnightly trip for business supplies. She quite liked it when he went out for long spells now and had planned on a pampering day by herself.

In the main house, she frowned when she heard the noise coming from upstairs. Bang, clatter, scrape. It was coming from Louisa and Richard's bedroom. Curious to know what was happening, she went to see.

The door was ajar. Louisa was emptying a drawer of her clothes.

'Go away,' Louisa said when she saw her standing in the doorway.

'What are you doing?' Sarah asked.

'What does it look like? I'm leaving, and I'm taking Daisy with me.' Louisa's voice was manic. 'You! You want Richard for yourself, don't you?'

'No.' She tried to show a little concern in her tone. 'Of course I don't.'

'You're playing me.' Louisa pointed at her. 'I saw you and Richard fucking in the studio. You can't deny it when I saw it with my own eyes. Besides, he told me it was true.'

'Oh, give over. Have you taken your medication?'

'Don't patronise me!'

'Stop moaning then. All you do is whine and whinge and sit on your lazy arse and do nothing.'

Louisa looked at her, hurt etched on her face.

'You know that Richard can't stand you any more? He gives you things to make you sleep. So he doesn't have to spend time with you.'

Louisa's eyes widened. 'I don't believe you.'

'You should ask him some time.'

Sarah turned to leave but Louisa grabbed her arm. 'Why would you let him do this to me? Don't I mean anything to you?'

'No, you don't. You had no right to call me a sister when you left me to rot when I was fifteen. You didn't care about anyone but yourself. You made that clear.'

'It wasn't like that!' Louisa gasped. 'I was young and trusting. I thought I had everything in Richard, but I didn't realise he was so abusive, most of which I think he thought was fun. He wanted me to have a child so he had a hold on me. So that I wouldn't leave. I don't know why he wouldn't let me because it's been clear he doesn't love me any more.'

'It's all you, you, you!' Sarah spat. 'Have you any idea what happened to me when you left me alone in Derby?'

'No, because you won't tell me.'

'You think I didn't want all this that you have?' Sarah went on regardless, running a hand around the room. 'Well, I did. And I tried so hard but it was all taken from me. I had a daughter too, but she died and...'

Louisa froze.

'She was nine months old.' Sarah took a breath. 'I went a bit wild when you left, hooked up with Jessie and then I got pregnant. When I had Poppy, I moved in with Jessie and his mum.'

'Jessie Davidson?'

'Yes, and you were right. He was a layabout. I thought he'd change when Poppy came along but he didn't. I had no choice but to go out to work and leave her with him. But I regret it every day of my life. Because he killed her! He murdered my little girl.' Tears rolled down her cheek. 'He left her in the bath and then he fell asleep. I came home to... to... He was supposed to have taken care of her. I left her. It was my fault.'

'Oh, Sarah.' Louisa didn't know what to say.

'She was beautiful. Daisy reminds me of her so much. I still can't believe she's gone. She was my life.'

'If I'd known, I would—'

'You didn't want to know, that's the problem! All you were interested in was your precious Richard, and his house and getting away from us all.'

'I never wanted to leave you.' Louisa reached for her hand. 'Richard was all-consuming and I was in love. Back then, he was good to me and yet I didn't see how manipulating he was. He isolated me from my family, from you, from making new friends here, before I even realised. He said he loved it just the two of us, but that he couldn't wait to start a family.

'But when Daisy was born, and I had trouble adjusting, he didn't like that. It was as if I'd lost my shine. As if I wasn't enough for him and over time I did lose myself. *He* made me into who I am today, and if you're not careful, he'll do the same to you. He's evil, Sarah. Let's all leave and go back to Derby. You, me and Daisy. We could get somewhere to live and—'

'You think I'd help you to get away?' Sarah turned to walk away again.

'What do you mean?'

'You left me to deal with Nigel!'

Louisa had the decency to look shamefaced.

'You knew what he was like and you left me there, to be molested by that – that bastard. Mum didn't believe me when I told her I didn't want him in the house. And unlike you, I had nowhere to go. So I had to tolerate it. For four months, Louisa! Every Friday night he would come into my room, drunk, while Mum was passed out legless downstairs. I tried to push him off but he was too strong. He'd hit out at me and it was easier to give in. But I never forgot a second of it. That was all your fault.'

'I'm sorry! I didn't really know.'

'You didn't care.'

Louisa paused. 'That's why you came here, isn't it? So you can get your own back on me?'

'Got it in one.' Sarah nodded.

'You shouldn't have come if you weren't going to help me. I trusted you to be there for me.'

'You left me to him!'

'You stole my childhood!'

Sarah and Louisa glared at each other for a moment before Louisa continued.

'I'd had to watch you since you were born. I was the only one looking after you. Mum was hardly ever around, and when she was, she wasn't capable. It was *me* who fed and bathed you. *Me* who got you ready for bed. *Me* who soothed you when you were ill. *Me* who took you to school and worked a Saturday job to pay for treats.'

Sarah went to speak but Louisa held up her hand and went on.

'It was me who sat with you when you were being bullied. Then when you got your own back, it was me who went to see your headmaster.' Louisa prodded herself in her chest. 'I did all that because I loved you. But I wasn't your mum. I *couldn't* be your mum, and yet I had to be because without me you would have been taken into care.'

'So you're saying I should be grateful to you?' Sarah laughed in disbelief.

'Of course not! I loved you. You were my sister and I thought we had a special bond.'

'Well, you proved that wasn't true when you moved here with Richard.'

Louisa shook her head in disbelief. 'I wanted a good life for myself. Was that too much to ask? I wanted less responsibility, to be wined and dined, treated nicely. Given treats, actually. I had all that with Richard.'

'To my detriment. You left me to rot in that house with Mum and I had to get out. It was your fault I met Jessie and he killed our daughter.'

'But I'm as much a victim in this as you! I had nothing before I met Richard.'

'And what do you have now?' Sarah scoffed. 'A half-life because he drugs you to stop you from moaning all the time.'

She turned on her heel and stormed out of the room with the slam of a door. Daisy was standing in her bedroom doorway, tears pouring down her cheeks, her little body shaking. But even the sight of her niece didn't make Sarah stop as she ran past her and down the stairs. She wanted to put as much distance between herself and Louisa as possible.

Because even though there had been some nasty accusations thrown around, there had been some truth in among the lies. It seemed she might have been wrong about her sister abandoning her all those years ago.

FIFTY-ONE

Louisa was exhausted. The argument she'd had with Sarah was playing on her mind. She wasn't sure they would recover from it, and she desperately needed her sister as her alibi.

She looked in on Daisy who was napping on her bed. She was such a good girl, always knowing when she should stay in her room, entertaining herself whenever necessary. But it worried her how much time she slept, most likely because she was bored on her own. It couldn't go on. They needed more out of life than this poor existence. She had to be strong, for both of them.

She made her way downstairs, hanging on to the banister as her legs felt heavy. She found Richard in the kitchen. His face was dark and he looked away as soon as he saw her.

'What's wrong?' she asked. 'You don't look pleased.'

'Who would be happy to see you?' he snapped.

She didn't retaliate. Richard in a mood was more than she could take right now. Instead she stayed quiet, hoping he would say no more. But he went on anyway.

'You've become unbearable, Louisa,' he said. 'You're always going on and on, moaning about this or the other. If I had wanted a nag, I would have married one. Why can't you be more like your sister?'

Louisa gasped. How could he be so cruel? Didn't she mean anything to him any more? Shocked by his reply, she answered back. 'You're not the man I thought I married. You're evil.'

Richard laughed. 'You're paranoid too.'

'I am not!' Feeling the need to defend herself after her recent argument with Sarah, she folded her arms. 'You're nothing but a bully, Richard. Ever since I met you, I've been loyal and faithful. Everything I've done was for you. Having Daisy was your idea and I went along with it. I have been a good mother and a good wife and what have you given me in return? Nothing! I know you've been seeing other women for years during our marriage. And I know you've been screwing my sister and you're hoping that she'll take my place. Well, don't worry because I'm—'

Richard punched her in the face.

The force of it made her drop to the floor heavily. Pain shot up her back but she was more concerned with the blood gushing from her nose.

'I fuck your sister because you are useless,' Richard seethed as he stood over her. 'You were never anything more to me than a glorified maid.' His laughter was taunting. 'I obviously chose the wrong sister when I met you. I should have gone for the younger one. Sarah is a breath of fresh air compared to *you*. She can't stand you, you know? She hates you as much as I do. But I have to put up with you because of Daisy. I will not lose her.'

Louisa struggled to get her breath. She tilted her head back to slow the bleeding.

'It was your own fault that happened.' Richard leaned in closer to inspect the damage. 'Clean up this mess before you leave this room. And I don't want to hear another word about any of this.'

He threw a tea towel into her lap and left her sitting there.

Louisa could barely understand what had happened. There had been no need for that, none at all. It was clear that Richard's temper was getting worse. That was the first time he'd hit her in months.

Tears stung her eyes as she realised what a mess she would

look. And she wouldn't be able to disguise it. Perhaps it would do Sarah good to see what Richard was capable of.

One thing was certain. It made her more determined to set her thoughts into motion. She had to leave with Daisy.

* * *

Richard went into his studio and sat heavily on the settee. He bunched his hand into a fist to inspect the damage. It was a little swollen but that would soon go down.

Recently, his temper was running away with him. But he couldn't stand Louisa's whining. How much longer could he put up with her? If it weren't for Daisy, he would have told her to sling her hook soon after Sarah came.

He needed a way out of his marriage.

Maybe he *should* tell Louisa to leave. It was his house, after all. He loved his daughter, but was it really worth the effort he had to go to, to keep Louisa placid just because he wanted to see Daisy every day?

It wasn't rational to do anything drastic just yet. Sarah was okay for a bit of fun on the side, but he didn't want to take things further with her. And even then, he could tell she'd become more reliant on him over the past few weeks, and he wasn't sure what to think about that.

Then he smirked. It seemed the sisters couldn't do anything without him. He had them both under his thumb. Stupid bitches.

It had been the same with his father. Jack had chosen women who were vulnerable, who fell for his charms and were browbeaten before they knew it. He'd watched his father control them all, except his mum. Jack had loved Patricia so much. Richard wondered how different his life would have been had his mother not died when he was so young. Jack had adored her. He'd gone to pieces when she'd withered away and eventually died.

And that's when he'd started drinking, changing from the dad he doted on, to the father he loathed.

He couldn't blame it all on Jack though. Nature versus nurture was to a certain extent the problem, but Richard could have changed when he was older. He could have chosen a nice woman to settle down with, have a family and be happy. But instead he'd taken this path.

And right now, he needed to stay on it. If he stepped off course too much, he would crack. And that wouldn't be good for anyone.

Perhaps he would be wise to get rid of both sisters, as well as Daisy. He could start again, easily enough. The woman who he was seeing at the moment would be better manipulating material than Louisa and Sarah. In hindsight, it had been a bad idea to get them together.

The balled fist suddenly reached out to pummel the cushion beside him. At least it would rid him of the aggression that was boiling up inside. For he wasn't certain he could contain his anger for much longer.

FIFTY-TWO

Louisa lay on the bed, her face throbbing where Richard had lashed out at her. She'd stemmed the bleeding, but she looked such a mess. How could he do that to her? Be so cruel verbally and then hit out physically. She sniffed away tears as she heard footsteps outside.

Sarah knocked on the door and pushed it open. 'Lou, I'm sorry about what I said earlier – are you okay? What's happened to your face?'

'Richard hit me.'

'That bastard.' Sarah came across to her. 'When did he do that?'

'Just now. Because for once in my sorry little life, I decided to stick up for myself when he said I was useless. I've had years of this. Sometimes I think all he wanted was Daisy so he could tie me to him forever. I have to get away.'

Sarah sat on the bed next to her.

'You don't know him like I do,' Louisa went on. 'He's got a split personality. He can be charming to your face yet when he's out of sight he's not a nice man at all. But he won't let me take Daisy. I have nowhere to go. I have no money, no job, no future.'

'Louisa.'

'He says he will prove I'm an unfit mother so Daisy has to stop here. It's the only reason I stay.'

'Louisa.'

'I have never neglected my child and if he thinks he can take her away from me, then he doesn't realise what a fight he'll have on his hands. She's all I've got. Someone who takes me for what I am. Someone who loves me, can make me happy with her smile. I will not let anyone remove her from this house.'

'Louisa!' Sarah cried. 'Stop!'

Louisa glanced at her. 'I wish I had somewhere safe to hole up where he wouldn't find us.'

'You could always go to the police and say he's keeping you both against your will. I think you have to get away if he's so dangerous. Me too, for that matter. I wouldn't want to stick around if you weren't here. I don't like him that much, if I'm honest.'

Louisa paused for a moment, wondering if it was possible that she could get away. It seemed so easy but...

'You don't think I'm imagining things? I thought you'd side with him.'

'Of course not. I would help you if you're certain. Despite what I said earlier, I care very much for you and Daisy. I want what's best for both of you. If you think it's good that you take her, then maybe you could pack some clothes when Richard next goes out for the day. Then you could leave and have a head start.'

'But I don't want you to be here when he comes back and sees us gone. He'll go mad.'

'I can handle him.' Sarah paused. 'Why don't you think about what you want to do and let me know later?'

'Come with me.' Louisa took her sister's hand in her own. 'I'm sorry about what I've said about you lately, but Richard has me thinking all kinds of stuff. I'd love you to leave with me and Daisy.'

Sarah nodded. 'Okay, then. But you promise not to breathe a word of this to Richard beforehand? Because if he finds out what we're doing, he won't be happy.'

'I promise.'

As soon as Sarah left the room, Louisa could think of nothing else. It could be her chance to start again, somewhere with Daisy that she felt safe and in control. Richard was an evil man yet she didn't have any proof of that. It was her word against his. He would talk the talk and people would believe him.

Yet she began to wonder about her sister's motives too. Was Sarah putting ideas into her head, getting her to do something that Richard would know about? Perhaps punish her for it at a later date?

No, Louisa had no reason not to believe Sarah would do that.

* * *

After speaking to Louisa, seeing her in such a state, Sarah wasn't sure she could go through with her plan. It was one thing to have no feelings for her sister, but a whole different ball game to see her come to any harm.

At first when she came to see Louisa, Sarah had wanted to seek her revenge for being abandoned. But now there seemed to be more to Richard ill-treating her than she'd originally known about.

Guilt coursed through her for hurting her sister when it was clear that she was living under Richard's control. Louisa was a victim, Daisy too. Sarah had to help them get away.

And Louisa was right. They might as well go together. It would be better than staying with Richard in case he became nasty to her too.

But then she thought of what her sister had left her to deal with when she was fifteen, and then ignored her for so many years, and her anger raged again.

Come on, Sarah, get a grip.

She needed to be stronger, get through this final push and then she would come out the other side, free.

Free from the feeling of being abandoned.

Free to be with Richard until she had no need for him.

And free to live in her perfect home. Where no one could make her feel unsafe, or unwanted ever again.

FIFTY-THREE

Louisa stared through the kitchen window. Sarah was sitting in the garden, Daisy at her feet. She wondered whether to join them, decided against it. She didn't feel as if she fitted here now, especially since the episode with Richard a few days ago. She didn't know who to trust any more.

From the very first day she'd seen her sister, she'd been protective of her. She'd been five years old and Sarah had seemed like a living doll. Of course, Mum let Louisa do as much as she could to help with looking after her, and at that age, she'd been happy to oblige.

She remembered rushing home from school when she was seven. Sarah's face would light up, her arms outstretched towards her. Louisa couldn't wait to give her a cuddle. They had such a special bond. It was something she couldn't hate her mum for. The rest of their childhood she could, but not that.

When she was eight and Sarah had been three, Dad had left. He'd hardly been around for them in the sense of being a parent anyway. He'd spent most of his life either in the pub or on short-stay prison sentences. He fancied himself as something of a thief but he got caught too many times. So when he left, for the first week or so they never even noticed. The first inkling was when the food started to run out and they had to go to Nana's for their tea.

Their mum got a job for a while then. She was nice at times, when she was off the booze. But it was when she started bringing home men that it became a problem for them. That was when the five-year age gap between them became more relevant. Louisa was old enough for the men to gawp at but equally she could hold her own. She tried to look after Sarah but was sure there were things her sister hadn't told her. Sarah had become withdrawn a few months before Louisa had left for Mapleton. She'd put it down to teenage hormones and the fact she was leaving, but she should have taken more notice about what was happening. It was probably then that Sarah had lost faith in her.

How Louisa wished she could turn back the clock to when they would have been happy. To when they wouldn't have become distant. To a time when there had been no blame, just fun and laughter and looking out for one another.

Sarah might think she knew Richard, but she didn't know all of him. And it would also depend on the side he wanted to let her see. When Louisa first met him, he'd been such a charmer. But she hadn't realised what was happening until it was too late. Richard controlled her. He didn't want what was best for her, like he led her to believe. Richard wanted her for his own entertainment. She perhaps wouldn't have minded so much if he hadn't been so cruel.

Over dinner with Richard, she tried to act as if everything was fine. But the first plate he handed to her slipped from her grip and clattered to the table.

'You're such a clumsy cow,' he muttered, leaning back in his chair with no attempt to help her.

'Sorry,' she said. 'I lost my grip for a moment.'

'I suppose you're going to blame that on your illness.' He rolled his eyes.

'Well, it could be. I often drop things and it is a condition.'

'Of what?'

'ME.'

'You don't have ME.'

'Well, it hasn't been diagnosed yet but Doctor Alliott said—'

'Oh, what does he know?' Richard's tone was snidey.

'You think he'd lie to me? He wouldn't.'

'He never said you had ME. You're making it up. Because you're a liar. You're a thief too. Don't think I haven't noticed money going missing.'

'What?' Louisa frowned. Even though she planned to take some with her when she left, she hadn't dared go into the box where he kept a few hundred pounds.

Richard grabbed her wrist and gripped hard. 'You've been stealing from me. As if I don't give you enough.'

'No, I haven't! Let go, you're hurting me!'

'There's two hundred pounds missing. The least you could have done was take a little at a time.'

'I haven't taken anything. It... it could have been Sarah.'

Richard raised his eyebrows in surprise. 'We'll go and ask her then.' He pulled her towards the back door.

'Please, stop!'

'No, you're calling your sister a liar. Let's see what she has to say about that.'

Louisa struggled but he dragged her along the path. She had to do something to stop him causing more trouble. Before they got to the annexe, she balled her hand into a fist and hit him on the side of his face.

He let go of her wrist, crying out in surprise. It gave her time to run back towards the house.

'Louisa.' Richard marched after her. 'Louisa!'

'Leave me alone,' she cried, glad she'd hit out at him, but realising she would be trapped in the garden if she couldn't get back to the kitchen and lock the door before he caught up with her.

Richard levelled with her in no time. He spun her round to face him with such force that she was lucky to stay on her feet. His lips were almost touching hers but there was nothing sexual about their encounter. He raised his hand and slapped her.

The force made Louisa drop to the ground.

'Get away from me,' she cried, holding on to her cheek. 'I can't take any more. I'm leaving and Daisy is coming with me.'

'You're going nowhere.' Richard reached for her hair and lifted her to her feet again.

'Please, let us leave,' she pleaded. 'We won't be any trouble. And you and Sarah can be happy together then. Maybe you could start a new family.'

He stopped. 'What has she told you?'

'Nothing, I saw you with her, in the studio. I'm happy for you but I want to leave now. You don't love me any more. You love Sarah.'

'Don't be so ridiculous.' He loosened his grip for a moment. 'You can go, but you're not taking Daisy.'

'She's my daughter.'

'And you're an unfit mother. I won't allow it.'

'Please,' she sobbed. 'Let me take her with me.'

'You don't understand me.' His eyes bored into hers. 'You're not leaving either.'

'You can't keep me here, against my will.'

'Oh, yes I can. Because you'll be buried in the woods.'

Richard's hands went around her throat. Louisa struggled but he was too strong for her to push away. Still she tried. Her breath became shallow, her lungs struggling to work without the oxygen they required. All her blood seemed to rush to her head, and her vision began to fade. Darker, darker. Then nothing.

She flopped to the floor.

FIFTY-FOUR

Sarah had been in the shower. She'd dressed and was sitting on the bed, only hearing raised voices when she finished towelling dry her hair. She went to the window, spotting Richard with his hands around Louisa's throat. Banging hard on the glass to get his attention, she watched in horror as Louisa collapsed.

'No,' she whispered, tearing down the stairs and out into the garden. 'Louisa!' She dropped to the ground next to her. 'Louisa, talk to me.'

It was happening again, just like it had with Poppy. Louisa had that same look in her eyes.

'Louisa! Oh, no, no, no!' She turned to Richard. 'She's dead! What have you done?'

He paced beside her, running a hand through his hair. 'Fuck!'

'You've killed her!' Sarah sobbed. 'You've killed my sister.'

'It was an accident.'

Sarah stood up, shoved him hard in the chest and went down on her knees again. She took her sister in her arms and rocked her. 'How can I believe you? You've lied to me since I arrived here. I saw how you treated her, and I let you! How could I have been so heartless?'

'I didn't hear you saying anything when we were fucking,' Richard said. 'You didn't think of your sister then.'

His words chilled her. She gasped as she looked down at Louisa again, looking for any signs of life.

'We have to call for an ambulance,' she said. 'They might be able to get her breathing again.' She pushed images of an unresponsive Poppy from her mind. 'They might be able to save her!'

'She's dead, Sarah.'

'Then we'll go to the police.'

'And say what?'

'That we found her here and she must have tripped and hurt herself.'

'There are already bruises appearing around her neck. They'll know what I did.'

Richard knelt down but Sarah still held on to Louisa.

'We need to get rid of the body,' he said.

Sarah turned to him sharply. 'We can't.'

'If I go to prison, you'll have to leave White Oaks and Daisy will be taken into care.'

'I haven't done anything wrong! It was you who hurt... who killed my sister! I can look after Daisy. She's my family. The authorities would let her stay with a blood relative, especially after what you did.'

'No, we're burying her. In the woods.'

Sarah held on to her sister's body. 'We can't.'

'We can. And we have to.' Richard got up. 'I'll go and fetch shovels.'

'No!'

Richard backhanded her.

She sat in shock, numb to the pain that was to come. But as he walked towards the studio, she took a few deep breaths. How could he have done that to Louisa? She'd known he'd hit out at her sister every now and then but she never imagined he would go that far. If she had, she would have got her away from him earlier, with Daisy. She would have gone too.

Richard was a psychopath. She doubted he'd meant this to happen. His temper had merely got the better of him. But that made it worse. For the first time, Sarah understood how much danger she could be in. And even if she hadn't wanted Louisa to be with Richard any more, she never meant for anything like this to happen.

She couldn't bury Louisa and pretend nothing had happened.

Richard was back in minutes, wheeling a barrow.

'We can't do this,' Sarah tried again.

'We have to.'

'But whatever we do tonight will have consequences. There's no going back. If one of us says anything to the police, the other will be charged with aiding and abetting. It's a jail sentence for us both.'

'Can you see any other way around this?' Richard snapped.

'People will miss her!'

'Really? Who?' Richard sneered at her. 'I chose you and her because no one cared about you. No one will come looking for Louisa, nor you for that matter. Louisa has no friends, no one except for you. And you didn't really care about her, did you?'

'I did!' It was a shame she was only now realising it. But she had loved Louisa once. She didn't deserve to be treated this way.

Richard pulled Sarah to her feet, Louisa rolling from her lap like a rag doll. 'You will do as I say.' His hands went around her throat.

Sarah pawed at his fingers.

'I could kill you too, burying you both,' he said, squeezing harder. 'No one would ever know. You're nothing, both of you. Nobody gives a shit about you.'

Sarah searched for breath, spots appearing in her vision. Her chest hurt at the effort to take in air. My God, he was going to kill her too.

And then, it was over as he let go.

She coughed as she inhaled too hard. Bending over, she rested her hands on her knees as tears poured from her eyes. Richard didn't even look at her as he took hold of Louisa's arms and pulled her towards the wheelbarrow.

'Help me get her in there,' he commanded.

She shook her head. She wouldn't do that.

While he cursed and shoved Louisa's body into it, Sarah's fingers rummaged round in the flower border, picking up a rock. Then with a scream she ran at him.

He turned in time to dodge it, pushing her out of the way. Then he bunched his hand up into a fist and hit her in the face.

'We are burying her in the woods and that is the end of the matter,' he growled.

She wouldn't show him she was hurting. With tears pouring down her face, she stood shaking as he pushed the wheelbarrow away. She watched him disappear into the woods. Minutes later, she saw him marching towards her again.

'We'd better get digging,' he said. 'It will take a good few hours.'

Still, she didn't move.

'Come on!' he shouted. 'Move.'

On autopilot, she followed him into the clearing. He placed the shovel in the soil and pressed the heel of his foot down into the ground.

She refused to join in, even knowing it would take him twice as long. When it was done, they stood over the grave.

'We never speak about this again,' Richard said.

'How can we after...?' Sarah sobbed.

'It's done now and we just need to forget about it.'

'Someone will know she's missing.'

'We won't tell anyone.' Richard's eyes were wide and white in the dusk. 'Think about it. There's her doctor that sees her once in a while, but only when she makes an appointment. We have no neighbours except that nosy bitch Linda down the lane. We can say that we split up, that Louisa has gone back to Derby.'

'But what about Daisy? She wouldn't leave without her.'

Richard paced the ground again. 'We'll have to keep her hidden for a while.'

'We can't do that!'

'Yes, we can.' He took hold of her upper arms. 'We can shield her from people. Until anyone stops asking about Louisa.'

'But what do we tell her?'

'That Mummy went away. After a while, she'll stop asking for her.'

'But that's cruel!'

'A few nights ago, you were wanting something like this to happen. For Louisa to disappear.'

'Not like this,' she shouted. 'I wanted her to leave.'

'Well, she's gone now.' Richard groaned. 'I never meant for it to happen.'

'Liar!'

'You need to know that I will stop at nothing to see that this doesn't get out. Nothing, do you hear? That includes harming you, or Daisy. Besides, do you want to go to prison for helping me cover it up? Daisy will go into care then.'

'She would go to my mum.'

'And you'd want that to happen? Really?'

Sarah couldn't speak but she shook her head in reply.

'Then we play it my way. I hate what's happened to Louisa, but it's done.'

Sarah sobbed. It was his fault, not hers. But they both had to live with it. Would it be easy to forget? Did she even want to replace her sister now?

So many questions were running through her mind. Many would go unanswered. Most could fade with time. But one thing was certain. Her sister was never coming back.

And right now, she wasn't sure how she felt about that.

FIFTY-FIVE

In the house now, Richard poured himself a neat whisky, knocking it back quickly before pouring another. His hands shook and he slammed his glass down once he'd finished.

Fuck! How had he lost his temper again? He'd sworn he'd never do it after getting away with it before.

He thought back to the night he'd shot his father. The thrill of standing over Jack with his finger on the trigger, while he snored oblivious to the danger. Jack had been arguing with him, throwing several punches Richard's way until he'd managed to push him off. He was always hard to get away from when he was drunk.

But as he'd lain back in the armchair and fallen into a stupor, Richard had seen his future mapped out. A lackey lad, farm hand. Never being good enough. Never doing anything right.

And the women Jack brought home. He always had one or two on the go.

Richard failed to understand what they saw in his father. At least *he* was a gentleman to the women he saw outside his marriage. He treated them well. Of course a little control didn't do any harm, but for the most part, both Louisa and Sarah had done as he demanded.

There was a single light on in the annexe, upstairs. It was no use going to talk to Sarah now. In the light of the day, things would look different.

He stared out into what was left of the night, the shadows playing tricks with him. His gut reaction was to run, but he couldn't do that. It would seem suspicious and, if he left Sarah here, who knew what she might say if questioned?

White Oaks was supposed to be somewhere he could forget his past. But now he had brought his violence here as well. Could he really get away with murdering Louisa? Would Sarah keep her mouth shut or would she crack? Would he end up killing her too?

There were so many things to think about. He'd have to get rid of Louisa's possessions. Slowly but surely over the coming weeks. Then if anyone asked after her, he would say she had left him. If someone called from the doctor's surgery, he could say she'd gone back to Derby.

That was the beauty of living somewhere so secluded. The house nearest to them had been empty for years and their closest neighbour was a good walk down the lane. No one would bother them, not for a while and by that time he'd be calm again, getting on with his life with Sarah.

He hadn't meant for it to happen but it did solve a problem. Maybe it had created another, he wasn't entirely sure yet. But he would do whatever was necessary to keep his secret safe.

He needed to keep Sarah on side.

* * *

In the annexe, Sarah was taking another shower. She was washing off the dirt, scrubbing at her skin as tears poured down her face. No amount of rubbing would take away the anguish of what they had done but she had to try.

Her sister was dead. Louisa, her beautiful sister, was gone.

When her skin was red and raw, she slid down onto the shower tray, wrapping her hands around her knees, and let the water pour over her. She squeezed her eyes shut to stop herself from seeing the images she knew she would never forget. Before Richard had started to cover Louisa in soil, she had pushed her eyelids closed. But all she could see now was them opening wide and Louisa trying to get out of the grave.

It had been cowardly not to call the police, but she'd seen what Richard was capable of, and his threats towards her were real. She was certain he would have killed her if she hadn't been compliant. His eyes were demented. She had never seen them so dangerous. Once she realised it was going to happen regardless, her first instinct had been to do as he said, then get away later. She had Daisy to think about too.

That poor child. She was an innocent in all this. She had lost her mother.

Sarah couldn't leave her in the hands of that... that monster. And how the hell did he expect her to be hidden away from everyone? Daisy was due to start at nursery soon.

As grief overtook her, Sarah's thoughts of revenge turned darker. She would get Richard for what he'd done, even if it took forever. In a matter of hours, he had destroyed any love she had for him.

She would also have to live with the things she had done to her sister – the selfish, callous actions she had taken before she realised how evil Richard was.

And she would look after herself too, cover her back in case he tried anything similar to her.

She needed to keep Richard on side.

PART THREE

FIFTY-SIX

Juliette sat at the breakfast bar, coffee in hand, and thought about what had happened. Last night had been surreal, the conversation she'd had with Sarah shocking. Sarah was being controlled by Richard. She was scared to leave because of what he might do to her. Juliette had seen first-hand how intimidating he could be. No wonder the woman was a nervous wreck most of the time.

More importantly, there *was* a child next door. She'd seen her, so there was no denying it now.

She'd thought she'd been going out of her mind. And now looking back on how Danny had been manipulated by Richard, the anger she'd wanted to keep in check began to boil over. Richard was tricking her, fooling them both. He was allowing her to doubt herself, putting it down to the grief of losing her own child by imagining another.

Locking a child in a room was barbaric. Sarah and Daisy were both in danger, which is why if Juliette was going to be of any help, it had to be over days not weeks. And if she couldn't find anything out, she would go to the police herself.

She'd do some digging about Louisa. Maybe someone local could tell her something that would lead to discovering if she had left of her own accord. But then why wouldn't she have taken Daisy with her?

What had been going on under everyone's nose? And what would have happened if she and Danny hadn't moved in when they did?

She thought back to the time when they'd had coffee in the garden and she'd been annoyed when Richard came to check up on Sarah. Had her own actions put her neighbour in danger? Had she antagonised things that time, by getting him to agree to Sarah staying for another half hour? She cursed aloud. She had to learn to play his game.

Once she'd finished her client work for that day, she walked into the village. The coffee shop where Louisa used to work was much busier than she'd expected, although it was nearing lunchtime. There were tables of elderly couples and groups of younger women. Over in the far corner, three new mums sat with their babies on their knees. Juliette couldn't help but smile, envious but joyful of the scene. Excited that she would become a mum again soon.

She joined the small queue at the counter, smiling as Barbara noticed her.

'Hi, Juliette. Lovely to see you. What can I get you?'

'A regular cappuccino please. How's business?'

'Busy.'

Juliette laughed when Barbara rolled her eyes.

'I was hoping to have a word with you,' she added.

'Sounds ominous.'

'It's nothing really. I—'

'Lots of these tables have been occupied for a while now. This place will empty soon. I'll join you then if you can wait?'

'Sure. Thanks.' Juliette collected her coffee and sat in a chair by the window. After a few minutes of people watching, she took out her laptop and began to work. She was engrossed with a spreadsheet when Barbara dropped down in the seat opposite her with two slices of cake. She slid one over to her.

'So, what is it that you want to know?'

Juliette beamed. 'Louisa who used to work here – what was she like?'

'She was a good worker.' Barbara smiled. 'She was funny too. She had a wicked sense of humour and used to make a lot of the old dears laugh.'

'How long was she with you?'

'About four months. It was strange actually. She seemed to be enjoying it, but one day she turned up and decided it was too much for her, that she wanted to help Richard out with his business and couldn't fit both jobs in. I missed her as soon as she left.'

'Do you know where she lived before she came to Mapleton?'

'Derby, I think. Why do you ask?'

'I found something of hers and I wanted to return it.' Juliette lowered her eyes hoping that Barbara wouldn't ask any more questions.

'The last we all heard was she and Richard had split up, and she left with Daisy. Richard told Linda. We all assumed as Sarah was still there that she was the reason.'

'So you know Sarah?'

'Vaguely. She's always kept herself to herself when she's nipped in for a coffee. I can count on one hand how many times though. She's not very sociable.'

Juliette made a note of that. 'I don't suppose you have any way of contacting Louisa?'

'I don't think so, and I couldn't share it with you anyway.'

'Sorry. I shouldn't have asked.'

Barbara waved to the young girl behind the counter to indicate she'd be with her soon. 'Between you and me, I do wonder if Louisa leaving here had something to do with Richard. She almost seemed scared of him by the time she left. I can't put my finger on what precisely it was, but I'm actually glad she's got away from him.' She moved her head closer to Juliette's. 'Carly too.'

'Carly?'

'She works at the estate agents two doors down. She was with

Richard for a couple of years. Apparently it wasn't an amicable split.'

'Oh!' Juliette was about to ask her more but Barbara got to her feet. 'I have to go. See you at the book club next week?'

'Yes, I might pop along, although I haven't finished the novel yet.'

'Don't worry about that. It's not all about the book, as you realised when you joined us.' She winked as she collected the used crockery. 'See you soon.'

'Yes, and thanks.' Juliette looked back at the spreadsheet but her mind wouldn't settle. Still, she had time to nip in and see if Carly was free.

FIFTY-SEVEN

As usual, the high street was a bustle of activity and Juliette found herself stopped twice before she got to the estate agents, by people she'd either met to say hello to in one of the shops or spoken to in the pub. It was lovely to be recognised already.

Finally, once outside their office window, Juliette studied the properties on display under the guise of looking for a new home while she glanced through the images and into the office behind.

There were two women at separate desks. One was on the phone, doing a lot of talking with her hand. She didn't look older than twenty so would be too young to have been with Richard for so long. The other woman, however, seemed in her early thirties. She had long blonde hair, was slim and wore rimless glasses perched on the end of her nose. The uniform of navy-blue suit, white blouse and red neckerchief made her look like an air hostess, but there seemed no airs about her.

The woman looked up at that moment, probably feeling Juliette's stare. She smiled and beckoned her inside. Juliette took a deep breath and went in.

'Lovely morning, isn't it?' the woman said. 'Although sadly, it's given rain out for later.' She held out a hand. 'My name's Carly. Is there anything I can help you with?'

'Oh, I—'

'Don't tell me you were just browsing. I always beckon in the wrong people.' Her smile was friendly as she teased, and Juliette felt herself relaxing enough to ask a few pertinent questions.

'Actually, I've not long moved in. A few weeks ago, with my husband. I live in Abbey Cottage.'

'I thought your face looked familiar. I must have seen you around the village. Oh, that's such a beautiful property. I lived next door for a while. The views at the back are amazing.'

'They are. I don't know why anyone would want to move out.' She faked embarrassment. 'Sorry, that was a bit rude.'

'It's fine. I was in a relationship with the owner. He's still there now, so I guess it's him you've come to ask me about and you're not remotely interested in a new property?'

There was no embarrassment to fake now. Juliette's cheeks turned red in an instant.

Carly went back behind her desk and sat down. She pointed at the seat in front of her, urging Juliette to do the same.

Juliette sat, thankful that she hadn't been thrown out.

'What is it you want to know?' Carly asked.

'There was a woman after you. Louisa. She hasn't been there for a year or so and I'm trying to contact her. I-I have something that I'd like to return to her.'

'Right.' Carly smirked. 'Richard was an arsehole of the biggest proportion. Is that what you're really after me saying?'

Juliette felt herself warming to Carly. Her nature was pleasant, considering what she was trying to find out.

'I met Richard when he first moved here,' Carly went on. 'As you probably know, he can be quite a charmer. Very persuasive too and soon after we started dating, he asked me to move in with him. Over the course of a year, he changed me completely.'

Juliette couldn't help but sigh.

'Coercive control. It's as damaging as domestic abuse but I didn't see the signs until it was too late. We became an item really quickly but by the end of the first year, I was solely with him all the time. I never went out with friends and I barely saw my family, even though everyone I know lives in the village.

'He wanted me all for himself, but when he got me, it was as if I wasn't enough.' She shuddered at the memory. 'He went with other women while we were together, and that was all right from his point of view. It seemed he really wanted a glorified house-keeper, to look after him and then he'd do as he pleased. I wish I'd had the courage to leave him earlier but I was so frightened.'

'Oh dear,' Juliette remarked, recalling seeing him with the blonde in the restaurant.

'He's a predator who played on my emotions. I'm sure he did the same with my mind too. I found out he'd been giving me sleeping tablets every so often.'

'No!' Juliette couldn't hide her surprise.

Carly nodded. 'But it came to a head when I finally couldn't take any more and I tried to leave. He threatened me with all sorts. Said he'd taken video footage of us in bed and would send it to everyone I knew. Then he said he would ruin my business. I believed all of this but one night after a pretty brutal attack, I left and never went back.'

'You mean he hit out at you?' Juliette blanched. 'I'm sorry that I made you bring all this up.'

'He punched me square in the nose,' Carly continued, never-theless. 'I looked a terrible mess.'

'Did you press charges?'

'He persuaded me not to. Like I say, he could be a charmer. Don't get me wrong, he's great at the beginning of the relationship. But once he's sucked you in, he stops with the acting and becomes extremely calculating.'

'I'm sorry you had to go through that. Did you ever see Louisa with him?'

'Only on her own, the times she was allowed to walk into the village for supplies. He was a bastard of the large variety. When I walked away, I went home to my parents at first. He kept pestering me to come back. He wouldn't take no for an answer, couldn't understand how someone had dared to walk away from him.' Carly sat a little straighter. 'Well, I had, although my dignity was half intact as he had broken me a little with each passing month. I had no intentions of returning to him. Luckily I had somewhere to stay. Why do you ask about him? Are you worried about the woman he's with now?'

'Yes.' Juliette said no more. She didn't want to betray Sarah's confidence. Besides, she had enough now to be getting on with. She was already building up a picture of Richard that she didn't much like.

FIFTY-EIGHT

Walking back from the village, Juliette turned to check the road as she was about to cross. A few metres behind, Sarah was walking slowly. Juliette waved and waited for her to catch up, wondering why she hadn't shouted to her. It was as if she hadn't wanted to be seen.

'Hey. How are you?' she asked.

'I'm okay, thanks.'

'I've been thinking about you since we had our chat. Figuring out how to help you.'

Sarah looked around as if Richard was going to jump out of the hedgerow and catch them talking.

'He's not here,' Juliette spoke softly.

'Sorry, I'm just wary.'

'I wanted to ask if you knew where Louisa used to live?'

'I don't know her exact address. Why?'

'I'm going to set out to find her family, see if they've heard from her.'

'You can't do that.' Sarah stopped. 'If Richard gets to hear about it, he might become suspicious.'

'But if I do find her, then we can figure out why she abandoned Daisy and I think—'

'No.' Sarah shook her head. 'It's too dangerous. What happens if you contact someone, they find out she's missing and then come here? Richard will go berserk. He'd probably keep me on a tighter leash.'

'Do you have any other suggestions? We have to get you away from him so that you and Daisy can live without fear.'

'I'm worried about what will happen if he finds out.'

'It's a chance we have to take.'

'No!' Sarah cried again. 'Maybe we'd be better leaving things as they are.'

'And you live like this, with a child stuck in her room?'

'She's not in there all the time. Mostly she has the run of the house. And the garden was okay until you came.'

'What he's doing to you both is wrong.' Juliette wondered why she was putting the blame on them. 'What he might have done to Louisa is wrong too. So for now, I need to find out where she is.'

'You can't, please!'

Juliette paused. 'You really don't want me looking into this now?'

'Not yet. I need more time.'

'Okay.' Juliette was lying. She would search for Louisa, but she wouldn't say anything to Sarah until she had concrete evidence.

'I shouldn't have brought you into this.' Sarah's shoulders drooped.

'You needed my help and I'm happy to provide it. Hey, I'd walk right out of here with you and Daisy if you'd come. I hate what he's doing to you.' She pulled a mobile phone from her bag. 'I bought this for you. It has my number on it, credit too. We can keep in touch by text instead of using your main phone. Keep it on silent, read what I send and then delete the messages so if Richard does find it by chance, there will be nothing incriminating on it.'

Sarah paused for a moment, as if she was wondering whether to speak or not. Finally, she did.

'There's a box of Louisa's in the annexe. Richard must have put it there when I moved into the main house, and I found it by chance. I could leave that out for you if I can get it down. It might have something useful in it. I don't know where anything else of hers went.'

'You mean her things have gone?' This was all too creepy for Juliette.

Sarah nodded. 'A long time ago.'

'Okay, I'll leave you for now.' Juliette touched the woman's arm. 'But if you need me, ring at *any* time.'

'I will, thanks.'

Once back in her home, Juliette was glad she'd offered to help Sarah. She seemed petrified of Richard finding out anything. A few minutes later, she received a text message from an unknown number. She opened it to see a message.

I don't think it's a good idea to pursue this any more. Thanks anyway.

Juliette baulked. What had made Sarah change her mind again so quickly? Had Richard scared her? Was he hurting her, or threatening to harm Daisy?

Whatever the reason, she was determined to help even more. Poor Sarah, why should she put up with such abuse? It wasn't right.

Juliette replied to the message.

* * *

Next door, Sarah sat in the kitchen as she read Juliette's reply.

You need to get away. Let me see what's in the box, see if I can help you.

She cursed out loud. She'd been reckless to get Juliette

involved. This change of plan couldn't work. It would do more harm than good. She should have continued alone.

It had taken her a whole year to get to this point. She had kept the secret of Louisa's death to herself. She had suffered the anguish of knowing her sister had been murdered, hadn't received a proper burial, that she'd rotted in the woods mere metres away.

She had internalised the pain she'd felt covering things up, the guilt of not going to the police when she could have.

Yet even though she knew it was harmful for Daisy, it was the right thing to do. Bide her time and wait.

She felt as trapped as Richard. He'd been right on that night. She would have implicated herself if she said anything to the police. She couldn't go to prison for something he had done. And would a jury really see it as self-defence, that she'd had to keep herself safe and do as he said, for Daisy's sake as well? She couldn't have taken that chance.

Still, she needed to keep things from Richard for a while longer before she set her plan into motion. Which meant either she got Juliette to back off, or they brought everything forward before what they were doing got out.

FIFTY-NINE

The following morning, Juliette received a message from Sarah.

The box is hidden in the hedge, a third of the way down, by the second rhododendron bush.

She texted back her thanks, got out of bed and took a quick shower. Then she rushed out to the garden, walking along to where Sarah had mentioned. She stooped down and there was the box. She pulled it out and, tucking it under her arm, went inside again.

She made coffee and then sat at the island. She had more room here and would be able to spread out what was inside the box. Carefully, she lifted the lid and placed it down beside her.

Inside were mementos of Louisa's life. Her passport, still in date by two years. Louisa Banks. Juliette frowned – why wouldn't she have taken that with her if she'd gone? Then again, Daisy wasn't on it, and it was in her maiden name, so perhaps it was out of use now.

In a tiny round tin, she found the first lock of Daisy's hair. It made her tears well up as she thought of Emily. She had a keepsake tin too.

There was a card with a tiny footprint on it, from a hospital no doubt. She ran a finger over the image.

There were several photos of Daisy from when she'd been born, laid out in a cot at the hospital, wrapped up in a blanket with her arms either side of her face.

Juliette's heart sank. These items were personal, things that shouldn't be left behind.

She picked up the first photo of who she assumed to be Louisa. Then she stared at the young girl next to her, her familiarity uncanny. It couldn't be. She took a closer look and then turned it over. Written on the back was:

Louisa and Sarah at home, Derrington Estate.

Juliette gasped. Her thoughts had been right. It was Sarah. If she wasn't mistaken, she and Louisa were relatives. So why was she showing her this rather than telling her? Why did she want her to find out now? She sent Sarah a message.

Why didn't you tell me that you were related to Louisa?

She waited for a few minutes and a message came back.

Because you might think I was in on her disappearance. She's my sister. It's the reason I don't feel safe here too. I know too much.

Juliette sat with her thoughts for a moment. She didn't understand the logic behind Sarah sharing this now. But she did realise that Richard was more dangerous than she'd imagined. She wasn't sure she wanted to face him again, not now she had this knowledge.

She couldn't let herself believe that anything had happened to Louisa. She had to think that she was alive and well, and perhaps not wanting to be found. She had to think that she might put Louisa in danger if she kept on looking for information. But Sarah was Louisa's sister, and that meant she wanted what was best for her sister too. Sarah was telling her for good reasons. She just hadn't worked out what they were yet.

She sent another message.

Everything is going to be okay. Trust me.

* * *

Sarah replied to Juliette's message with a thank you, then looked at the two mobile phones that were in front of her. They'd been inside the box she'd found hidden in the annexe a few months ago. Richard must have put them there and forgotten about them.

She'd charged them up and looked over the messages that were stored. He'd tricked both her and Louisa. All those months she'd tried to get in touch with her sister when she'd first left, Richard must have pretended to be her on the phone. He'd wanted to isolate Louisa away from everyone she knew.

She recalled Louisa mentioning she had lost her phone and Richard had given her a new one, saying he couldn't retrieve the previous contacts. Sarah had known that was suspicious and had thought Louisa was making it up through embarrassment. Most people stored their information via cloud so that they could get a new phone or gadget and everything would be transferred over.

There were messages from lots of people, always excuses from Louisa. And in the end, even those had dried up. It had made Sarah angry and more determined than ever to go through with her plan. Richard really was a piece of work. Had she known that before the fateful night, things could have been very different. She almost wanted to be angry with herself too, for letting him trick her, but also for poisoning her mind.

Richard was more cunning than she'd given him credit for. But he had met his match with her. He wouldn't be allowed to get away with this.

And at least Juliette now knew that she and Louisa were

sisters. It must heighten things dramatically, she suspected. Juliette would want to know all the whys but she wasn't willing to tell her yet.

She sent another message to Juliette.

I realise now that Richard must have had Louisa's phone and sent me messages making me think they were from her.

She waited a moment for a message to come back.

That's so cruel. And heartless. I think we need to meet again to discuss what you know. I can understand why you didn't tell me that Louisa was your sister but I wish I'd known earlier.

Sorry, I was scared you wouldn't believe me.

Of course I believe you! I have been researching some places where you and Daisy could go. I could even take you to Derby, somewhere safe where Richard can't get to you. I want to help.

Thanks.

I need Danny to see Daisy though. Do you think you can get Richard to invite us around for a meal?

She typed back.

I'll try.

Sarah sighed as she put down the phone. It was good of Juliette to offer to take her to Derby and look for alternative places for her and Daisy to stay. But Sarah couldn't go anywhere. She couldn't leave Louisa behind.

Not without doing what she'd set out to do to Richard.

SIXTY

Juliette logged on to Facebook and typed Louisa's name in the search box. Nothing came up. She tried the name of the estate mentioned on the back of the photograph she'd got from the box. A neighbourhood group came up and she clicked on that. It was set to private so she clicked to join and her request went to pending.

When she next logged on, she had been approved. Once inside, she scrolled down the posts. She noted a few names and made a few friend requests. Then she decided to add a post.

Hi, I'm looking for anyone who knows Louisa Banks.

Juliette waited, then a comment popped up.

I knew Louisa. How do you know her?

She's a friend of mine and I'm trying to contact her. I haven't seen her for twelve months.

She left the estate when she got married. We lost touch, sorry.

Juliette sighed. She made coffee and when she returned, there were three more messages.

I haven't seen her in ages.

That's a blast from the past. Sorry, me neither.

The last I heard she was living in Mapleton.

A friend request popped up. Suzanne Ridley. She wasn't one of the commentators. Juliette accepted it and seconds later, there was a direct message.

I used to be Louisa's friend at school. Can I help?

I'm trying to locate her. I'd like to invite her to a reunion.

A school reunion? I went to school with her at the same time. Do I know you?

No. I live in Mapleton and she used to work with me in a coffee shop a few years ago. The coffee shop is closing and we're getting together all the staff for a farewell party. I was hoping that Louisa might join us.

As far as I know, she still lives in Mapleton. Although we haven't kept in touch really.

Juliette decided to bite the bullet.

I'm over your way for a meeting in Derby tomorrow. I was wondering if you had time to chat to me over a coffee?

* * *

Juliette headed along the A50 at a steady pace, the roads quite free of traffic for the time of day. The satnav informed her it was an hour's drive to the address Suzanne had given to her.

Finally, she pulled up outside a row of shops on a tiny high street. From the outside, The Coffee Pot looked small but inviting, especially after a long drive. Inside, she glanced around the few tables. Only two were unoccupied. A woman raised her hand and said her name. Juliette smiled and went over to her.

'Suzanne?' she said, offering her hand.

'Hi, that's me.'

'I'll grab a drink and be right back.'

'No need.' Suzanne beckoned a waitress over. 'What would you like?'

'I'll have a latte, please.' Juliette thanked the young girl and then turned back to Suzanne. 'Have you lived around here long?'

'All my life. It's not so bad if you've been born and bred here, but I bet Mapleton is much better.'

Juliette was stuck for words. Whatever she said about the area might offend Suzanne, but equally she wasn't the type of person who judged people before she got to know them, no matter where they came from.

Once the coffee was brought over, Suzanne got out a small photo album. She flicked through a few pages before turning it around to face Juliette.

'This is me and Louisa when we were at school.' Suzanne pointed to two young girls, all smiles and pigtails in school uniform of black pinafores and white shirts. 'We met when we were in the juniors and became inseparable.'

Juliette could see the affection in Suzanne's smile. 'What was she like?'

'She was the boisterous one, always up for an adventure. We'd often get into trouble because she wanted to push boundaries. But she was sweet. She gave me an identity. I have four older brothers and was a tomboy but I was shy too. She brought me out of my shell, and she taught me how to be more feminine without trying. I had no real role model and, through Louisa, I learned a lot of how life would be if I moved off the estate.' She snorted. 'I never did though. Louisa was much braver than me.'

Juliette frowned.

'Don't look at me like that,' Susanne mused. 'Leaving this estate to visit Mapleton was like travelling from one end of the country to another if you've ever lived in a place like this. Of course, as a child, I wanted to move out. But now, I'm settled and I can never see myself living anywhere else.'

'Do you have children?'

'Two boys.' She pointed to the photo. 'I married him, Peter. His parents owned the shop two doors down from here. It's ours now.'

'When did you lose touch with Louisa?' she asked next.

'When she married *him*.'

'Richard?'

Suzanne nodded. 'I barely saw her then, tried to keep in touch but you know how these things go. Once someone isn't in your life as much as before, it becomes harder to fit them in. I did try to see her but she was always busy.'

'How did you contact her?'

'Mostly by text. I'd ring often but it was never answered. Shortly after that I'd get a reply to say how wonderful everything was and that she would meet me soon. But there was never anything more concrete than that.'

'What about when Daisy was born?'

'I saw her once, when Richard played the loving father. But when we were alone, he told me to stay away from Louisa as she was with him now and didn't need any friends interfering. He's a control freak.'

'So when she went missing, what did you do?'

'I didn't know until you got in touch. I just thought she didn't need me, like he said.'

'And you never checked?'

'I had no need to.' Suzanne grimaced. 'I wish I had now though.'

'And Richard, have you seen him at all?'

'No, nor do I want to. But if I find out he's done anything to harm Louisa, I'll rip him apart limb by limb.'

SIXTY-ONE

Sarah watched as Richard came into the living room and sat across from her. Something hung heavy in the air. She waited for him to speak, praying he hadn't somehow spotted that the box with Louisa's belongings had gone missing.

'Things are getting out of hand,' he spoke eventually. 'Juliette's getting a little too close for my liking.'

'What makes you think that?' She trod carefully. 'Has she said something?'

'Not in as many words.'

Sarah was confused. Richard shouldn't know about Juliette speaking to people, if that's what he was referring to. How would he have found out? Unless someone had spoken to him?

Then she went cold. Had Richard got access to a social media account? Had he seen what Juliette was up to? She looked over at him, his brow furrowing as he was deep in thought. He didn't seem annoyed enough for that. Besides, he'd have to be good to search out where Juliette had been looking, although she knew she was using her own name.

'What shall we do?'

'I'm not sure. I'm going to think about it.'

'If you're that concerned, why don't we invite her and Danny around for a meal, to see exactly what they know?' she ventured, thinking back to Juliette's suggestion.

He turned to her then and she tried not to shrink under his stare.

'Don't you think that's risky?' he said eventually.

'Possibly, but like you say, we have to do something.'

After a moment's thought, Richard nodded before standing up. 'Text Juliette, see if they're free this weekend.'

Once Richard had left the room, Sarah let out a sigh. She checked her watch: half past one. There were a few hours before she'd have to think about dinner. She'd better not waste a minute.

She cooked fish fingers and beans and cut the crusts off a round of bread and butter. Then she popped the meal on a tray along with a glass of orange juice and an apple. Steadily she went upstairs, trying not to spill the liquid.

Inside her bedroom, Daisy turned to her with a smile. She had Richard's eyes but the hair colouring was light to his dark. Like her sister Louisa's.

She stepped inside, the child knowing better than to try to get out. Conditioned to life with just the three of them for the past year had made her even more compliant, considering. She was a pleasant child, none the worse for it in Sarah's opinion. And it wouldn't be for long now.

The room was hot: she must remember to open a window before she left.

'There you are, poppet,' she said. 'Auntie Sarah's here with your lunch.'

Sarah picked up the carving knife she'd hidden inside a napkin and while Daisy tucked into her lunch, she discreetly popped it on top of the wardrobe. It was the third one she'd managed to hide around the house over the past few hours.

* * *

Juliette had collected Danny from the station and was in the kitchen when he joined her after taking a shower. The text message from Sarah with confirmation of their meeting had come through.

'Richard has invited us next door for a meal tomorrow,' she said, trying to sound casual about it. 'I wasn't sure if I'd be up for it or not, but he's said he'll show you his studio and I know how much you're dying to see what he's working on.'

'I'd prefer a night in just the two of us.' Danny came up behind her and gave her a hug. 'What did you say?'

'I said I'd ask you first.'

'Then I'm going to be the party pooper.'

'I'd put him off but I like seeing Sarah. You know how I worry about her.'

He sighed. 'Tell him we'll be round about seven.'

Relief flooded through her, although she was nervous too. She turned to face him. 'I can't wait for you to come home for good next weekend.'

'Me neither.' Danny kissed her. 'I can keep an eye on you.'

She pressed her face into his chest. 'There you go again.'

'What?'

'Worrying about me. I'm okay. Things are settling down now.' She yawned.

'Have you started dinner yet?'

'No, I've just got the mince out of the fridge. I was going to cook spaghetti bolognaise.'

'Indian takeaway?'

'Sounds like a good idea.'

While he rang the order through, Juliette picked up her phone, popped it in her pocket and headed upstairs. When she was there, she sent a message to Sarah.

So pleased you managed to persuade him to go for it.

It took a while. He was suspicious but I said it would be good to do as Danny is coming home soon.

Will Daisy be in her room when we come round?

Yes, I'll have a think about how best to do it. Thanks for this.

Happy to help. Hopefully it will all be sorted soon.

Juliette put her phone down. Although she was nervous about what might happen, this was an opportunity to prove to Danny that Daisy was at the house. Once he saw her, then they could go to the police and start looking into why the child was being hidden, and Louisa's whereabouts. She couldn't wait until Richard was out for a full day before she did something about the situation next door. Someone would believe her and Sarah eventually.

Because it was looking more likely Sarah had been right about Louisa's disappearance.

SIXTY-TWO

The next evening, after a nap, Juliette came downstairs just before seven. In the kitchen, Danny was looking at two bottles of wine, deciding which one to take next door.

'Oh, you're ready on time!' he exclaimed with a snarky grin.

Juliette slapped his arm playfully. 'Don't be cheeky. It's usually me who's waiting for you when we go out.'

'How are you feeling?'

'A bit better.' She'd been nauseous for most of the afternoon, but she couldn't tell him why. Even now she was trying not to show how nervous she felt.

'You seem a bit peaky.'

'I didn't have much of a rest, that was for sure.' She yawned.

'We don't have to stay long, do we?'

'I'll let you know if my head droops in the dessert.' Juliette smiled. She followed him out, her hand in his as they walked round to their neighbours' home.

Richard was at the side gate before they had reached the back door.

'Welcome,' he cried. 'Come on through. Aren't we lucky that the weather is good again?'

Danny handed the bottle of wine to Richard and he took it from him.

'Thanks, not my usual tipple but it will do.'

Danny threw a look at Juliette but she ushered him inside.

They noticed the atmosphere as soon as they entered the kitchen. Sarah was at the oven. She turned around as soon as she heard them, her cheeks flushed.

'Hi!' Her voice was too high, her smile too wide. 'Do help yourself to nibbles while I finish off here.'

Juliette took the chair that Richard had pulled out at the table for her and sat down opposite Danny. He gave her the glare, the one that said, *have we walked into an argument?* She shrugged a shoulder discreetly in response.

'How're your last few days at work going?' Richard sat next to Danny, handing him a bottle of lager. 'Is it next week you're moving here for good?'

'Yes, that's right.' Danny nodded. 'I can't wait, to be honest. Everything is tied up in London now.'

'Here's to new beginnings.' Richard held out his bottle for Danny to clink.

While the men chatted, Juliette helped Sarah with the food.

'Everything good?' she whispered.

Sarah nodded slightly. 'I can manage here, thanks. You sit yourself down again. I'm dishing out now.'

'If you're sure.' At the table, Juliette took a sip of the orange juice she'd been given.

Sarah popped plates in front of them and sat down too.

'Enjoy,' she said.

The small talk dried up halfway through the main meal. It was excruciating sitting there. Sarah was timid, almost to the point of not contributing to any conversation, which made matters worse.

'That was delicious,' Juliette remarked, putting down her knife and fork.

'I thought so too.' Danny wiped his mouth with a napkin. 'Was it your own recipe, Sarah?'

'Of course not.' Richard shook his head. 'She's not that talented.'

Richard had moved on to the wine and as he reached for the bottle to top up his glass, Juliette could already hear a slur in his voice. He'd been knocking it back quickly, the rest of them refusing top-ups.

She glanced at Sarah but she wouldn't catch her eye. When she looked again, Richard was leering at her.

'You think you're so smart, don't you?' he sneered.

Juliette froze, hoping not to show any guilt. 'Sorry?'

'Anyone for pudding?' Sarah shot to her feet and reached for Juliette's plate.

'Sit down!' Richard roared.

Sarah did as she was told.

'Steady on, mate,' Danny said. 'Is something wrong? You've been a bit off since we got here.'

'Why don't you ask your wife?' Richard replied. 'She's been snooping, asking people lots of questions about me.'

Both men stared at her. Juliette dropped her eyes.

'That's not very neighbourly of you,' Richard added.

'Oh, I—'

'You could have asked if there was anything you wanted to know. I haven't heard from Louisa in a good while but I spoke to her a few months ago. She put Daisy on the phone to me and it was good to hear her voice.'

'Who's Louisa?' Danny asked.

'My ex-wife.'

'That's great,' Juliette said, not giving Danny the chance to reply. 'Are you meeting up with them soon?'

'I don't think so.' Richard looked at Danny and rolled his eyes. 'The reason we split up was because Louisa was having an affair. Daisy was a result of it. She isn't my daughter.'

'I'm so sorry,' Juliette said.

'So whatever crap Sarah has been feeding you with' – Richard switched his gaze back to Juliette – 'it's all lies.'

Juliette sat still. Had he found out that she'd been to see anyone? Had Sarah told him, and if so, had he hurt her to get the information?

'I suggest from now on you keep your nose out of my business,' Richard went on.

Juliette held Richard's stare. She wasn't standing for that, no matter how much danger Sarah might be in if she spoke out.

'I've seen her,' she said.

'Not this again,' Danny sighed loudly.

'I've seen her!' Juliette repeated.

Richard's eyes narrowed. He reached across the table, grabbing Sarah's arm.

'What have you been up to?' he demanded.

'Hey, now,' Danny started but Richard held up a hand for him to stop. 'What's going on?'

But Richard kept staring at Sarah. Then he laughed.

'You don't really think we keep Daisy locked up in a room, do you?' He clicked his fingers at Sarah. 'You, come with me now.'

'Where are you going?' Juliette glanced at Sarah, seeing the look of panic on her face.

'We'll be back in a minute,' Richard said.

As she followed Richard out of the room, Danny rounded on Juliette.

'What the hell is going on?'

SIXTY-THREE

Juliette swallowed. Suddenly, the reality of what she was doing sank in.

'I'm so sorry,' she said to Danny. 'I've felt really deceitful not telling you, but the little girl I thought I saw and Richard denied does live here. She's four years old and her mother, Louisa, is missing. Louisa is Sarah's sister.'

Danny's mouth dropped open.

'I couldn't believe it either, but it's true.' Juliette explained what had happened the day she'd met Daisy. 'I've been trying to find out more about Louisa before Sarah goes to the police. I went to Derby, where she's from, and I spoke to a friend of hers. She says she lost contact with Louisa because she thinks Richard is—'

'You've been to see people about this?'

'I wanted to tell you but I knew you'd try and stop me.'

'Too right I would, because it's none of our business.' He shook his head in exasperation.

'There's a child's life at stake!'

'Wait a minute.' Danny paused. 'You said you've seen her?'

Juliette nodded. 'Last week. I made Sarah take me to her. I thought I was going out of my mind seeing things and all the while it was Richard playing tricks on me, to stop me from finding out the truth.'

'Are you sure?'

'Yes! How many more times do I—'

'Christ, Jules, I would never have agreed to this meal if I'd known all this was going on!'

'What do you expect me to do?' She hissed. 'Walk away and pretend I haven't seen her? You know I can't do that.'

'She isn't your responsibility.'

'So you think it's okay living next to a child that's locked up away from people? A child who hasn't seen her mum for a year?'

'You don't know that for certain.' He glanced towards the door but there was no sign of Richard or Sarah. 'Did Sarah say anything about Richard's part in all of this?'

'Richard told me he'd seen Louisa and Daisy a few months ago. I now know he's lying. Plus he's just said he *hasn't* seen either of them. He only spoke to them on the phone.'

'You've spoken to Richard about this too? I can't begin to understand why you wouldn't confide in me.' His tone was sarcastic as he threw her a thunderous look.

'He said there was nothing to worry about. But I didn't believe him. I got us an invite here for dinner, so that you could see Daisy. And now you're doubting me.'

'It's not that I don't believe you. It's the reasoning – why would they go to such lengths to hide a child?'

'Exactly. Something is wrong. I can't let it go, not with a child involved. I can't leave her there, not after...'

She couldn't say the words but Danny knew what she was getting at.

'That's a low trick to use Emily,' he muttered.

'I'm sorry,' Juliette said. 'But this is important to me. If you can see Daisy, we might be able to get her and Sarah away from Richard.'

'But he's just said she's not here!'

'He's lying.'

Danny gnawed his bottom lip. 'Do you think they're both in danger?'

When Juliette nodded, he continued.

'You should have called the police if you have suspicions.'

'I couldn't, don't you see? Sarah says she's tried before but you know Richard and his smooth talk. She said he had officers believing Sarah was making it up. She's scared to do anything now because he hit her after that.'

'He hit her?' Danny's face darkened.

Juliette nodded, feeling her cheeks burning. She wasn't sure if that was entirely true. She reached for his hand.

'Please, do this one thing for me. I have to try and help them. If things get out of hand, then we can call the police. But for now, I need you to believe me. I want you to see Daisy.'

Danny shook his head and stood up. 'I think we should leave, right now. I don't want anything to do with this.'

Richard appeared in the doorway. 'I think you should stay where you are.'

Danny's legs gave way as he thumped back down.

Juliette gasped. Richard was holding a shotgun and he was pointing it at them.

'Richard? What's going on?' she asked, glancing from him to Sarah and back.

Neither of them spoke as Sarah moved into the kitchen.

'Sarah has been putting things into your wife's head,' Richard said to Danny. 'She thinks Louisa isn't missing. She thinks she's here on the land. Buried in the woods, no less, don't you, my love?'

Juliette saw the blood drain from Danny's face.

'I can see your mind ticking over,' Richard added. 'But she's lying.'

'I don't know what to believe right now,' Danny replied.

'So all these things that have been happening to me were all *your* doing?' Juliette questioned.

'Some of them, yes.'

'The cries of the child in the garden?'

Richard nodded, sniggering to himself.

'He used to do that to Louisa,' Sarah spoke quietly. 'He recorded Daisy crying on his phone, then would pretend it was her during the night. Louisa would get to Daisy's bedroom to find her asleep. Richard would repeat it once she was in bed.'

'But why?' Juliette asked him.

'I like playing games. Like the trip to the woods we said you'd done that morning?' Richard shook his head. 'That never happened.'

'And the toy that was left on the bench; the photo that was missing from my phone? The note pushed through the door? The doors being left open?' Juliette couldn't meet Danny's eyes, fear of the hurt she might see because she hadn't confided in him. 'Do you have a key to our home?'

'We do. I used to look after the old dear's cat.' Richard sniggered. 'But that wasn't me. That must have been Sarah. She's always been a joker.'

Juliette was struggling to keep up. 'I don't understand.'

'Why don't you explain to her, Sarah? Because if you hadn't meddled, none of this would be happening.'

'Don't you dare blame me!' Sarah yelled.

'It's your fault *she* found out about Daisy.'

'Well, obviously that wasn't part of the plan. And neither was this.' She pointed at Juliette and Danny.

Richard glared at Sarah. 'Shut up.'

'Oh, come on. You haven't thought this through very well. What are you going to do? Shoot them? And bury them in the woods too? Somehow I think people might get suspicious and start asking questions. Because it was you who murdered Louisa as well!'

Juliette thought that Sarah was brave to come out and say what she was thinking. She wondered if it was because she and Danny were there to protect her. But that all changed in an instant when she saw Richard swing the gun round and aim it at Sarah.

Danny jumped to his feet but Richard turned the gun back to him.

'No, please!' Juliette stood up too.

'Stay where you are! In fact' – he waved the gun around – 'Both of you on the settee.'

They moved across the room and sat down again. Juliette pleaded with Sarah, then Richard.

'Please,' she said, her voice a tremor. 'Whatever is happening here, let us go. We've done nothing to you and I promise we won't—'

'I found the phone this afternoon with your text messages to Sarah.'

Juliette paled.

'Can someone tell me what the fuck is going on?' Danny looked at them all in turn.

SIXTY-FOUR

Danny had thought Richard and Sarah were a strange couple but this was beyond anything he could imagine. They had deliberately set out to trick Juliette about the little girl who lived with them. Make her think she was hallucinating so that they could continue with the misconception. But he couldn't fathom out why. Unless Sarah was right when she said Richard had murdered his ex-wife.

Richard and Sarah were arguing.

'You can't keep doing this, Richard. It's insane,' Sarah cried. 'No, *you're* insane!'

'Sarah, Sarah, Sarah.' Richard sighed. 'Why do you have to spoil the fun? I was going to set it up as a murder-suicide. So, let's see.' He looked at Danny. 'That baby your wife is carrying? It isn't yours. It's mine.'

Despite the situation, Danny couldn't help but scoff.

'It's pretty obvious to me but I'll spell it out to you,' Richard went on. 'While you were in London, Juliette and I have been fucking on a regular basis. I've had more fun with her than you, so.' He shrugged. 'What are the odds?'

Danny sat stunned. Not because of what Richard was telling him about his wife. But because he didn't believe a word of it and was wondering why he was playing this card.

Richard raised the gun an inch and aimed it at Danny's chest. Juliette screamed.

'Look, whatever has happened, we can talk about it,' he said, trying to calm the situation.

'Sure we can. But I'm still going to kill you.'

Juliette shook her head, using her eyes to plead with Sarah. But Sarah was silent now. Staying still.

'That's what I'm going to tell the police when they find you,' Richard went on. 'I'm going to say you came round to confront me. I wasn't in, nor was Sarah. Juliette followed you in here, where you argued and then you grabbed this gun. There was a fight and you shot her. Then you shot yourself. Murder-suicide. I have it all planned.'

'That wouldn't work. You'd still be charged with murder because you left your gun out of a locked cabinet.' Danny shook his head. 'And how would we even get in if you were out? Plus neither of us is going to be willing, so one of us could get away before you have the chance to kill us both.'

Danny couldn't believe his voice was so composed, as if there wasn't a mad man standing in front of them with a shotgun. But the circumstances dictated he stay as calm as possible.

'I'll make it work.' Richard nodded. 'Because if I let you go, you'll send the police. They'll start snooping round too and I don't want them to find out what happened to Louisa. Sarah was right, I killed her.'

Juliette burst into tears. 'Please let us go and I promise we won't interfere any more. No one will know that we've even been friendly with you and I could—'

Hearing the distress in his wife's voice, Danny got to his feet. He had to do something.

'No!' Juliette grabbed for his arm but it was out of her reach.

Before Richard could react, Danny grabbed the barrel of the gun and pushed it up into the air.

Juliette screamed again as the men grappled with the gun. Richard managed to get it from Danny and he pushed him with such force that he fell backwards onto the table. Losing his balance, he tumbled off its side, cracking his head on the marble worktop. He dropped to the floor.

* * *

'Danny!' Juliette rushed across and knelt beside him, ignoring the danger she might have put herself in if Richard came at them. Danny's eyes were closed, he was out cold. 'Call for an ambulance! Danny? Danny, ohmigod.'

When she heard no movement, she glanced up again. Sarah was still standing there.

'Ring for help! Please.'

'I can't,' Sarah replied.

Juliette cried out in frustration. 'Where is your phone?' Why was Sarah being so obstructive?

Richard rummaged around in the drawer. He pulled out a piece of thick rope.

Juliette frowned. 'What's going on?'

'Move over to that chair,' Richard demanded.

She looked up at them both. 'Please! You have to help Danny.'

'On the chair,' Richard roared.

Sarah pulled her upright and it was then Juliette caught her eye. Sarah was pleading with her to do as she was told. Did she have a plan?

But Richard grabbed Juliette by the chin.

'Do you really want to know what happened to Louisa? Well, I'm going to tell you before I kill you too.'

Juliette was sobbing openly now as Richard tied her hands together.

'I killed her, and then Sarah and I buried her in the woods. Your friendly neighbour, your new friend was in on it too.'

Juliette froze. That couldn't be true. Could it? Had they both fooled her all along?

'Louisa was such a liability. I was glad to get rid of her in the end.'

As Richard ranted, Juliette saw Sarah reach behind the bread bin and pull out a large kitchen knife. Watched as she raced across the room towards Richard.

'You bastard,' Sarah cried, plunging the knife upwards into his chest.

It went in so hard that Juliette heard Richard grunt. He came out from behind her, his face creased up in pain. And then he was stumbling as he made his way across the kitchen.

'What have you done?' He held his hand out to Sarah. 'You mad bitch.'

Sarah stayed where she was, the knife with Richard's blood hanging down by her side. When he fell and didn't get up again, she came towards Juliette.

Juliette cowered, for a second thinking Sarah might attack her too. But then she was cutting her loose.

SIXTY-FIVE

'How's Danny?' Sarah asked, dropping to sit next to Juliette. 'I'm sure the paramedics will be here soon.'

'I think he's going to be okay.' Juliette looked down at Danny who was cradled in her arms. He'd woken up a minute ago, although he was groggy and his eyes were closed.

'I'm so sorry. I didn't want it to turn out like this. I tried to think of a way around anyone getting hurt.' Sarah was shaking, as if she was in shock too, but there was something not quite right.

'What is it that you're not telling me?' Juliette asked.

'He was going to kill you both. We talked about it before you arrived.' Sarah looked at her with so much guilt it was hard to comprehend. 'You know I haven't been straight with you, but you don't know all the reasons. Before Richard murdered my sister, he made her life hell. He dragged her down so low, he hit her constantly. He had affairs too. And yet he wouldn't let her leave. I think he must have seen it as a kind of failure, although why he didn't say he wanted Louisa to go is beyond me. I guess that was control too.'

'Do you think he loved Daisy too much for her to go?'

'I honestly have no idea. But he didn't love Louisa. He made her think she had ME. He drugged her daily, to keep her tired, docile, something he could use and manipulate to make himself feel better.'

'He told me you have ME too.'

'It's a lie. I let him believe a lot of things about me over the past year. I needed him to think I was on his side. That I would live with what he'd done and hidden away. He had me over a barrel really. I'm an accessory to murder, and my sister didn't have a proper burial, which is against the law. It's the reason I could never go. I couldn't leave Louisa here.'

'Oh, Sarah.'

'I had no choice. We made a pact on the night he... I could stay here if I never talked about what happened. I made him add my name to the deeds of the house in return for my silence.'

'Did he agree?' Juliette was beginning to see how clever Sarah had been.

She nodded. 'I needed something for Daisy. She's the innocent victim in this.'

'So are you.'

'No, I'm not. Because I manipulated you. When you moved in, I reached out to you because I needed to tell someone else without Richard knowing. He murdered my sister. He threatened to murder me and Daisy if I didn't help cover for him. He murdered his father too.' Sarah told Juliette about Jack. 'He's a psychopath because of that man.'

Juliette disagreed. 'He has his own mind. He didn't have to take after his father.'

'I suppose not, but he's still a manipulative, arrogant, evil, twisted killer. Although I was at fault too. I put the idea into his head that you knew too much, that we had to talk to you and then you suggested we meet for dinner and—'

'Why didn't you just leave?'

'Because I wanted justice for Louisa.' Tears dripped down Sarah's cheeks. 'I couldn't leave her out there a minute longer than necessary. I was horrible to her and she deserved so much better. When I first came to work here as Daisy's nanny, I had this mad idea that Louisa had abandoned me. When she came to live here with Richard, we fell out as she became distant, wanting to spend all her time with him. I realise now it was his way of controlling her. But I-I'm afraid to say I wanted to hurt her and I wanted her life. I wanted to live here in luxury with a handsome man and I wanted Richard for myself. So I slept with him. It was okay at first but the longer I was here, the more I could see what he was doing to Louisa. And yet I still didn't help her. I was a terrible sister.'

'He'd obviously manipulated you too,' Juliette said.

'He was so nasty to her but I couldn't see what he was doing. Until one day, I saw him adding drugs, sedatives I think, to Louisa's drink. He said he'd been doing it for years, to keep her under control. I pretended I thought it was a good idea but I hated it.'

Danny stirred. Juliette cried out but his eyes closed as quickly as they had opened. She squeezed his hand, thankful to feel its warmth.

'What about Daisy?' she asked Sarah.

'It's her I did this for and yet I'm going to lose her now.' Her voice was quiet, defeated. 'But I had to do it.'

Juliette knew what she had to do too. 'It was self-defence, Sarah.'

'No, it wasn't and you know—'

'It *was* self-defence.' She stared at Sarah ensuring she understood.

Sirens in the distance alerted them there was help on the way. Juliette looked down at Danny who was regaining some of his colour. She glanced fleetingly across the room where Richard lay next to a puddle of his own blood. His skin tone was already turning grey.

'You had no choice,' she went on. 'He was going to tie me up and kill me, then Danny. Okay?'

A silence fell on the room, the only sound laboured breathing. A little girl appeared in the doorway.

'Auntie Sarah, I heard something and I woke up.'

Sarah rushed to sweep Daisy up in her arms. 'Come on, poppet, back to bed. There's nothing to be scared of.'

SIXTY-SIX

If it wasn't for them needing an ambulance straight away, Juliette and Sarah might have had more time to talk things through. But both men were bleeding on the floor and despite one of them being dead and the other groggy after regaining consciousness, two paramedics tried their best to revive Richard, to no avail. He was pronounced dead on the scene. The police then arrived in their droves.

Now it was nearing eleven o'clock the following morning. Juliette was sitting in the living room, curled up in a chair. Still in shock, she was trying to piece it all together. She'd gone with Danny to the hospital, where two police detectives had taken a statement from her, plus a short one from Danny as he waited for stitches in a gash at the side of his head.

They'd arrived home in the early hours. A police cordon had been set up at the front of White Oaks, an officer on guard at the front door. Despite the late hour, several police vehicles were in the lane.

They were due to start digging soon. Juliette shuddered just thinking about it. She was dreading hearing the news, knowing that Louisa could be found at any minute.

Danny popped his head around the door and came into her.

'Hey, how are you feeling now?'

He kissed her on the forehead. He'd been a bit groggy this morning. He'd had five stitches and she'd been asked to keep an eye on him regarding concussion for the next twenty-four hours. Luckily the scar would be covered by his hair.

He sat down beside her and placed an arm around her shoulders. 'I'll survive,' he replied. 'Besides, I'm going to play on your sympathy over the coming weeks. Have you heard anything else?'

'No.'

'How's Sarah?'

'I've left a couple of messages but she hasn't replied.'

After the police had questioned them, Sarah had taken Daisy to stay in a hotel, away from the house while the police did their work. She was sure Sarah would have had to complete a statement in writing like she had.

'You can't hold yourself responsible,' Danny soothed. 'Richard was a psychopath. How were we to know he'd murdered his father, as well as Louisa? I was flabbergasted to hear that.' He paused. 'No, actually I wasn't.'

'But I led you into danger.'

'It wasn't *Game of Thrones*.' Danny sniggered. 'You only had an inkling of what was going on. And at least that little girl might get a normal life now.'

Juliette nodded in agreement. 'The police said we might be swamped by the press for a few days.'

'We can book into a hotel too if you prefer, if it gets too intrusive.'

'Let's see how it goes.' Juliette raised a hand to Danny's face and stared at the man she loved so much. The man she hadn't confided in. The man she may have lost because of her stupidity.

But she would do it all again if a child's welfare was at stake. Too much went on behind closed doors that never got talked about. Never reported, often to the detriment of someone who couldn't defend themselves.

Thankfully, Danny would make a swift recovery, although his

wound would go beyond skin deep. They were both going to be traumatised by the events of last night.

'So how are *you*?' he asked her, resting a hand on her tummy.

She smiled. He was checking up on the precious life growing inside her. Their child.

'Everything seems to be fine. Unlike you.' She ran a finger over his hand before grasping it.

He cocked his head to one side. 'Do you still see this as our perfect place? I'd understand if you want to move.'

She shook her head. 'We're not going anywhere. This is our home.'

SIXTY-SEVEN

SIX MONTHS LATER

Juliette stared at the baby in her arms. Jordan Elliott Ansell was ten days old now. They'd settled into a routine as if he'd been with them forever. Danny was taking a month's paternity leave. He was besotted with his son, just as she was. Like any parents, really. But Jordan was special. He felt like a gift.

She was sitting in the kitchen waiting for Danny to come in. He'd popped into the village for a few essentials. A few minutes later, she heard the car pulling up in the drive.

'Daddy's back,' she said, standing up carefully. Jordan had not long woken up and was a little grumpy.

'Hey.' Danny greeted them both with a kiss as he joined them. 'How's my lad doing?'

'Very well, thanks.' Juliette grinned. 'His mama is doing fine too.'

Jordan stirred and they both looked down at him. From the moment he was born, they could see Emily in him. Tears welled in Juliette's eyes at the thought of them being given a chance to start another family. Neither of them would forget Emily, but now it was time to celebrate her short life by the arrival of another.

They went out into the garden and sat on Emily's bench. Juliette had moved it slightly so that it wasn't facing next door's rear garden now. Even so she turned her head and looked at the house. White Oaks was up for sale, and quite frankly she was glad about that. She didn't want to be reminded of what happened every time she came outdoors and saw Sarah.

But at least Sarah and Daisy were free to do as they pleased. It was strange to think that little girl had lived mostly inside that house for the past few months. Now, thankfully, she might be able to live a normal life.

Danny passed her a glass of champagne and fresh orange juice. 'Thanks.' She smiled her appreciation.

He sat down beside her. 'To Emily.' He raised his glass to the sky. 'Whatever you're doing up there, I hope you're tidying up after yourself.'

Juliette giggled. She raised her glass too. 'To Emily. May you make as many people happy there as you did here.'

Danny popped his arm around Juliette's shoulders and pulled her near. She felt safe, protected, even after all they'd been through. It was over. It was time to move on.

* * *

At the cemetery, Sarah walked with Daisy's hand firmly in her own. It was the first time she had visited her sister's grave in a while. When Richard had been killed, the press intrusion had been enough to drive her from White Oaks. Richard, after all, was a well-known artist.

But after a month, she'd returned and started to integrate herself into village life. People must have been shocked to see Daisy, but no one had said anything. Besides, no one would ever know the real truth. Because Sarah had secrets of her own.

Postnatal depression ran in the family. It had happened to her mum as well as Louisa and, looking back, she could see it had happened to her too. Or maybe they were a family prone to mental illness.

When she'd found Poppy dead that day, she'd been in such

shock that as the paramedics worked on trying to resuscitate her, she'd tried to knife Jessie. Luckily she hadn't been able to succeed. She'd been spoken to about it but there'd been no police there to witness anything at the time.

Jessie had been jailed for two years. Sarah had moved back to her mum's. How she'd hated Louisa at the time. She'd wanted to find her one day and break her. Let her see how horrible it was to be let down, left to fend for yourself. To make mistakes with big fat consequences. And all the time Jessie had been behind bars, it had made her think more about her sister. If it wasn't for her leaving, she wouldn't have been with Jessie.

So she'd been surprised to receive the text message from Richard asking her to call and talk to him. She hadn't meant to fall for him, but when he killed her sister, she hated him in an instant. Of course he hadn't known that. With a body hidden in the woods, they'd been stuck living in the house. She'd seen the place where her sister was buried every day and yet she couldn't grieve for her until now.

During that time, she'd tricked Richard into thinking she was okay with what had happened to Louisa, that she would keep their secret. But when she found out he was seeing other women, well, that made her see red.

Juliette and Danny arriving next door had worked out in her favour. She'd been able to fool Juliette into thinking her home life was worse than it was. Her neighbour had taken her word for it that Richard was abusive to her, that Daisy was indeed kept mostly in her bedroom. She'd set her up to find out the truth about Louisa, getting snippets of information from people, looking at the photos.

Plunging that knife into Richard hadn't been anything to do with self-defence. Sarah had instigated it all so that she could kill him. Get away with it, just like he had when he'd shot his father, and strangled Louisa.

Luckily, during their time alone in the kitchen while they waited for the emergency services to arrive, she'd managed to get her story across, ensuring that Juliette came out in sympathy for her. They'd changed the truth slightly, guaranteeing the police thought Richard had come at Juliette first, and that Sarah had acted bravely to save her life. With Danny out cold and no other witnesses, the evidence couldn't say any different. And more importantly, Juliette sided with her.

It really had taken some planning but she'd got there in the end. Richard was dead. Louisa's death was avenged. Some of the monies raised by the sale of the house would be put in trust for Daisy until she was an adult and, once White Oaks was sold, Sarah would buy the perfect home for the two of them in Dorset by the sea. For now she had sourced a cottage to rent.

'This is the last time we can come and visit Mummy for a while, Daisy,' Sarah explained as she stooped to her level by the side of Louisa's grave. 'She was very brave and loved you so much, and you know she had to go to live with the angels.' She pointed up at the sky. 'Can you see the sun?'

'Yes.'

'And the clouds, and the blue sky?'

Daisy nodded.

'That's where Mummy is. When you're sad, wherever you are, look up and she will be with you.' She pointed to Daisy's heart. 'And she will always be in there.'

'Will you look after me now that Mummy and Daddy are gone?'

Daisy seemed a little tearful so Sarah gave her a hug.

'You try and stop me, poppet. You're family and we always look after our own.'

A LETTER FROM MEL

First of all, I want to say a huge thank you for choosing to read *The Life She Wants*. If you'd like to keep up to date with all my latest releases, just sign up at the following link. Your email address will never be shared and you can unsubscribe at any time.

www.bookouture.com/mel-sherratt

I hope you enjoyed getting to know Juliette, Louisa and Sarah as much as I did. It's the seventeenth crime novel I have written. I always enjoy writing about sibling characters and the rivalry between them. With Louisa and Sarah, there was a bond that had been broken but finally healed itself, so be it too late for Sarah to make amends to her sister.

If you did enjoy *The Life She Wants*, I would be extremely grateful if you would write a short review. I'd love to hear what you think, and it can also help other readers discover one of my books for the first time. Or maybe you can recommend it to your friends and family.

Keep in touch,

Mel

www.melsherratt.co.uk

facebook.com/MelSherrattauthor
twitter.com/writermels

ACKNOWLEDGEMENTS

I started my writing career in December 2011, after twelve years of rejection from publishers. To say I am grateful to the hundreds of thousands of readers who have invested their reading time in my books since then would be an enormous understatement.

Thank you to Team Bookouture, in particular to Peta, Laura, Janette and Noelle. Particular thanks must go to the friends I am very lucky to have – Alison Niebiezczanski, Caroline Mitchell, Talli Roland, Louise Ross and Sharon Sant. Thanks for the long lunches, shopping trips, coffee and cake, Pimm's and cocktails and many, many book chats.

I'd like to say a huge thank you to anyone who has read my books, sent me emails or messages, engaged with me on social media or come to see me at various events over the country. I've been genuinely blown away with all kinds of niceness and support from you all. I love what I do and hope you continue to enjoy my books. Your faith and support mean so much to me.

Likewise, my thanks go out to all the wonderful book bloggers and enthusiasts who have read my stories and taken the time out of their busy lives to write such amazing reviews, I am grateful to you all. A writer's job is often a lonely one but I feel I truly have friends everywhere.

Finally, to Chris. Without your support I know I wouldn't have got this far. Love you to bits, fella.